the chan

Damian Lanigan was born and brought up in England. He now lives in New York City. *The Chancers* is his second novel. His first was the highly acclaimed *Stretch, 29*.

Praise for STRETCH, 29:

'Heartbreakingly funny, Lanigan charts Stretch's downward spiral with masses of style. Debut novels don't get much better than this.'
Daily Mirror

'The novel is lit by some truly fine writing and observation . . . moments of Dickensian greatness.'
Independent

'The humour is kept jet black as Stretch descends into further realms of misery, and the result is a three-dimensional comic character we really feel for, as original and affecting as Billy Liar or Lucky Jim were to previous generations.'
GRUB SMITH, *FHM*

'Nick Hornby, Tim Lott, Tony Parsons . . . [Lanigan] might just be the best of the bunch. Very funny and strangely touching, the book is a vastly entertaining satire on modern manners and manhood, and works wonderfully.'
Big Issue

'The book's warmth and honesty ensure that it is more than simply satire. Frank is an engaging character, and as he gropes his chaotic way towards redemption and reconciliation, one not only laughs but sympathises.'
Daily Telegraph

by damian lanigan

Stretch, 29
The Chancers

damian lanigan

the chancers

HarperCollins*Publishers*

HarperCollins*Publishers*
77–85 Fulham Palace Road,
Hammersmith, London W6 8JB

www.**fire**and**water**.com

Published by HarperCollins*Publishers* 2003
1 3 5 7 9 8 6 4 2

A catalogue record for this book
is available from the British Library

ISBN 0 00 226122 7

Set in Meridien with VAG Rounded Display
by Palimpsest Book Production Limited
Polmont, Stirlingshire

Printed and bound in Great Britain by
Clays Ltd, St Ives plc

For my brother

part one

Today I discover that the second line of a tax-return form is capable of provoking an existential crisis:

Name: *Patrick Moon*
Occupation:

Every year for a decade I have written 'ACTOR' in this space. However, for the fiscal year 99/00 this statement would carry a controversial implication: namely that in that year I actually did some acting. I didn't.

My pen hovers for a moment while I think things through:

- *An actor is a person who acts*
- *Patrick Moon doesn't do any acting*
- *Therefore Patrick Moon is an actor*

I am aware that this argument is somewhat flawed. What about:

- *An actor is a person who is available for acting jobs*
- *Patrick Moon is available for acting jobs*
- *Therefore Patrick Moon is an actor*

My pen nearly makes contact with the paper but not quite. The problem here is that it offers too broad a definition of what an actor is: nowadays *everybody* is available for acting jobs. I try something more specific:

- *An actor is a person who derives paid employment from acting*
- *Patrick Moon no longer derives paid employment from acting*
- *Therefore Patrick Moon is no longer an actor*

No way. Accepting this would mean leaving my tax-return form blank. It would mean that as far as the wider world is concerned, I am no longer an actor. Which would mean that I am no longer an actor. This would be unbearable. I need to invent some new way of thinking. So:

- *An actor is someone who thinks he's an actor*
- *Patrick Moon thinks he's an actor*
- *Therefore Patrick Moon is an actor*

The argument is perfect. A delusional premise pursued to its logical conclusion – which in fact is a good description of my entire career. I score the paper deeply:

Name: *Patrick Moon*
Occupation: *ACTOR*

1

I'm on the threshold of a doctor's surgery, clammy and anxious. They're piping in classical music to make me feel better.
It makes me feel worse. I walk over to the reception desk,
trying to look confident. The receptionist ignores me. I look
at a poster on the wall behind her – Prostate Health. The
cross section of the male genitals makes them look fronded,
lush and beautifully balanced, like a hothouse orchid. She
doesn't look up, but can obviously sense me hovering:

– Been here before, sir?

She aspirates the aitch as if it's not her normal practice.
The Margate whine is overlaid with the breathy tone of
administration.

– Not to my knowledge.

She looks up at me. I am jaunty and unembarrassable;
the only man ever to visit the dick doctor who's got nothing
wrong with his dick.

– Do you have your referral, sir?

– Yes. Dr Olswang sent me.

I produce my referral. She studies it as if it's much more
difficult to understand than it really is.

She's got this stewardess thing going: brass buttons,
scraped back metallic hair, porn star make-up. Comfortably

fuckable, but I bet she doesn't date patients – 'Enough about me, let's talk about your chlamydia.' She solves the riddle of the referral, a brief unsettling smile.

– Lovely. If you'd like to take a seat. Help yourself to fresh fruit juice or coffee. Decaf or reggerler.

The atmospherics are Business Class. There is another Prostate Health poster over the table where the coffee waits in black fishbowls. The cross section on the poster is compelling. Ruled lines link the different elements to their names. Shouldn't I have been told that I have a Cowper's Gland? Actually, I may have two; it/they are like two leaves of a fleur-de-lys on either side of the urethra, which branches at the top to the seminal vesicles, which in turn are linked to the testes by the vas deferens. Suddenly I'm back at school, in the refectory after double biology, the pipes in the chewy liver being compared to seminiferous tubules. Urethra Franklin, there's a vas deferens between your penis and your balls.

I am compelled by the poster; it makes me realize how little I know about the way I'm assembled. The prostate gland hovers behind the branching urethra like a hot-air balloon or a seedpod. The whole arrangement has an impossibility to it: the fragility, complexity, delicate interdependencies; the symmetry intricate and unlikely, beyond sci-fi. Again, I'm back at school, but in Divinity now: The Argument from Design – it's all so impossible some super-intelligent being must have put it all together; or the Cosmic Accident – it's all so impossible that it can't be anything other than chance.

– Mine's the size of a tangerine now.

A man in a mac sits on one of the orange plastic bucket chairs, his hands knitted on his lap. His voice is midway between pride and regret. He points at the poster.

– Prostate. A tangerine. I piss like Christmas all day long.

– Oh dear.

6

– Piss like my old grandma, fifty-eight years old.

That to look forward to, as well as so much else. I make a commiseratory grimace and move away with my mug of coffee. I sit opposite a man in a pinstripe suit. He is reading *Condé Nast Traveller*, trying to look blithe; no cock complaints on the Côte d'Azur. I pick up *Golf Digest*. I look at an article on resorts in Arizona, which is illustrated with aerial photographs. The fairways are like green finger lakes against the baked desert. In one picture ('The 5th – A sporty downhill par 4') the cart path drapes around the hole like a vas deferens, the fairway a penile shaft, the green's slight outward swell like a moderately engorged glans. I think about the dimpled texture of a golf ball, and check my mental image with the poster: testes seem to be more the texture of rambutan or lychees. Still, it's no surprise that the dick doctor's a golf freak.

He comes into the reception area, whistling nonharmonies to the delicate strata of music that fall from their invisible source. He whispers something to the receptionist ('this guy's got a *really* dodgy dick'?). She sniggers.

– Mr Moon? I'm Dr Fineman.

He is fifty-ish, bearded with badgery hair and googly tortoiseshell glasses. His mouth is deeply embedded in the clean, glossy beard. He shakes the one hand that isn't still gripping *Golf Digest*:

– Golfer?

– No. Bullfighting.

– Interesting. Let's go through.

I throw the magazine down and follow him along a small corridor to his surgery. He's still whistling, a sprightly blackbird trill. He is obviously delighted at the prospect of inspecting my gonads. He leaves me alone for a moment. The windowless surgery is panelled like a lawyer's study. Heavy, presumably obsolete leather-bound textbooks line the walls. There is a picture of Fineman surrounded by six

7

or seven children. Each time I try to count them I forget where I started. The boys wear yamulkes and red velvet bow ties, the girls velvet dresses in bottle green and midnight blue, with puff sleeves. They are photographed against a background of rouched velvet curtain. It's either a picture of his family or a publicity shot for the Velvet Information Council. Fineman returns with a buff file into which he peers, scratching his beard. He starts drumming a couple of pencils on the edge of the desk and smiles almost coyly.

– Come on, then. Let's have a look at you.

– What? Here?

– Where else?

– It doesn't feel right. It's not very clinical.

– That's right. That's how I like it. Homely.

If you live in a medieval library.

– Trousers and undies only.

– What, keep them on?

– No, no. Take them *off*.

I stand and start to strip. I feel as if I'm getting undressed in public, which I am. He drums away, whistles on, the rhythm section to my approaching humiliation.

– Why this, doctor?

Everything has become gluey and stretchy, I may be over-balancing. Note to self: *Take shoes off before trousers.*

– Why what?

– Well, it could have been kiddie cancer, geriatrics, I don't know, psychiatry.

I have to sit to take my shoes off. I am bare-buttocked on the patient chair. This is maybe the first time I have felt the sticky kiss of vinyl on my backside, maybe the last. I am slightly out of breath – horrid danglings everywhere.

– I never ask myself the question, to be honest. Sometimes I'm glad I didn't choose proctology. What do you do?

– I'm an actor.

I stand up, naked from the waist down, still with my

8

jacket on. A soft breeze from somewhere is bringing home to me just how naked I really am.

– That must be fun. Any particular type of acting?

– Anything going.

– Excellent, fine, now come to me.

I stand, move round the desk, tousling my cock and balls to give them a bit of extra volume and mass. Fineman pushes towards me on his chair and moves in. I hold my T-shirt and jacket at belly-button height so that he can get an un-restricted view.

– Have you been in anything I'd know?

– Almost certainly not.

– Very good, very good.

He's right up close now.

– I've mainly done theatre.

– I don't go to the theatre. It bores me to death.

– You're seeing the wrong theatre – acch!

– Sorry, cold hands, doctor's prerogative.

Fineman is breathing heavily through his nose and I feel a tepid jet of air on the tip of my bwana. He then chokes my scrotum where it meets the body and clasps my balls, manipulating them like worry beads with his cool, dry hands.

– Balls OK. Balls good. You did what – you were just saying?

I'm too glutted with pride at the quality of my balls to say anything just now. He takes my cock between index finger and thumb and rolls it around like a slug of plasticine.

– You've been seeing the wrong type of theatre.

– The type that happens in a theatre. That's the type I don't like.

Although lacking curiosity about the dramatic arts, my genitalia are to him an inexhaustible source of fascination. He's getting in really tight, head moving from side to side, examining from every angle. He makes a noise in the back of his throat and moves in even closer. He looks up at me,

9

eyes bulgy and keen behind his glasses, my cock pincered in his fingers like Groucho's cigar.

– No pain?

– No. Just discomfort.

– Physical discomfort?

– Psychological discomfort.

– Because . . . ?

– There's a grown man holding my dingus.

– I see. Dingus. You don't hear that very often. I might write it down.

He resumes his grisly study, pursing his lips. I get a premonition he's going to pop it into his mouth – da dick doctah gonna cure you good, Mistah Moon – but instead he starts to whistle again, pulling me around like putty. With a sudden definitive throat-clearing, he drops me and pushes back behind his desk.

– Well, everything seems fine. Get dressed if you want.

– Actually, I'd rather just stand here with my balls out.

– Of course, anything you like.

Fineman's gone back to his buff file, he's humming again, drumming pencils again.

– Right, so when did they start?

– What?

– The erection problems?

– Can't put a precise date on it. It's been ongoing. Few months maybe.

– It's all very normal, by the way.

I'm pulling on my trousers. A shudder runs through my shoulders, zapped in late by the shame gods.

– Normal, really?

– Very, very normal.

Now clothed, I feel more naked than ever. Fineman makes every mannerism possible to indicate how normal my sexual problems are: mouth downturned in its neat nest of beard, hands moving out in smoothing gestures.

– Not for me, it isn't.

He resettles his glasses and leans over his desk towards me. His thumbs twiddle. He's constantly in motion, resettling in his chair, pushing his glasses up his nose. I figure it's related to some kind of existential uneasiness with his career: the infinite chain of genitals he has seen, will see, looks at in books, looks at in specialist periodicals (*Bollocks Today incorporating Cocks Monthly*), imagines under people's clothing, dreams about night after night, and then his own, rudely present and immutable to him every day. For a normal man his dick is the spindle around which the world spins. What must it be like for a professional, with not only his own to worry about, cajole, keep fed and watered, clean and functional, but every other bastard's? It's a dick dick world for the dick doctor.

– Well, describe what happens.

– It's fairly simple, I can't . . .

– Summon?

– Sustain.

– You can't sustain . . .

– An erection. I can get one of a certain quality, but I can't sustain one. Throughout – intercourse.

I can't say sex for some reason, or fucking, or boffing, swiving or whatever, so fall back on the vocabulary of those biology lessons. I'm looking him dead in the eye up to this point, but now I have to look away. The photo, the Fineman family, all three and a half million of them: no erection problems with Doctor Tackle.

– This is all good stuff. We can get you straightened out in no time. The hard part's over, coming here.

The faint suggestion of double entendre is somehow annoying, as if I may be the unknowing nun/Frenchman in a 'Carry On' film. He takes a yellow legal pad from his drawer and starts to write, with the left-hander's exaggerated arc over the words.

11

– Now, I need to ask you a few questions. Are you taking any drugs at the moment?

I decide to be honest with him, and start to tick off my drug use, evading clarity on quantity and frequency.

– Well, cocaine occasionally. Ecstasy. A bit of spliff, obviously. No speed any more – not very much, anyway. Shall we treat alcohol separately?

Fineman is staring at me strangely.

– I meant prescription drugs.

– Oh sorry. No, never touch them.

– Alcohol then?

– Well. Bits and bobs.

– Can you put it in units a week? A unit being a glass of wine, half a pint of beer, whatever?

I put on a mental arithmetic face. He is looking at me open-mouthed, pencil awkwardly poised. I'm still struggling. What's plenty times too much, squared?

– Just roughly, that's all I need.

– Hmmmm, I don't know. Let's say sixty-ish?

– Sixty. Right. I'll put down ninety.

– That's probably closer to it.

– Yes. High blood pressure?

I once felt as if I had high blood pressure. When I was at drama school we did an exchange with an acting troupe from Kiev. They only stopped drinking to start smoking. Dancing was no impediment to either. I had a whirlwind affair with a chain-smoking theatre director with a sopping, peaty crotch. She was furred from inner knee to sternum. 'There are only two questions in Russia, Patrick: Who is to blame? and, What is to be done?' – this while I was still in my post-orgasmic twitch. She lit a cigarette that smelt as if it could easily be made of hair. Well, you've got to find some use for it. As was our wont, we shared a post-coital mug of tepid vodka and a rollmop herring. Anyway, it was a long tough week, and I wore a high flush for a

12

month afterwards. Dead people would have come back pumped.

– No. No high blood pressure, I don't think.

– Depression? Any history of depression?

– None whatsoever.

And then I remember I've always wanted to try Prozac, Paxil, Wellbutrin, Zoloft, lithium, any of them, all of them, so I curse myself. Maybe I could get away with qualifying my negative with 'although I hear strange voices very often, in my shattered mind', but I've missed my chance. Fineman's moving on.

– Do you smoke?

– No. Not during the days anyway.

– Meaning . . . ?

– You know: I smoke a bit of draw, and sometimes a few fags if I'm out drinking or whatever.

He frowns, his mouth puckering into an anus within the thicket of beard.

– How does the thought of a day without any artificial stimulant make you feel?

– I don't know.

– Why not?

– I'd just never consider it.

– Hmph.

He rubs at his temples.

– Stress?

– Well, I've never been a great believer in stress.

– Do you feel under pressure at work or in your personal life in any way?

Apart from the career fall-off and my little chunk of the global low-level anxiety, then I'm OK. Of course, there are some issues surrounding the engagement ring in my jacket pocket. And then there was that piece in *The Guardian* about the crisis in Rhenish capitalism, the other one about Israel getting punchy again, inflation trending upward, the ozone hole, the rising seas, England having no bowling, the increasing incidence of motor neurone disease, the long, cool freewheel towards death. But apart from those things, and everybody's got those things, I'm doing just fine. I move my hand back into my jacket pocket to feel the gnarly irregularity of the ring against the satin lining. It is like a loose tooth, the shape nuggety and sensuously interesting, asking to be nagged at.

– I honestly don't think I am stressed. Actors like me don't get stressed. We don't have much to get stressed about.

Fineman pushes the pad away. He jams his right index finger into his ear and rootles around, grimacing.

– And these . . . problems. Are they always with the same woman? I mean, are you married, Mr Moon?

– No, I'm not.

– So it's been with a variety of women, these . . . problems?

– No, just one.

– Your girlfriend.

– Yes.

– And how long have you been with this . . . girlfriend?

– Eight years.

He sniffs like he's snorting a rope of coke off a stripper's haunch, suddenly on to something.

– And do you ever wake up with erections?

Erections plural. I'd love to wake up like that, erect in multiples every morning like some Hindu cock god, sprouting and lolling everywhere.

– Every now and then.

– So it's probably not totally a physiological thing.

– That's a relief.

– Well, it shouldn't be. Just because it's not physiological doesn't mean it's not difficult to deal with.

He enjoys saying this; it sounds pat and over rehearsed,

14

some new bit of received wisdom deployed to scare the lupins out of his patients.

– This . . . girlfriend. Attractive woman is she?

– I think so, obviously.

– Obviously. On the way here this morning, Mr Moon, did you look at women at all?

– Of course, a bit.

– Did you have libidinous feelings for them?

– Some of them.

– How's your masturbating currently?

– Jesus, doctor.

– You don't have to answer.

– Well, I have a – masturbate occasionally, like anybody else.

– And no problems there sustaining . . .

– Sometimes, I suppose. I'm not quite as keen as I once was, but who is?

– Have you experimented with pornography? Magazines, erotic novels, videos, internet, cd-rom, dvd?

– It depends what you mean by 'experimented'.

He sniffs again – just clearing up the last dregs from her belly button – then turns his eyes back to his pad.

– I can only think of one thing I could *possibly* mean by 'experimented'.

– Well, yes, I've experimented.

– And no . . . problems there?

– No. Not really.

– So you could say that your libido is all right, but your current . . . context for its expression may not be.

– What else did they teach you at euphemism school?

– Ever used a hooker?

– No.

– Would you like to?

– I don't know, what do you think?

– Two hookers, maybe – a Jap, a Swede, whispering 'fuck

me harder' in broken English – maybe three, a Bangladeshi, a redhead, a Latino. Three-fifths of the Spice Girls pawing at you for mouth action?

– What?

He shrugs.

– If you don't like the euphemisms.

– I may be recording this conversation.

– If you are, I advise you to listen very carefully to what you've said, and draw your own conclusions.

– What, like for instance book myself a hooker?

– Or three.

I gesture at the velvet portrait.

– And how does your wife feel about this?

– My ex-wife? She couldn't care less. She sunk her erotic energy into interior design a decade ago.

– Ahh, I'm sorry.

– Don't be, Mr Moon. I've never felt better.

He smiles briefly, raises his eyebrows cheekily.

– Are you being *serious*?

– All I'm saying is, it may be worth a try. I can give you a number if you like.

– Does my insurance cover it?

– Patrick, I've been a doctor a long time. My diagnosis of the human condition? We're all killing ourselves by not doing the things we want to do. My own solution: divorce and paying for sex three times a week.

He leans back in his chair.

– It's an interesting philosophy.

– It works for me.

– I'm astonished.

– And of course there's always Viagra.

– I won't touch it.

– Why not?

– It's cheating.

– It's cheating.

16

– I like doing things the right way.

He opens his mouth to speak, then doesn't bother. I prompt him:

– Yes?

– Nothing, off you go. I've got another appointment.

– Is that it?

– Two things: Dr Fineman says lay off the drugs, do some exercise and have a good, solid think. Benny Fineman says get yourself a hooker. What's to lose?

He slides a business card across the desk to me. I take it without reading it. I stand and think about shaking hands with him, but don't. I'm almost light-hearted. There is a poster on the back of Fineman's door: 'Anatomy and Physiology of Erection', with a series of three drawings: 'The Flaccid Penis', 'The Tumescent Penis', 'The Erect Penis'. It's a kind of torture, all these representations of perfectly healthy organs in the house of genital agony, like having Mars Bar posters in the diabetes ward. There is a paragraph on the poster, linked to a picture, a vertical drawing of a 'glans' which looks from above like two bloodshot blue-bottle eyes. 'The engorged corpora become rigid with trapped blood – the rigid corpora are hard enough for insertion of the penis during intercourse.' It reads like a hard-nosed précis of all pornography ever written. The only difference is that the accompanying picture is of a feasibly sized dick, not some Spam-coloured rolling pin. Which gives me a thought.

– OK, Doc. One last thing.

Fineman looks up from his pad and squints as if to say, 'Haven't you gone yet? I've got dicks to think about.'

– Put me in a decile.

– What?

– Well, you'd know better than anyone. What decile am I in, size-wise?

– A decile?

17

– Top ten per cent, bottom ten per cent.

– Oh, I'd say you're about average.

– *About* average.

– Yes. Common-or-garden size. Let's just say you won't feature in the textbooks for either reason, big or small.

– Thanks.

I walk back into the reception area, approach the exquisite Laura, for the moment in lacquer, foundation, tights and a sensible worsted suit, but surely underneath a filthy, seething riot of working-class squirm and urge.

– Everything's fine. Just a quick check in three weeks' time.

She flicks through the desk diary, obviously speculating about my herpes, thrush, gonorrhoea, crabs, warts, non-gonococcal urethritis, scrotal gangrene, leprosy, whatever.

– Fancy a date?

– Three weeks' time, then, the thirtieth all right?

– For the date?

– For your appointment.

Mr Softee, I mean, Mr Moon.

2

The question is, then, how do you end up impotent and unemployed simultaneously? I try not to dwell on this too much. History is pretty much bunk. All that: 'If I had taken a left turn on Regent Street, got on the Underground the day I met Susie rather than going to The Circle I would now be either a) a shop assistant, b) playing third base for the San Diego Padres, c) about to be inaugurated as the new Shah of Iran.' To hell with it. Wondering about your past turns out to be as much an exercise in fantasy as speculating about your future – if anything more futile, because what's done really is done. Even Stalin scratching non-people from the negatives only changed history for other people, not for himself.

What if I'd pursued my piano? What if I'd kissed Martin Houlihan, as I so nearly did one watery sunlit morning after an all-night strike party in 1988? What if I had become a Rosicrucian? Then the only thing I can be sure of is that I'd still be asking 'what if', each question sprouting infinite future 'what ifs', 'what ifs' multiplying at light speed like cracks whispering across an infinite ice-field.

So as the past is just the world's most difficult probability puzzle, I'd rather think ahead: a gratifyingly simple, rising gradient, or an image, say, of an escalator reaching up into a glassy atrium with my scrawny-assed silhouette receding towards the ball of light at its apex. However, these pictures don't currently have much credibility. Instead, the future currently looks murky and complicated. I realize I've got some explaining to do. So 'what if' may not be the right question, but 'what happened' really should be addressed.

July 1991, Derek McCandless, the theatre critic of *The T——*, lead review, page 3, headline: 'Must-see Macbeth'. I read and re-read it until I knew it better than the 'Our Father':

Patrick Moon's Macbeth is a tour de force. First of all, he is an inordinately tall, thin young man and brings an aston-ishing restless, gawky energy to the role. The director, Graham Furnish, uses this physical conspicuity to great effect. One gets the feeling that almost nothing could ever fit him properly. His body is gangly, parts of it appearing to move independ-ently of others. All this nervy physical energy expresses with ample eloquence the unspeakable, unmotivated ambition that dwells within the character.

Indeed, such is Moon's scale and so dominating his psy-chotic energy that it is difficult to imagine that there are many parts in the repertoire big enough for him.

Blah blah blah, lighting this, supporting cast that, then:

Moon gives credibility and grandeur to his character's tragic predicament. A fundamental truth explored in the play is that we are not always who we choose to be. To this truism, Moon adds the nuance that we never can be who we choose to be because we have different plans for ourselves than our conscious mind is aware of. He is subtle, a brilliant verse speaker, literate and has tragic scale. There is so much more to say about this production. The only important thing is: see it at your earliest convenience, if not sooner.

Suddenly, then, two years out of RADA and from nowhere I was 'hot'. Ask me what it feels like to achieve everything you've ever dreamed of, and I am one of the few people who can tell you. I am convinced that my preconscious mind was aware of its desire to act. It could have started when I emerged from my mother blue, glutinous and mute: they slapped me on the back, I emitted a perfect middle C and the room applauded. Or even before that, when I was a ricocheting, gin-fuelled tadpole, colliding with the soft ball of potential inside my mother. The skies cracked open, Saturn entered Uranus, the fairies sneezed, Jesus wept and Patrick Moon was an actor.

Aged three I'd clip-clop round our flat in Marylebone in my mother's cork-soled platforms and a feather boa pretending to be Tallulah Bankhead. My parents never discouraged me because they knew what I was going through: they're both actors too. There was no possibility of escape; it possesses you, you can't fight it.

Aged six I played Joseph, the Holy Spirit *and* Harold Wilson in a school nativity play audaciously scripted by Miss Darby, our crypto-communist art teacher. I was a ham, I hogged the stage, I stole fruit gums from the Magis' crowns, on stage, for laughs. I had Wilson's hunch-backed pipe-sucking sneer to a tee. The audience loved me, and I loved them back, which made them love me more. At eleven, installed at an all-boys Catholic school, I was a tiny winsome Desdemona. Tommy Grady, blacked up and boiling with savage nobility, cusping six feet and nearing fifteen stone, broke me up like a sparrow's egg. The women wrung pints from their handkerchiefs as they limped out into the Dettol-stench of St Augustine's corridors.

21

At sixteen, perhaps overstretching, I persuaded Mr O'Malley, the English teacher who ran our drama society, to do *Lear* as the summer play. O'Malley was a quiet, feeble-willed man who spent a lot of time before curtain-up standing in the dressing room, smiling wanly as the young boys affixed their codpieces. I, of course, was to be Lear, tall now and having started shaving at least once a week. 'You could do him in a loincloth?!' was the phrase which accompanied his capitulation, but I had more on my mind than wardrobe. I decided that I could play Lear *and* the Fool, the latter as a voice in Lear's head, or – making concessions to the philistine nature of the audience – present the Fool as Lear's glove puppet. O'Malley concurred, and spent many hours with me after school, refining my verse speaking and stroking my hair.

Three years after I left St Augustine's, they found O'Malley hanging from a door frame, trouserless, head in a sack, a slice of tangerine between his teeth and a dead macaw clinging to his face. Perhaps it was an image of me in doublet and hose that accompanied his acidic, squawking exit from life. Such is love.

But anyway, I continued to act. A school play every term, the West London Children's Theatre four times a year, auditions for commercials, bit parts on TV. Every other belief, in the Catholic Church, in QPR, in my parents' infallibility, was lost or fatally weakened, but this one remained: Patrick Moon is an actor.

There was never any question. Until, that is, I met Tim Donachie. Nature does its casting sessions early: juve leads to the left on the dais, character actors to the right, in the pit. Donachie was a luminous, glossy-haired, beautiful, energetic, gravely talented juve lead. I was a looming, jug-eared character actor who he could blow off stage simply by pushing back his hair. The looks and the talent, he had them both, and of course he knew it. He tore up women

22

like wet tissue paper, his teachers loved him as if he was an only son, other boys tried to hate him while barely able to suppress their love. Hence, the gaze of rapt ambivalence so many of them wore as they watched him at work. If he'd only been equipped with the looks, then his talent was obviously open to ridicule. If he only had the talent, then he could have been just another one of the boys. He had both; we were in awe. Now, as he reminds me often in his pithy yet riveting e-mails, he's in LA, on the verge of something spectacular. So after two years of drama school, the existence of Tim Donachie made it clear to me that I was in fact a civilian, nose pressed to the invisible membrane that separates the proscenium from the crowd. The mathematics are simple. If you have the looks and the talent, there is a one in a hundred chance that you'll make it as an actor. If you have either one of the two, the odds increase by a factor of fifty. If you have neither, go into telephone sales.

And whereas the talent is one thing, the looks is quite another.

Physical appearance is a difficult subject for me. Those minuscule distinctions – half an inch on the nose, quarter of an inch between the eyes, a mouth so big rather than so big, the head shaped like this rather than like that, the teeth straight and true or too big with the tendency to rest on the lower lip, unmanageable ears – these are the tiny, accidental outcomes, scripted way down in the DNA boilerplate, which separate character actors from juve leads, or love from indifference. It doesn't matter how much we prize diligence, bravery, kindliness; these qualities recede instantly in the face of beauty. You can forgive bad character in someone who is beautiful, because everyone has bits of them that could be described as bad character, but so few people are beautiful. This is why there are so many films about loving the inner person rather than the outward appearance, and

23

why they always feature beautiful actresses. They fulfil two fundamental desires simultaneously: our need to be told that appearance doesn't matter and our need to look at beautiful things.

I still look at Donachie and think 'wow'. I am also striking anyplace, of course: six foot five and a half, the generic crew-cut, ears on stalks, the heron-like angles badly concealed in monochrome clothes, my wrists always bonily visible. Not 'wow' though. 'Eek!' perhaps.

But thank God I'm not a woman. The ugly actress is consigned to playing spinsters in commercials, the Ugly Woman as opposed to the Beautiful Woman in bad comedy, the witch, the lesbian, the born-again Christian. The ugly actress must become acquainted with unhappiness and psychological deficits, because that is what people will assume her ugliness signifies.

And a large part of my talent was my desire to succeed. I imagined that the sheer intensity of that desire could override my appearance. In addition to this, ugly men have got Shakespeare. Straight out of RADA, I was Macbeth in Graham Furnish's 'landmark production'.

Now that he's disappeared into obscurity I feel that I can be honest without jeopardising any future job prospects: Furnish is a hideous mimsy little queer: mannered, pretentious, manipulative, abusive, and bloated with a sense of his own fabulousness. He also had the best theatrical sense of anyone I have ever met. I hated him and loved working for him.

Maybe his talents were too old-fashioned. Firstly, he was obsessed with speaking verse correctly, that is as if it is being extemporised in the mouth of the actor. In order to do this, you have to know the lines so well that they live like bacteria in your guts, bubble up through your being into the facial cavities and are spoken before they are thought about. You also have to know what the words *mean*. I spent hours and days and nights with Furnish buckling my mind to fully grasp his preternaturally subtle understanding of what my character was saying. Furnish cared nothing about anything but the play, the words, and how his ego could feed on the way he got the cast to act it, speak them.

This kind of stuff is work like no other. I would emerge from my sessions with Furnish feeling battered, dismantled, cleaned out, re-wired, reassembled and pristine, exhausted but in possession of some curious, jagged, masculine energy.

We opened quietly then we got the review I excerpt above. Within a week (when it happens it happens so fast), we were as hot as the surface of the sun. We were sold out so bad that when people rang for seats the ticket agents burst out laughing. Furnish primped and preened and was magnificent at parties. I walked on air, my jaw set at an imperious aspect, talked passionately late at night at private drinking clubs about the language, the language that's what it is, you know, plain and simple, the *words*, don't you see?

It may or may not be right to mention that at this time I was screwing like a ravening panther. The recipients were reduced to asthmatic husks nightly, barely capable of getting their come-down cigarette into the correct orifice on account of the tears and trembling. Post-coital *tristesse* as Hamas funeral.

We secured a transfer to the West End. Furnish threw a party at The Circle, which at that time was writers, actors, artists, directors. Strict rules: no PRs, no TV riff-raff, and no, I repeat, *no* advertising guys. Susie was a friend of someone who knew the actor playing Macduff. She was buzzed at getting into The Circle because she'd heard all about it and hoped soon to become a member as her first novel had just been published to gaudy reviews and respectable commercial success. She looked superb, Spanish or Italian (though actually Home Counties via Yorkshire), black hair, wet, black eyes, aggressive Jewish-looking nose, clean mouth always on the verge of laughing, that ass!

The night we met I was flying. Not cocaine, because I had no need: the smallest amount of alcohol would impact with the chemicals fizzing round my body and transform me into a social magnifico, expansive, devastating, relentless (it's what success feels like). We were introduced and heard everything we needed to know from each other in the first exchange:

– I'm Patrick, I'm an actor.

– I'm Susie, I'm a writer.

We spoke for half an hour, the conversation barely disguised foreplay, nearly full sex, no kidding. I was cantilevered over my hard-on by the time we hailed the cab; she was twisting in pre-orgasmic distress before we'd given directions to my place.

She was drunk, the mania and velocity of vodka. I tried to slow her down, stroking the stiffness and hyperactivity out of her arms in the back of the taxi. All the while, I still can taste it almost, the desire. It was like a thin burning skin, screaming to be slit. As we kissed she laughed into my open mouth.

– Sometimes kissing's the silliest thing.

– Oh yeah, if you think about anything for too long.

– But that doesn't mean I want to stop.

We stumbled up the stairs to my Bayswater studio, me in front, her breathing heavily, rummaging in her handbag.

– Wankers.

– What is it?

– I can't find my keys.

– But this is *my* house.

– Oh my God, you're so right.

As soon as we were inside she attacked, bumping me up against the wall, bracing her legs around mine, forcing me

26

to kiss her against my natural angle, head cocked to the left, not to the right. I caught sight of us in the plateglass mirror, twined in a double helix, and winked at myself. We staggered into the bedroom in a barely pre-orgasmic three-legged race, banging our heads, laughing, snorting and snuffling, our clothes suddenly unremovable.

– Are you on the pill?

– Yeah, but you're using one anyway.

I asked her to try to put it on with her teeth, but she was too impatient, so I rolled it on myself, arrogantly eschewing foreplay, and moved straight into it. The first time she pushed me off and wriggled from under me before I came.

– Come on here.

She clawed at her glistening breasts and neck.

Surprised but grateful, like getting a Christmas present that wasn't what you wanted but was arguably better, I obliged. Afterwards, she went straight to the toilet for ten minutes.

– What was that all about?

– Quadrilateral contraception: me on the pill, you wear a condom, come on the outside.

– That's only three things.

– I had my toes crossed as well.

I giggled. Good sign, laughing with a girl.

– I've always wanted to ask this question: how different are they? The feeling inside?

She sucked her cheeks in and stared at the ceiling. I could see her eyes gleaming in the dark like black raindrops.

– It's like when you use a new toothbrush. Same but different.

– Not what I was expecting.

She turned towards me and curled her head under my chin.

– You realise I don't even know you; you might chop me into bits and flush me down the sink.

27

– I'll order you a cab then.

– Don't be stupid. I'm staying.

My theory is that people don't change, just reveal more of themselves to you over time. They start off easy to figure out, get more difficult, become easy again, then get tougher and so on – new levels of complexity revealed, then everything made simple for a moment before you wander back into confusion. People are like foreign languages or like chess. People are like *Macbeth*.

And words don't help, because words are general, meant to apply to anything: there are no words that get close to describing her. People don't have their own words or even their own set of words: forget even trying. She's really Susie, she is driving at eighty miles an hour through Glencoe with the roof down, talking on the phone, in headscarf and Jackie O shades, scrabbling for a camera to get a shot of herself in the side mirror while trying to change the tape to *Songs for Swinging Lovers*; she is dancing to 'Satisfaction' with my father at his sixtieth birthday, stomping round him like Mick Jagger, pelvis forward, fist pumping the air, chin held high as he does the twist eyes half-closed; or she is standing on a bed in a hotel in Vientiane wearing only a shower cap, smoking, screaming at me to kill a lizard that is in fact one of her pop socks; or she is lying in bed in the dark with a terrible hangover saying that it's weird that people stopped wearing hats in the late Fifties; or she is in evening dress thrashing me with a wooden spoon in the kitchen of her parents' house because she found me outside the party hugging an ex-girlfriend, laughing like a drain; or she is in her pyjamas, running on the spot in our bedroom to work off the lager she was 'forced' to drink at some book launch she went to:

– I'll look like Natalie Wood's waterlogged corpse.

However, there is one word that gets close to what she's about: that word is ambition. In her personal life she is singularly unambitious, or it's unlikely she would have settled for me. In her professional life, though, there it is, coursing through her body, intrinsic to her like spinal fluid or something gently spinning at her core: the need to feel that her influence is increasing, pulsing out into the atmosphere like radio waves, being received by people. It's what keeps her eyes blinking in the dark of our bedroom when she should be fast asleep, makes her flirt with middle-aged men and not feel any shame. Late at night, if you listen close enough, you can hear her ticking.

She doesn't want global idolatry. She doesn't want to be a thing in herself, a Madonna or J-Lo or Cher. Regardless of the talent and the looks, she wouldn't want to be that lonely, and how terrifying to be marooned in one's own myth. All she wants is prominence in her peer group. She'd like to have herself quoted back to her on afternoon radio or late night TV, to be a darling of the literati, mediati, arty-ati. It's a limited and not very admirable ambition, but I don't think she can help it. She just wants her friends to think more of her: if she can't have love, then admiration and envy will have to do.

But to go back again, to eight years ago, the simple phase, or the phase when ease and difficulty alternate ten times every day. The name of this condition used to be sexual love, now is called 'fancying the arse off someone'. The quality of the emotion itself probably hasn't changed, nor have its manifestations. I would leave the taste of her on my face all day, until the stage make-up was caked over it, then re-anoint from the bowl of her pelvis at night, first thing, mid-morning, whenever. She was typical of her generation in that her blow job was nuanced, intricate and strikingly constructed. I had the feeling it had been brought to this pitch of perfection through many hours of study, certainly some desk work, probably some practice on inanimate objects, probably in front of a mirror, possibly with the use of recording equipment. And the investment paid off. She could have got a patent on it: The My Sweet Lord.

But more, much more.

The desperate, ugly, semi-violent arguments, always about some other girl, some other boy, jealousy, possession, neediness, fragility, fury, beatific peacefulness, redeemed or cemented by one of those involuntary internal swoops of love, chromatic and vertiginous like bad romantic music, the first and most debilitating symptom of the condition that is, I'm going to go ahead and say it, sexual love.

And more, the external aspect, the way we were in the world: the parties where we cast ourselves as amazing and amazed, watching each other hungrily as we worked the rooms, separate but on the verge of cleaving back together at any point; the sense that we were in some kind of aura of invulnerability. The fact that, despite the frequent crippling spasms of jealousy (that we liked to glut ourselves on so that their abatement was so much sweeter), we were each other's. Like everyone else (we imagined), we were in love with the image of us, but unlike everyone else, only I went home with her, and only she went home with me, and only we knew what it felt like to be the two of us alone.

And for that brief time, more than a month, less than a year, we thought we were special. Of course, we weren't television/movie/pop music special, but that wasn't what we wanted, anyway. We were a hangover from another era in that we affected to despise pop culture. Susie, I discovered early on, would rather have had dinner with Milan Kundera than Mick Jagger. We had a dated notion of London literary parties at which editors, authors, actors and musicians talked brilliantly about art and books, didn't get too drunk, plotted affairs that would consist of Continental sex and beautifully written dialogue. And it seemed almost palpable because we were a special couple, in love and *doing good work*, and when everything else fell away love and

30

good work were all that mattered to us. We had replaced what a previous generation had derived from political idealism with a kind of artistic equivalent: good work, rather than good deeds. What we hadn't yet realised was that an even newer idealism was emerging that was entirely concerned with appearing on TV. For that time, however, success in the wider world was a side-effect of doing good work, which in itself was sufficient. We occupied the intersection of the almost mutually exclusive force fields of credibility and success. It couldn't last. As it was, we lived in that slender ellipse for perhaps one hundred and fifty days.

Her novel disappeared, buried under the rubble-pile of newer novels. The ones that replaced hers were not that dissimilar in style and theme, and were greeted with equally histrionic reviews: 'staggering', 'strikingly mature', 'the emergence of a considerable new talent', 'sensitive, subtle and wildly, wildly funny' (why not three 'wildly's? why not three 'funny's?). *The Breakdown Heart* was perhaps an over-candid reworking of her childhood and adolescence, with the statutory child-abuse sub-plot and climactic wedding in Paris to leave the appropriate romantic glimmer in the minds of readers who didn't necessarily believe in happy, glamorous endings but need them because all the alternatives are intolerable.

This mild and, it transpired, brief period of success came at the lasting expense of her relationship with her father. He was understandably appalled by the portrayal of the father in the book as an insidiously silent tyrant, with his liking for 'extra special goodnight kisses' ('kisses can hurt more than hits, didn't you know this, Daddy?') and 'Daddy's favourite cuddles'. When the book disappeared, the estrangement remained. In fact, it increased, driven by a shame and sadness on his part and a stubbornness on hers that baffled observers from outside the family. I tried for a while to talk her round – 'It's not worth losing a father over', other soap-opera bromides – but it was no good. She is as obstinate as is he, and ultimately, inevitably, I went quiet. And anyway, other people's families are no place for strangers: their power-balances are too intricate and subtle, their atmospheres too humid.

Her second book was never finished. This fact only served to alienate her from her father even more. His argument was that it was proof that the first book represented her true feelings because, when required to, she actually found it impossible to write something that wasn't as an allegory on her childhood, or a parody of it, or vengeance for it. She pretended to stop caring, and rarely speaks to him, never talks about him. I stopped trying to make her even talk about it years ago. It's just some deep-down, hard, unchangeable part of her, and we all have those.

So, discouraged by the harsh and mysterious operations of the fiction market, she started writing features for teen magazines and tabloids and became good at it. Eight years later she writes a column for *The T——*, does celebrity profiles, occasionally gets a gig on talk radio, riffing about bad TV and sex: 'So, Susie, what is it in the *zeitgeist* that makes this show succeed? What does this say about England now? No, no, but tell me what do men *really* think about cunnilingus?' She swims with it all now. She's a soap addict, reads *Sleb*, occasionally re-reads it, only looks at a novel if it's become compulsory, says that Britney's awesome and sort of means it. On balance, I now know, she'd rather have dinner with Eminem than Saul Bellow. In many ways she's happy.

As for me, after the Furnish *Macbeth*, something happened which my agent described as 'unusual if not entirely unprecedented': I stopped getting work. That is, I was offered theatre jobs I thought I didn't want or need – in Bolton, St Albans, Chichester, Norwich – and I turned them down. By the time it became clear that this was the only kind of work

I was likely to get, I had lost my confidence and started to get fewer auditions, and often when I did I just didn't bother to turn up at all.

What happened? I still don't know. My feeling is that maybe the early success wrecked me, raised expectations that it was improbable I could ever meet, given the raw material. Spoiled for the work that I deserved, under-qualified for the work I expected, I occupied some actor's purgatory, where time moved forward but I did not. Soon I was irrelevant; not long after that I was superfluous. In 1993, Furnish cast me as Richard II in his new production at The Donmar, but it never happened. The money disappeared, then he disappeared. Over the years, I've noticed his name attached to some tiny thing at the Edinburgh Fringe or off-off-off-Broadway, always Shakespeare or at least Jacobean, always unremarked upon: *King John* or *Measure for Measure* or *Volpone*. The thought of the years of constant study fills me with sadness and admiration.

After I stopped getting the work I wanted I became convinced that I was right and the world was wrong. At some point I managed to disassociate the ensuing melancholia from a feeling that it was caused by my status as a misunderstood world genius. I think this may have occurred during my first season of panto. Walking on stage dressed as a 400-pound Marie Antoinette lookalike can certainly instil a feeling of melancholia, but this feeling is difficult to confuse with the cosmic, non-specific gloom of genius. In fact, one can be all too specific in identifying its cause: it is a rainy Saturday afternoon in an eighty-per-cent-empty theatre in Blackburn, Lancashire. You are living in digs above a tobacconist's with a gaunt widow who insists that you call her Lady B and every day makes you flasks of Bovril you have not requested. You are being paid Equity minimum. You are about to say, 'Ooh goodness, not in those booties,' and your girdle is killing you. You can see out of the corner of your eye a child on the front row gently, rhythmically flicking you the Vs.

This was the melancholy of mediocrity. It is like a kiss on the cheek at the end of a sweet evening with a girl who doesn't love you, or a municipal worker sweeping up confetti from the steps of a register office, or calling your mother from a phone box in Stoke to tell her you won't be home for Christmas. It is the feeling I had on an early spring afternoon a year ago as I performed my one-man show, *Who is This Guy Shakespeare Anyway?*, at an old people's home in Norbury, South London.

I had persuaded myself that my life had been greatly enhanced by Shakespeare, and I retained the belief that he could do the same for others. The fact that my single acting success had been in Furnish's *Macbeth* of course had something to do with this, but it went back further than that. My first encounter occurred as a ten-year-old boy when my father took me to see *Julius Caesar* at The National. I watched from the front row, by turns transfixed, astonished, terrified, aroused and finally exhausted but replete. Shakespeare for me was what sucking butane from a canister was for most of my classmates.

I thought that I could bring sublimity into the lives of others, and of course also imagined two or three eulogising features in the colour supplements. A photoshoot – me in the middle of a crowd of young people now wired for the Bard, a caption along the lines of, 'Patrick Moon with friends and admirers: "If people can't go to Shakespeare, then I'll take him to them."' I was thinking maybe a simple white dress shirt, jeans and sneakers, perhaps a crewcut, the get-up of the artistic Evangelist. Maybe a Yorick skull for comedic potential. Me on a barstool, chin resting on hand, probably smiling so I don't look too monomaniacal.

I spent three months getting the show together. My idea was a kind of stand-up summary of the life and work, done chronologically. Humble beginnings in Stratford, early career as actor, quick trot through the early comedies, marriage to Anne, maybe small gobbets of *Venus and Adonis* and *The Rape of Lucrece*, the big sonnets, return to personal life with the death of Hamnet, then into the ensuing tragedies, lots of *Lear* and *Hamlet*, a look at the genesis and development of The Globe, his role at King James's court, a brief survey of contemporaries, and cap it off with highlights from the Romances and a coda on influence through the ages.

My first draft came in at seven and a quarter hours.

After some drastic surgery I got it down to a highlights reel of about three and a half, three if I omitted the collaborations with Beaumont and Fletcher and the examination of the working methods, which was a little dry in places anyway.

With this new abridgement, I secured several engagements – mainly, it must be said, from nursing homes – and set out on what I thought would be a few months of work that would nourish the soul not just of my audience but mine as well.

Which brings me to this afternoon a little over a year ago. The performance space was a semi-circle formed in front of the fireplace in the lounge of the Bridewell Oaks Retirement Community in Forest Hill. Mrs Leacock, the boss of the place, was a very pleasant, somewhat harassed-looking woman who offered me the following advice:

– No sudden movements, don't worry if they start milling about a bit and keep the tempo up.

I had acclimatised to the smell of piss and hairspray and the gentle but insistent humming of a hundred massed hearing aids and had begun to relax into the gig. A man who called himself Captain Arthur Burroughs had been ushered back to his quarters after he spent the first half-hour of the show getting up from his seat, wandering up to the stage area and offering me directions to Stroud.

I was about a third of the way through the show, just out of Feste's song (which I accompanied on the ukulele, played for laughs, as we were about to enter a somewhat dark passage: the death scenes of *Hamlet*, *Lear*, *Coriolanus* and *Macbeth* done back to back) when a woman two rows from the back turned to her neighbour and said in a rather loud, clear voice:

– Can we switch over now? It's awfully boring.

To which her friend replied, in a deafening stage whisper:

– No we can't. Mrs Leacock said he was from the special school.

I continued, somewhat disconcerted, through Laertes and Fortinbras, recovered some brio as Lear crouched over the dead Cordelia, and was embarking with considerable vigour on Othello's last speech, when I heard from centre-left a small, desperate voice say:

– Oh please, please, somebody make him stop.

The confidence was sucked out of me like shit from an aeroplane toilet. I halted in mid-sentence, bowed and packed up in heartbroken silence. I left to the sound of one arthritic hand clapping, enclosed in a bubble of grief. I haven't worked since, and am beginning to think that I won't work again. But hey, I'm getting over it – like the universe is getting over the Big Bang.

The escalator climbing to the sun keeps moving on up but I can't get on. I stare upwards into the light, with a limp dick.

3

I leave Fineman's and am unsurprised to find myself with nothing to do. I mooch round town and drink a quart of cappuccino, which makes me skittish, so take half an e, which mongs me out, pick up a *Sleb* and look at the pictures over and over again over more coffee. We're all killing ourselves by doing things we don't want to do. Got to get out of W1 before the rush hour starts.

Home now to the Islington flat (she pays, of course). I go up to the bedroom, take the ring from my jacket pocket and tuck it into a pair of winter socks deep in the back of my underwear drawer. I hear Susie opening the front door and the slide and scrape as she throws her car keys onto the kitchen worktop. Then the soft unsnap of the fridge door and the long delay as she filters her genuine need for refreshment through the more complicated demands of her eating disorder. Hers is not particularly severe as eating disorders go, no worse than mine, probably, and a damn sight better than most of her friends'. Her pattern is consistent: start with health food, lo-/no-fat yoghurt maybe, or fruit or even some celery, then graze a little on cheese, using a sharp knife to shave off just one or two slender curls, then bigger lumps, interspersed with a fingerful of stale tortilla chips, perhaps, or if she's being really good, a few grapes. Read a magazine so it feels as if it isn't really happening. Then back into the fridge, but nothing's quite right, so pull off a corner of pitta and chew on it, wondering what to have for supper, then finally open the freezer, take out the Ben and Jerry's, microwave it for twenty seconds then eat the entire tub in eight minutes while watching *EastEnders*. A robust dramatic structure to her food problem: Good Intentions – Evil Thoughts – Escalation – Apocalypse. Lately, my disorder is simpler. I just don't eat. It's getting more difficult by the hour to tolerate the thought of things passing through my system. I'm nervous, fractious, disconnected, preoccupied. I've got the symptoms of a man deeply in love, but I'm not. I'm deeply in something, though.

I go down to the kitchen where she's at the cheese-paring stage.

– Oooh. Who's a quiet Moonman?

– Just mooning about.

– Well, you are the Moon.

The tone, the dated love talk too easy, too difficult to change now.

– What've you been up to?

– Upstairs.

– What happened at the doctor's?

– Apparently I have the most amazing balls.

– Ah, Mr Gatsby, all of New York is talking about your balls.

She runs the blade of the knife down the face of the cheese, thumbs the curl into her mouth. She's focused on this, doesn't look at me.

– My cock, on the other hand, still has a low profile.

– Indeed, it hasn't been around in ages.

– Thanks for that.

– Sorry.

– No, thanks, really.

38

I see her shake her head, annoyed. I open the fridge door; there's never anything to eat.

– So, what's wrong?

– He spoke in riddles. Thinks it's probably just a phase.

– That's what *I* said!

– So, why did you force me to go then?

– Oh, stop it.

– It was a farce. It's all in my mind.

– Just because it's in your mind doesn't mean it's not real.

– That's what *he* said.

– HA! It's so easy, this doctor thing.

– I thought we might talk about my medical problems rather than exult in how very clever you are.

– Oh, fuck off.

She's been at the gym. She's not built for cycling shorts and lycra tank tops. The top has a starburst on it and the acronym 'JFDI'. Everybody loves Susie; she's so funny, so 'feisty', a 'good laugh', and I love her too, there is no question about that. I close the fridge door, lean against the counter, arms folded, hands tucked into my armpits, look into the middle distance. It has an uncertain meaning. I've seen this pose in many movies. She looks at me and tips her head to one side. This means sorry. She puts her arms out, inviting a hug. Her arms bend oddly at the elbows. I kiss her but with prim lips. She smells of Parmesan, sour-sweet and sicky. We're still coiled together, her arms loosely on my shoulders, her smiling up at me. I notice not for the first time that slowly she is beginning to resemble her father, something about the relation between her nose and mouth. I can't bear this thought, so I pull her close and press my nose into her hair, a shaggy bob. Now I can smell grease, sweat and vanilla.

Still looped together, I start to grind my hips a little, but become quickly discouraged and push away.

39

– What about you?

– Oh humdrum. Did a couple of starts at a column, got nowhere.

As she says herself, she's a newspaper columnist who used to be a journalist. When she first mooted the idea to her editor for her current job, she thought she'd never get away with it: a weekly 600-word column called (ironically, or at least self-consciously) 'Me, Myself, I' about, well, about whatever Susie wanted it to be about. 'The travails of an urban thirty-something woman', 'The ups and downs of love and life in the big city', 'The noxious keening of a solipsistic nymphomaniac', 'English journalism at its lowest ebb'. The first two quotations are from women, introducing her on radio chat shows, the latter two from men in broadsheet diary pieces. It has been running for over a year, and has become, according to reader surveys, the favourite bit of the newspaper for young affluent women, exactly the demographic where *The T*—— has struggled, and exactly the type of readership the cosmetics, fashion and car advertisers want. It should be the easiest thing in the world to write about yourself, but in fact, 'Me' isn't about the Susie I know. It's about this character called Susie who looks like her, lives her life, has her boyfriend, her job, her friends and family, but who *definitely isn't Susie*. In fact, she never made mention of her real life until recently. Until recently, Column Susie was a character; now the two are converging. I can't identify precisely the difference between Real Susie and Column Susie, but it's something to do with the voice: in real life she thinks of herself as serious-minded, considered, reasoned; in *The T*—— she's 'spunky', 'trilling', 'neurotic', prone to exclamation marks and gabbled asides, though still with 'something to say'. She's looking in the freezer now.

– I'm starving.

Just Fucking Do It, Patrick: run upstairs, get the ring and with

banging heart just blurt it out to her here and now when it's least
expected. Make it funny and incongruous and 'would you believe
he proposed to me in the kitchen', and then fuck her on the counter
because the decisiveness of the act will untangle you sexually and
you'll come like a shire horse and then again ten minutes later on
the bed and then once more in the bathroom five minutes after
that and the whole thing will be settled and on we go. Kids next,
just like their mother.

She takes out a basin of ice cream, removes the lid and
stabs at it with a fork. I leave the kitchen and hear the beep
and hum of the microwave. She comes into the sitting room,
turns on the TV. Is she so sure of me that she can afford to
turn herself into some fat bitch? But where the hell would
I go, with my body of work ancient unrecorded history and
a permanent soft-on?

– Do you have to watch *every single* soap opera on television?

– Oh, piss off. What the hell does it matter?

– It doesn't matter. But every single one, for God's sake?

She is considering saying something, almost stops herself, then:

– Do you have to visit *every single* porn site on the internet?

– What are you talking about?

– Next time you use my laptop, maybe you should
remember to delete the history file.

She carries on spooning the viscous sugar soup into her
mouth. I have to respond.

– Look – the doctor said I need to experiment.

She waves the spoon at me, keeps her eyes on the screen.

– Very good. Go on then and I'll watch TV. There must
be one Latino bitch-slut you haven't experimented with.

I watch her watching TV, have nothing to say. I go to the
spare room, fire up the laptop and check my e-mail.

*   *   *

41

I have a fan. Her name is Hillary and we have been corresponding for two years now. She writes about how much she admires me. Her tone is usually awkward, semi-literate, reserved, over-formal, but sometimes becomes slavish and embarrassingly sycophantic. I suck it up, of course, try not to get *too* embarrassed.

She saw my Macbeth – 'it is not saying too much, to say that in many respects this night changed my life, Mr Moon'. She continued to follow my career during the slow, excruciating descent to C-list panto, and touchingly still holds out hope for me now that I no longer exist. She found me on the Hotmail directory, her first contact tentative and sweet, and I responded with cool gratitude. We now exchange over-polite messages maybe once every two months. She is outraged and astonished that I'm not currently jetting between an Ibsen rehearsal at the National and the set of the new Scorsese movie in NYC. A recent e-mail consisted of a long essay on the history of the theatre, which blamed my slow period on the establishment of the Arts Council. Her thesis was prolix and not always clearly developed, but it appears that public subsidy ends up encouraging conservatism in choice of repertoire, casting and direction. I responded with hauteur that in my opinion the theatre was dead – too expensive and too poor at the same time, too uneven, too long, too flat-out *crap* – but thanked her for all her work, to which she replied that she 'could never regard efforts expended on my behalf as work'.

I try not to reply to her. The spasms of weird sycophancy have become more prevalent. It's all giving me a bad case of the spookiness.

Fans are spooky anyway. The panicky, dripping teenage girls pressed screaming against a boy band's limo windows are spooky. The quiet, pot-bellied thirty-year-old man with four thousand nine hundred sci-fi novels in his council flat in Sunderland is spooky. Women in velour tracksuits lining up peacefully at psychics' book-signings with photographs to have signed are spooky. Middle-aged men in sky-blue windcheaters, Marks and Spencer jeans and box-fresh HiTecs swaying and stamping arrhythmically at Elton John gigs, then voiding themselves of emotion as he sings 'Candle in the Wind': spooky. That lot, the Diana people, they were really spooky: the lonely flower-bearing pilgrims in Kensington Palace Gardens, milling in the dark, each hoping she was more distraught than the next, superstition born of bewilderment, worshipping her loveliness but also the gawkiness that kept her human. The placard outside Westminster Abbey: 'Wills and Harry – We Want to See You Cry' – those people were *really* spooky. Then, of course, the next year, when they tried to arrange an anniversary spook-in, no one turned up, because there was something on TV.

It can only be humbling to be presented with your fans. I once 'met' De Niro at a movie premiere (she got the tickets). Towering over him, his face approximately level with my elbows, I proceeded to drip a single chilly bead of sweat into his empty glass. I hung on his every statement, which was: 'Man, these cocktail waiters are *slow*.' The spookiest thing? I don't even particularly *like* De Niro. That night for half an hour he had my unconditional, spooky love.

Anyway, this is Hillary:

From: Hillary Kelly
To: pmoon109@hotmail.com
Subject: [No Subject]

Fear the stillness

Then, ten minutes later.

43

From: Hillary Kelly
To: pmoon109@hotmail.com
Subject: [No Subject]

Do not fear the stillness, Patrick. Fear the faint, peripheral stirrings.

I have not yet given her my home address.

To be fair to her, this was her spookiest ever set of messages and they were sent at three-thirty in the morning when the world is at its spookiest. But nor have I given her my phone number.

Hillary – I don't know. I imagine her as a mousy, stick-thin woman with big square specs, a born-again Christian perhaps. Maybe she lives above a Chinese restaurant on one of those Sixties shopping/residential strips: an off-licence, a tobacconist's, the Ho Lee Fook, a knick-knack shop, going bust, a greengrocer's going bust, three granny customers with their weekly basket of one parsnip, one cabbage, three tangerines each. Hillary sits in the one-bedroom flat sandbagged with showbiz biographies, and when she's not reading about Coral Brown or Noel Coward, watches BBC2 all night, probably the silver-framed Diana headshot on top of the telly. The bedroom overlooks the car park, aged Novas and Rovers; she stubs out one of her infrequent cigarettes in a Silver Jubilee ashtray, listens to Sondheim, treats herself to a couple of chocolates from the bedside box of Just Brazils. She lives in Bexleyheath, Hayes or Wembley 'just a hop on the train to the West End!', and when she's seen the show she'll have a cocktail in a hotel bar and read the programme. Once in a while, she gets a cab home – *What the hell, I've got nothing else to spend it on*. Maybe she keeps a scrapbook: photos from the papers stuck into a big, red album, a few notes about her favourite performers and performances

44

scribbled underneath the pictures. There are a few pages dedicated just to me, although it's so difficult to find recent photos.

I think of her out there in the shadowy ranks of the crowd, the box of light reflected in her specs, the ardent eyes unblinking, the unconditional love. I sigh, and gratitude and pity compete for primacy in my mind as I read:

From: Hillary Kelly
To: pmoon109@hotmail.com
Subject: [No Subject]

Just checking in! Thank you for your last note, but I don't think you should be so despondent! There are many many examples of fine actors (like yourself) rebuilding their careers in their 30s and even 40s! Also, kindness is rewarded always. Your kind words store up their reward on Broadway!!!!!!!!!
We will one day have that lunch!
Love
Hillary

I re-read it a couple of times, daring to believe that there may be truth in it. Oh Hillary, you don't know what you mean to me, you beautiful spooky thing.

4

No matter how much I want to pretend otherwise, lunch with one's agent is about money. Oh, the time is spent discussing who's up, who's down, which casting director is sucking which cock, which cock is narrowly evading being sucked by which actress, which actress now has a cock – all the usual. But eventually there is a moment when all the trivia recedes and you notice that money is standing front and centre.

There is only one person who understands this better than the actor: the actor's agent. She knows: through the mist of cliché and hyperbole she can discern with utter certainty that this 'celebrated performer', this man who 'has physical presence and energy', this 'fine verse speaker' actually turned in less than a thousand gross last year, net to agent perhaps one hundred pounds. The agent has no elitist qualms about equating talent with financial production because that is actually a pretty good description of the job. It is debatable whether I am even a going concern: when you factor in the phone bills, stationery, the man hours, the wear and tear on the office furniture, the decaff, the psychic toll, other depreciations, I am in all probability an expense. Which will explain the following telephone conversation:

46

– Hi, Patrick, it's Mary.

– Great, Mary, what's going on?

– About lunch on Wednesday . . .

– I'm looking forward to it.

– Can we reschedule?

– Because?

– Or make it a quickie?

– Because?

– I've got something at two.

– Then I'm happy to meet at twelve.

– I've got something at eleven-thirty.

– Let's make it twelve. Say Asia de Cuba?

– Twelve-thirty, Patrick, can't get there before that. Let's say twelve-thirty at Fredo's.

– Fredo's?

– No need to book, get us in and out quickly.

– All right, all right. Twelve-thirty at Fredo's.

The downward spiral of an actor's career expressed as a list of lunch venues. On signing out of drama school, it was L'Escargot, where I tried to appear rather grand and got caned on three carafes of Beaujolais and four tumblers of calvados and coke. Over the next few years a maintenance in standards, either in terms of credibility or menu quality: Joe Allen's, Veeraswamy, an aberrant Christmas lunch at the Connaught, then Odeon, The Gay Hussar, Atlantic, the Chelsea Arts Club, Odette's. In 1996 something happened: Pizza Express on Hyde Park Corner (twice), then the ten quid all-you-can-eat buffet at Melati's. More recently tapas, eaten at the bar, still tolerable, especially the albondigas and pollo ajillo, and the rioja that kept on coming. Now Fredo's: a sandwich bar on Beak Street with no drinks licence. The ketchup is in squeezy plastic tomatoes. Behind the glass counter, tandoori chicken lies in blood-edged piles, mushed egg agglomerates, prawns curl up in a sickly mayonnaise sweat. I am yet to break all three rules of having lunch with one's agent: 1) always go somewhere where you don't get to see the food before you order it, 2) never go anywhere without a booze licence, 3) be glamorously late and hungover.

I turn up at twelve fifteen. At least I have the hangover.
– Decaff cappuccino. Scratch that. Mineral water. Still.
– Anything to eat?
– I'm waiting for someone.

I go to the toilet, take out my Altoids tin and snap off half an e and let it melt under my tongue. I look in the mirror.
– Come on, you motherfucker.

I sit at a table near the window. Someone's left an old *Sleb* on the chair. My favourite section contains aerial shots of sleb homes. Gosh, don't all those tiny little people need such big houses. There's one here that I particularly like: crenellated, rich in courtyards and lemon groves, teetering on a forested Californian cliff. Such an affront to the San Andreas fault! But the owner's never there of course, just the cooks, the chakra coaches, the maids, the swamis, pool guys, landscape gardeners, motor mechanics, French polishers, fluffers, vista consultants and gadget folk. When the entire Alhambra-styled arrangement slips into the ocean, we'll only lose some wetbacks and a few super-specialised homosexuals; the star's at a premiere downtown, perhaps meditating on the fleeting nature of worldly accomplishment.

A hand on my shoulder.
– Patrick, darling.

Mary Learmont will be delighted if in ten years' time she's referred to as a 'grande dame'. In fact, I note as she enters Fredo's, despite years of effort, her hair isn't big enough, and she lacks the sentimental core, the pneumatic bosom, the patent leather stilettos and nascent throat cancer of the true 'grande dame'. She is in a neat black suit, hair rigorously layered and feathered round the long face with the sinking cheeks. She wears make-up on her neck to disguise the deep lines. It occurs to me that she looks like a lady executive, or a lady executioner. She sits down, craning over the Formica to give me a whisper of a kiss. She smells of dead roses.

– Am I late?

– No, no, no.

It isn't that she won't look me in the eye, or that she seems restless, or that she continues to flip through the plastic-backed menu despite the fact she only ever eats green salad, but I suddenly get the impression that she wants to tell me something bad, ie: 'Maybe it's time you considered another career.' That is the only sentence that can destroy the actor, because there is no other career that can give the actor what acting can: hope. Despite the fact that almost all actors are not doing any acting, the idea remains within every one that tomorrow they may go supernova. This is the building block of the actor's imagination: 'Tomorrow I may go supernova.' The day before you'd heard of your favourite actor he was about to go supernova, and he had no clue. In fact, he was essentially delusional, because to all intents and purposes, statistically speaking, *nobody* goes supernova. I do not walk around thinking that tomorrow I will die in a freak angling accident, but that's more likely than me going supernova.

The only way to end this delusion is for somebody to mention some other career you should be pursuing. And of course, you hate this somebody, because what he is really saying is that you should become a member of the audience. Imagine that! Snuffling, coughing, uncomfortable on your seat, half a mind on the rent, the phone bill, mother's arthritis, the MOT. Only when the credits start can the willing suspension of disbelief kick in. The problem with being a member of the audience is that they are only deluded when they're watching TV or at the cinema. No, I'd much rather be an actor and be deluded all the time. I start the conversation, as she doesn't seem to want to.

– Anything happening at the moment?

– It's pretty slow over the summer.

– And such a slow spring we had this year.

– True.

– Not to mention the winter.

– Please don't mention the winter.

She flips through the menu, gives off an air of evasiveness.

– Just because I'm being self-deprecatingly humorous doesn't mean I don't want to work any more.

– Of course not, Patrick.

She frowns as finger traces down the list of diet specials. Mary has an eating disorder.

– What happened with that costume drama thing?

– They went young.

– What, for the older characters?

– No, for the leads. They started off thinking older, then they went young. You know what they like nowadays, the TV. They need young girls.

So the TV's like everyone else. Now her finger traces down the beverage list. She drinks caffeine-free diet coke. No slice of lemon, of course, in case the citric acid makes her upper arms saggy or the rind gives her cancer.

– What do you say to people about me?

– What do you mean?

– When I'm not around. What do you say to people, when you're trying to get me up for something?

– I just tell the truth. Talk about how talented you are.

The waiter is a dandruffy young Italian. Mary scratches her nose, orders her Greek salad, no olive oil. I get the same.

– Talented. So what evidence do you use to back up this assertion?

Now a little flurry of synthetic indignation.

– Look, Patrick, are you saying that I don't try to get you work?

– No, I'm saying you should try a different approach.

– Don't tell me how to do my job. I've been loyal to you for ten years.

One of the downsides of Fredo's is that you can't have a row without everyone hearing. You can't unpeel your scrotum from your inner thigh without everyone hearing.

– And I've been loyal to you for thirteen years.

– Right. So why get aggressive now? I always try with you, Patrick. Not for any sentimental reasons, but because I think you can do it, I think you've got it. I think in the right part, or even not in the right part, you could be truly good.

I believe her, despite the fact that I know that she knows that I have to believe her.

– You're sweet, Mary. I'm sorry.

– I'm not sweet. I'd tell you if I thought you were doing the wrong thing.

– Would you?

– Of course. I do it all the time.

– No you don't. You people can't bear saying no.

I wonder why agents and casting directors ever end up doing their jobs. Both species are pathologically incapable of saying the only word that they really need in their vocabulary. But then they do have its synonym: dead silence.

– That's unfair. I told somebody only two weeks ago to hang them up.

– Who?

– Jeremy Houston.

– He's ninety-one.

– He's seventy-eight.

– He's had two strokes, he can't speak.

– He was still getting the odd commercial.

– Thanks for putting me up for them.

– He's eighty years old, for God's sake.

– Are you saying I can't do old either? I'm too old for one thing, too young for the next?

– You're being silly now. And, besides, you're the only actor left on earth who won't do commercials.

– I won't do commercials.

Advertising, the collision of art and commerce: where art is on a tricycle and commerce is in a ten-ton truck.

– What about a Japanese commercial?

– And what would I tell my children? 'I did some of my best work as the spokesman for anal powerhoses.'

– It's just money. You're career isn't ruined by one Japanese commercial.

– No, it was ruined by something else.

– You're just so frigging difficult sometimes.

– I just want to do some work.

Our salads arrive, we push them around for a few moments. Mary separates out the feta, looks unsure for a moment about the olives, for God's sake.

– You never would have left her, would you?

– What do you mean?

– Susie. All that time you kept saying that you'd leave her once the work started coming through, but you wouldn't have, would you?

Why start this now?

– Listen, Mary, I don't know. You're older than me. You didn't want me really. You needed someone richer.

She married a Tory MP who made big money in aggregates but who now positions himself as an expert on Early Mayan art. Translation: he is an expert on aggregates who *bought* a lot of Early Mayan art.

– Peter drives me insane *because* he's so rich. He falls asleep after dinner and he just looks full of money. My mother said don't marry older, Mary, you'll either break his heart or he'll suffocate you.

52

– When did she say that?

– Ten minutes before the service.

– But he is *so* rich.

They have a Nash house in Regent's Park, a place in Sicily. Also he's in Central America a lot, presumably screwing adolescents two at a time.

– Oh but rich is boring, Patrick. It's not real. It's like everything's one continuous sweetspot; it's tiring and dull and disgusting. And we don't have sex any more.

He has to save himself for the Nicaraguan slum girls, Mary. Do you know how tired you can get towards sundown?

– So what you really need is someone like me.

– Why don't we go now? Why don't we go to some hotel now?

I never thought I'd done anything wrong. At the time it was frictionless and not remarked upon. We'd got into it and out of it so easily but now it all feels such a shame.

– I thought you had a two o'clock.

– I can be late for people now.

– I noticed.

– Come on, one for the road.

– No, Mary, I can't.

– I wouldn't expect anything more.

– I can't. In lots of ways.

– All right, I won't ask again.

We're not eating, we're not drinking, neither of us has sex any more. Are we breathing?

– Look, I'm serious. If you don't think I can still do this job, let me know.

– I'll tell you as soon as I think it's true. But I know you'll be waiting some time.

– That's OK, I'm not doing anything.

I have to leave now, I have an urgent appointment with *Sleb* and a latte anywhere but here. She puts her hand on my forearm and tries to look urgent.

53

– I can't help it if I'm still kind of in love with you.
– Oh Mary. No.
I withdraw my arm, scratch my cheek and half yawn.
– Why not?
– Look, I'm sorry.
– Well, it was worth a try.
– Just get me up for something. I don't care what, really I don't. If nothing happens, if we really can't turn anything over the next few months, I'll get out of your hair.
– Look, you're not in my hair.
– But it's all becoming too embarrassing.
– Let's talk about something else. You know I won't give up on you. And I'm not embarrassed.
– We should never have become friends. It always makes it more difficult.
– Not for me. I'm glad we became friends.
– Do you always squeeze them in between your eleven-thirty and your two o'clock?
– That's exactly what I do with them, that's why they're my friends. They understand why sometimes I have to do that.
– Then maybe we're not friends after all.
She has become more eager and humorous now, kicks me under the table.
– Come on, one more time.
– Do you do that to them as well?
– OK, let's drop it. Let's talk about something else.
– I can't think of anything to say after what we just talked about – sex, death, everything else would be a come-down.
– We didn't talk about death.
– Sorry, did I say death? I meant my career.
Olives taste like poison, how did we ever get to like them?

Another actor's afternoon of newspapers and public transport. It's five o'clock and I'm opening the front door,

54

beginning to enumerate my achievements so far today. By the time the door closes the task is completed.

Inside, the stairs and then a narrow hallway. Even outside the front door the air is infused with a sweet flowery smell. Susie's having a bath. I open the door and creep in, burglar quiet. All the lights are off. I pad into the sitting room, the uncertain late-afternoon light rendering the room unfamiliar. I enjoy the stillness for a moment, an intruder in his own home.

There is a new picture over the fireplace (which is a square white aperture in the white wall – my idea – in which one of those lights consisting of fibre-optic fronds where the tips change colour has been installed – her idea). The picture is of an African couple raving and grooving round a campfire. I remember that she told me that she'd bought something online. I rotate the dimmer switch so that I can see it better. A naked black man is dancing with a naked black woman, both with gigantic tree frog hands raised high, no eyes, crazy semicircular white smiles. White half-moon slices. The black man's dick is caught in a graceful upsweep left. To scale it's a foot long. I hate everything about it: the dick, the picture, my hating it so much.

I leave the sitting room and walk up the narrow stairs to the bathroom, into the thickening aroma of bath oils and scented candles. There is a trickle of music, which sounds slightly tinny because of the hard surfaces in the bathroom. It is reedy and, from this distance, wordless. Enya? Joni Mitchell maybe, the Cocteau Twins? Then as I get to the door I hear her voice, a low atonal drone, picking up shreds of the melodic line seconds after they disappear and taking them off into her own inner soundworld accompanied by the gentle slap and wash of the bath water. I'm freaked by my own stealthiness. Now frozen at a snoop's angle, torso leaning forward, ear an inch from the door, I breathe in through my nose. Sweet: roses, apricots, apples, tangerines.

55

She has a medium-term plan, for just after she gets famous: she wants to grow fruit and vegetables; she wants pastel walls; she wants a house by the sea.

Susie often bathes like this, thirty or more scented night-lights ringing the tub. I can hear the music more clearly now, it's on low. The singer's voice is Middle Eastern-sounding, but the background is partially Westernised, a lazy drum machine underpinning synthed Arabesque swirls and waverings. The sounds of the water have become rhythmical also, her voice now like whalesong, continuous but languid and seemingly disconnected from the taped music, sexual in the perfumed nook of low light she's created for herself. I focus on the slow splooshing noises and picture her moving: the round belly, dark orange flicker, surfacing and then submerging, her breasts swimming in sympathy with the tide, taking water into her mouth and slowly spritzing it out, perhaps one hand lazily massaging between her legs, these made picturesque and cinematically lustrous by the candlelight as she lifts them above the water line.

I pray that this image might create a reaction in my groin, but it doesn't, of course. The music changes, as does her voice, now a diva parody, swoopy, wordless and larded with vibrato, and she starts to laugh at her excesses and the singing breaks down in a flurry of splashing. I love her, and this makes me feel soppy-sad, because there are other things.

Do it now, break in while she's in this cocoon, throw the ring into the bath and get in with her and say flamboyantly, 'Will you marry me, Susie Fisher?' And there's no way she can say no and she laughs again, but through tears this time, and the light and the tears and the bubbles and my sodden suit and the trashy ballad blend into one of those perfect, unique moments that movies tell us accompany decisive moments of sexual love, and we try and fuck in the bath but it's hopeless and we keep knocking lighted candles into the water and onto the floor but we fuck anyway and the sur-prise, the strange irruption into the domestic routine, makes me

forget everything and I come like a blue whale and then again on
the bed ten minutes later, drenched and slippy and spotted with
clumps of bubble bath, and everything is better than fine and the
house by the sea comes nearer, baby-gros flapping in the salty wind.

I go back to the sitting room, stare at the new picture to inoculate myself against it, take an e.

I don't know why, but I've been getting this feeling that she's seeing someone else. It is currently resurfacing as I drive us out of town and I sense her settling into her motorway trance. We have decided to take our lunch in some ancient arena of quiet desperation, boredom and shame, i.e. a country pub. She's so quiet, so miles away, something must be going on. None of the signs is conclusive, but they build into a pattern which when interpreted correctly can only mean one thing. First of all, why is she often so preoccupied? Of course, there is an almost convincing explanation. Her job requires considerable inward examination. She, after all, is in the process of making her career out of her own life. The two things are indivisible, if it is true that you are what you do, well, she's taking this notion to its logical conclusion. What are you? I am a writer. What do you write about? I write about myself. What do you do for a living? I write about myself in the newspapers. What do you write about in the newspapers? Myself. So, yes, maybe this causes the deep brown studies over dinner, the hair twisting, the constant chewing of the inside of her mouth. It's a full-time job, being Susie.

But there are other things. Our general slow drift apart, her neediness, the multiple opportunities she has, the nonsex. The obvious conclusion: she's screwing someone else. Or she's overdressed for a normal workday, and why change her shoes four times before she goes out? Why is she a little more affectionate than seems appropriate when she's back a little later, a little drunker than usual? She's screwing someone else.

And finally, I can put myself in her shoes – the loafers, the sandals, the sneakers, the fuck-me boots she finally settled on – and find that if I were her I'd be screwing someone else too.

Oh no, the dead grey noise of a motorway drive. I try to start a conversation to take my mind off things.

– What are you thinking?

– Oh, just nothing.

– You can't think of nothing.

– Look, I wasn't thinking of anything.

– That's not possible.

– Give me a break.

– I can't imagine what it was that makes you so defensive about it.

– I don't even know what it was. I was probably thinking about work.

– That's the easy thing to say.

– Honestly, Patrick, I don't know what it was. And, anyway, you don't have any right to know what I was thinking.

– I'm not saying I have a right. But why should you want to conceal it? What's there to worry about?

– How can I even remember now? You've put me in such a terrible mood.

– Which is strange, because I only asked you a simple question.

– You've missed the fucking exit again.

– Again? I've missed it again?

– You missed the exit.

– Don't shake your head at me like that. What does that mean?

– Don't take out your petty anger on me. You missed an exit.

Men hate missing exits. Men back up along midnight motorways to pretend they haven't missed an exit. They instantly extemporise a superior route that involves coming off at the next exit, which is why they didn't come off at the last exit. They will do anything to ditch the blame or draw attention away from the fact that they just missed an exit. Even conciliate.

– I'm sorry I'm in a mood. Mary hasn't called even after I made that big fuss.

– It's only been, what, a week or two?

– But I said this is it, if we don't get anything soon I'll quit.

– You can't say that.

– It's how I feel.

– Well, I'm not having that.

– What else, though? How much more of this?

– 'When it happens it happens so quick.'

Which is what we said to each other for a while, because it had happened to us.

– And when it doesn't it seems to be taking for ever.

– That *nearly* works.

– The story of my life, Susie.

We're side by side, speeding towards the next exit at eighty-five, and her hand comes to rest on mine while she speculates on the bittersweet, the chiaroscuro of being in love with two people at the same time.

5

Mary finally called. She was self-justifying rather than happy for me, but whatever, I'm now sitting in the corridor of a loft apartment in Spitalfields on the verge of doing an audition. The film is a small independent item co-financed by a British TV channel and 'a rich American individual'. There's also some quango involved, redistributing lottery money from the council estates to where it's really needed. They didn't send me a script, just told me that they thought I had the right look. What, they're remaking *Day of the Triffids*?

It's the first time I've been up for anything for a long time, but because my expectations are so low I don't feel nervous. The moment just before death is apparently peaceful.

I always try to forget how to act when I'm waiting to do an audition. It's my only ritual, and it doesn't work. I never read the books on technique nor bought the little I understood about method. I've never had a theory about how to do the job, but that doesn't mean I don't feel strongly about it.

Acting is speaking and moving: speak the words naturally and lightly, as if they're your own. Move quietly and clearly so that each movement has impact: don't declaim as if you're addressing a rally, or wave your arms around, or clasp your head, or pound the table. Graduates of the Mussolini school of acting dominate the way Shakespeare is acted in the English theatre, which is why Shakespeare in England is now only watched by tourists who don't speak English, the elderly who are deaf, or businessmen who are asleep: they see a man in a dress shouting at the rafters and mistake it for great theatre. It is, in fact, pantomime.

Something else: comedy is the most difficult thing to do. Funny things aren't funny if the audience is told that they're funny. It's like when people say when they tell a story, 'Oh, it was hysterical.' The act of saying that means that it can't be. That's all there is to say about comedy, because you can either do it or you can't.

Finally: as in anything worth doing, the only opinions of your work that matter are the ones that come from yourself and those who you think have good judgement.

That's everything I believe.

I carry a rucksack that contains a copy of *Sleb*, a copy of *Ulysses* a bag of low-fat salt-and-vinegar crisps, because I haven't eaten all day. I always carry a rucksack in the hope that it will look as if I've got something to do. I carry a copy of *Ulysses* because I know that one day I should probably read some of it. For now, however, I graze the pictures of premieres and launches in the front of *Sleb*. There is a UK/NY page: Tim Donachie is pictured at a restaurant opening. I thought he was in LA. He looks as if he's having a really good time.

A door opens and a small woman with a suedehead and pale blue lensed sunglasses addresses me in a Brooklyn accent:

– Hey, you can come through now.

I adopt what I think is an American accent:

– Great, I'll do that.

She double-takes, moves her shades down her nose with

pincered fingers. Her eyes are squintily quizzical, almost aggressive.

– You're English, right?

– Why, yes.

– So what's with the 'Great, I'll do that'?

– I thought it was American.

– Right. No, we cast that part. Can you do, like, English guys?

– I should think so.

– You're the stage actor, right?

– Yes, sort of. I'm Patrick Moon from Mary Learmont.

– Hi, I'm Carver, I'm line producing.

– Great.

– OK, let's schnell, baby. The schedule's tighter than a quail's ass.

Talking of asses, following her into the room, I notice that Carver's is approximately the size of a boxing glove. It is bunched into what look like a pair of Barbie's pedal pushers, a kite-shaped chink of light at the crotch. Each buttock can be no larger than a bread roll. A tattoo snakes up her ankle. It is a tattoo of a snake. She has another peeking from the top of her micro-trousers, stylised licks of flame, like the markings on a Harley-Davidson's petrol tank. She could be twenty-five, could be forty. Either way . . . but ah, don't even think about it, Patrick. You would imagine that incapacity would lead to a waning of interest. It doesn't, maybe the opposite, in fact. Who's to say that theory is less interesting than practice?

Carver sits cross-legged on the floor next to an empty director's chair and consults a clipboard. I remind myself that I may be underemployed but at least I'm not in administration; timings, who to be where when, reconciled budgets, the ticked-off list. Items must accumulate, be written down, checked and carefully filed. What's with people who want to do that shit? I stand with my hands behind my back, positioned on a gaffer-taped X in front of a white screen. A digicam is set up on a tripod. *Stretch the spine from the ceiling, feel a looseness in the pelvic region, breathe with the stomach.* I try to check myself out somewhere but there are no reflecting surfaces. You can't see your distorted reflection in the lens any more. You don't hang round on videotape these days. Now your image can be eternally erased in a nanosecond, an infinite, instantly forgettable series of 1s and 0s. Once the button is pressed, not even the zeroes remain. Digital rubs you out.

Gideon Fryman enters the room accompanied by the sound of a toilet vigorously clearing its throat. He is tall and looks borderline malnourished, his body barely making contact with his dirty jeans and rip-necked black T-shirt. There can't be more than three ounces of fat in the entire room, and most of them are in the bag of crisps in my rucksack. I notice he has bare feet: they are long, animalish, tanned but with a pale V of flip-flop thong. He sits on the director's chair, mantis legs arranged, and pushes his hands through his long, black corkscrew curls. He looks at me, exhaling through his nose, eyes flickering. Without averting his gaze from mine he speaks in a soft transatlantic accent, an arresting amalgam of Mockney and LA. He closes his eyes.

– Carver? I need my purge.

Carver gets up and approaches a trolley upon which there is a large blue cooler. She takes a plastic jug from the cooler and decants some of its contents into a tumbler. The liquid is the colour of canal water. She gives it to him as if she were passing the communion chalice and he drains it with appropriate priestliness. He nods at her courteously, moves his head slowly from side to side, ear to right shoulder, ear to left shoulder. In an instant he leaps to the floor, adopts a lotus position and begins to hum, hands clasping his knees. I remain in pure Alexander technique stance. Carver is inscrutable behind the shades, her head turned towards the

63

middle distance. Gideon's hum begins to sound like silence. This quail's ass apparently has remarkable elasticity.

At some point in the near future I am confident that history will recommence its forward drift. In the meantime I try to think of pleasurable things. Just this morning, I finally acted on Fineman's suggestion and visited the website of Las Vegas Escorts. I spent an enjoyable, almost ecstatic half-hour running through my criteria with the site's elegantly user-friendly customer interface. First I selected ethnicity (Caucasian), specifying though not mandating a Mediterranean preference. I was then requested to choose a physique from the drop-down menu: ultra-petite, petite, small-framed, average, large, jumbo. Petite. I decided to submit an additional preference on the optional breast-size criterion (Smaller than Avg–Avg), although fully aware that 'selecting too many qualifications would possibly limit the pool from which my final selection could be made'. I then progressed to the 'Fantasies, Fetishes and Other Fun Stuff' section. The options on clothing were extensive to the point of provoking choice-freeze; in the uniforms section, I expected nurses, chambermaids and schoolgirls, but bus conductors? The armed forces broken down into regimental and combat dress? Dinner ladies? Two types of? Under 'Historical' I wasn't entirely confident that I'd be able to distinguish between Georgian and Early Victorian, nor between The New Look and 1950s. Prehistoric sounded promising, but I concluded after some ardent consideration that Raquel Welch in *One Million Years BC* presented an unrealistic benchmark. If I was going to spend close to one thousand pounds on a single night of pleasure, I didn't want buyer's remorse to set in as soon as I opened the door. The consequences on blood flow of a substandard cavewoman might turn the whole evening into an exercise in making conversation with someone in an otter-skin bikini – comfortable for neither party. I eventually selected Elizabethan. A dialogue box alert appeared commenting that there were a limited number of Elizabethan costumes, so I might want to select a back-up option, and it prompted me with Pre-Revolutionary France. I checked the box.

Once I'd gone through all the protocols, I was presented with an animated revolving representation of my choice. She looked like an extra from a BBC costume drama. I was reminded of Sunday evenings in the Marylebone flat watching the TV, Dad making inaccurate but passionate remarks about the great actors of his generation:

– Gielgud's a fucking amateur and he knows it . . . and if I see Dench do that little pursed-up look one more time I'll tie her to a tree and kick her twat in . . . The thing about Olivier is that he just can't bloody do it . . .

I didn't want my ultimate sexual fantasy to remind me of the hollow feeling related to the fact that you haven't done your weekend homework, so I hastily went through all my choices, removing any pretence that I was engaged in something by which others might judge me. From the top, with feeling. The big-titted Nubian tennis player who now rotated before me filled my soul with exultation, but I heard Susie come through the front door of the flat and, singed with remorse, I pressed 'delete all' and she spun off into cyberspace in a trillion digital flecks.

Fryman is now in an unconventional position, palms and feet flat on the floor, scrawny rump way in the air, long hair falling to form a straggly pool on the parquet. Carver studies a French-language version of *Madame Bovary*. I almost offer to help her translate it: we obviously have the time. Gideon is now in Islamic pronation, I am seemingly Mecca. Obviously bored, Carver watches him. The quail's ass expands and the early afternoon slips through it, like quail shit in slow-reverse.

Eventually, Fryman stands. Not as I might stand – that is by standing up – but rather in an elaborate sequence of events involving, in no chronological order, forehead touching the shins, arms rising outward with palms upturned, buttocks clenching, hands meeting in prayer way above the head and an exhaled murmur possibly including the word 'shantih'. He then folds himself elegantly into his chair.

– I'm sorry about that. My aura was kick-fucked.

– No sweat.

– Let me tell you a little about me, then we'll spin it around.

– OK.

– As you might know, I won the graduation prize at NYU film school, which is seriously impressive as I was their youngest ever graduate. I made videos with Nein Danke, Gorbydolls, The Jismaires and the Fingerbobs while I was still in school. Then I made a short called *Griffey Sluts*? Do you know it?

– I'm sorry, no.

– It was about baseball groupies in Seattle?

– Really, I don't think I saw it.

He waves his hands airily.

– Baseball doesn't travel. Then you might have seen *Logarithm*?

– I don't think so.

He is still unfazed.

– It won something at Sundance. I don't remember what. Fucking sound editing maybe. So anyway, what we're doing now, we're doing this movie and it's called *The House of the Mind*. We're shooting mainly in Scotland. It's cheap, and some of the money's Brit, some American. I wrote it.

– Great.

Carver takes care to make a note on her clipboard: 'chk what we won at S/dance', maybe.

– It's a psychological thriller based on that riff about the American innocent in Europe? But I flip it, flip the whole thing right around. So it's the English guy, the Old World guy, who's the innocent and the American guy who corrupts him. Like America's such an accelerated culture that in a hundred years it's absorbed all the cynicism, paranoia, bizarreness of the world and now it's throwing it back wrapped in a ball of dollars as movies and TV and politics. But I'm being way too meta. The story's basically part thriller, part comedy, without the gags. Gags suck. Gags died on the day the talkies started.

I nod, trying to make some sense out of this last statement. This happened recently, I noticed, the phenomenon whereby you can now say precisely the opposite of what is true and get away with it. So I join in:

– No gag comedy, I like it.

– Yeah, you get it, you get it. So anyways, the Henry James shit isn't explicit, but it underpins. It's a thriller, where you wake up and you're an English guy who's lost his memory. That's all you need to know right now.

Carver, scribbling, says:

– Yeah, it's all I know and I'm producing the fucking thing.

This time Gideon looks a little strained, but he carries on anyway.

– So, I don't want you to read anything. I thought we'd try improvising the type of dialogue, the feel of it we want in the movie, if that's OK.

Of course it's OK. I'll clean the toilets as well if you wish, master. Oh, the pliancy and eagerness of the actor. He will do anything for anybody, because what he wants he wants so bad. There isn't even a question. I am always surprised that people find it sad that Marilyn Monroe did most of her auditions on her knees. That was the no-brainer bit. As they slipped down, those oysters tasted of fame.

Gideon tips his head back, stretches. The larynx looks suddenly muscular pushing against the skin of his neck. I notice his toes splaying, too: reptilian, clean and smooth. He gets to his feet, pads over the polished wood, searching the corners of the room for inspiration. Gideon closes his eyes, apparently sees something on the inside of his eyelids.

– Right, talk to me. I'll try to guide the character with my questions, OK?

Clouds move somewhere in the north-eastern sky, the room is filled with slanted, sharp-edged sunlight. I let my shoulders drop, sense my synapses beginning to crackle and pop. I like this. This is what I do, I think.

– Let's go.

– So you're a defence lawyer?

– Am I?

– No, but let's just do it. Improvise, right? So you're a defence lawyer?

– Am I?

– I thought we'd just been through that.

– No, that was my response in character that time.

– Well, let's try again.

– So you're a defence lawyer?

I am a cool-minded lawyer. Or rather I am a combination of all the cool-minded lawyers I've seen in films and on TV. I have never met an actual cool-minded lawyer. I imagine they try to be like the cool-minded lawyers they've seen in films and on TV.

– Yes. I defend criminals.

Nothing else comes. Fryman looks at me and scratches his head. I check Carver. She has laid Flaubert down. There is a word written in diamante on the lower corner of the left lens of her sunglasses. That word is 'Pussy'.

– Let's move it on. Why did your wife marry you, Mr Moon?

– I believe she was attracted by my fundamental masculine decency.

– What do women find attractive, Mr Moon?

– I don't know: soldier-scholars in aprons, pioneers pushing strollers.

He's running his tongue around the inside of his mouth, nodding, walking round with a perhaps over-enhanced look of intensity.

– What do you remember?

– I remember very little.

– You must remember something.

– The taste of blood, a collision.

– Anything else?

– The feeling of intense heat, my face and neck.

Better, but maybe a little too strange. Fryman looks at me and pincers the end of his nose between the finger and thumb of his right hand. He's trying to look intelligent as he walks around me in a semicircle. I look back at him as if I am a Jet and he is a Shark.

– What did you say you've done?

– Is this in character?

– No.

– The usual. Never done a movie.

– Back in character. This is the opening scene. You wake up in a strange bed one morning and there is a young woman lying next to you, asleep. You have never seen her before. You don't recognise the room, but it takes you only a second to realize that you don't have a hangover. What do you do?

– I make a phone call.

– There is no phone.

– I get up and wander around?

– Very dramatic.

– OK, I wake the woman.

69

– And what do you say to her?

– 'Where the hell am I?'

– And her response?

– 'You're at home.'

– And your response?

– Who's going to make the tea then?

– What?

– Just a gag. Sorry, I know gags are dead and so on. Fryman's shoulders drop.

– You know this is low budget, right?

– So I hear.

– You won't get a trailer.

– Will I get coffee and cigarettes?

– You'll be living on coffee and cigarettes. Listen . . .

He stops pacing, steeples his fingers, his toes wriggle on the dusty parquet floor.

– The piece is about people not fitting, do you know what I mean? People not feeling comfortable in their skin. That's the issue. It's identity.

– Right.

– Do you really understand this concept? Displacement, discomfort, the idea that your psyche is under someone else's control?

I feel a sudden brightness, a sense of risk, but before I know what I am doing:

– If it were done when 'tis done, then 'twere well it were done quickly . . .

It's still inscribed in my innards, it emerges unaffected by ten years' incubation in my brain, word perfect, perfect rhythm, the whole convoluted, tortured speech full of love, doubt, fear and anguished self-knowledge. I stare into Fryman's eyes as I speak, he stares back, unblinking.

– '. . . I have no spur to prick the sides of my intent, but only vaulting ambition, which o'erleaps itself, and falls on the other.'

70

I hold a silence for five seconds, breathe hard.

Carver does nothing. It's possible she looks a little embarrassed. Fryman nods slowly and murmurs, 'That's OK.'

I am excused.

6

Susie and I in the car (she pays) on the way up to a party at The Circle. Someone's leaving *The T——*, going to the same job on *The G——* or *The I——* or the other *T——*, I can't remember. The deal is I drive there, she drives back, or we leave the car and get a cab, or drive home drunk and bickering, whatever.

My music choice this time, so Radio 3. It is an act of rebellion. When 'get money, kill, fuck bitches' is Top Ten, then Radio 3 is the counterculture. Also, you've got to try to hold it back, the slow creep of garbage into every corner of the world, never give in to their insane demands. We're listening to something called the Glagolithic Mass, which is even worse than it sounds. It's hideous but compelling, like a bad traffic accident, which, in fact, I narrowly evade while reaching for the volume dial.

– God, this music blows.

– Because it doesn't yield all its mysteries in eight seconds.

– No, Patrick, this is just horrendous.

– It's interesting.

– It's the purest embodiment of filth in sound.

– Because it doesn't rhyme 'maybe' with 'baby'.

God, it's bad, though, there aren't words to describe. Actually there is one: it's Glagolithically bad.

– Let's stop this, Moon. I don't actually mind whatever's on.

– No, let's not stop this. Why do I get criticised for trying to understand things and trying new things?

– I'm not criticising really, honestly. You keep it on.

– How can I now? How can I enjoy it when I know you're just sitting there brooding?

– Really, Patrick, don't get worked up. I don't mind. I'm sorry.

I get the desire to injure. Nothing serious, just a flesh wound. It'll be a little sore for a while, but she'll make a full recovery. So I go back in, what the hell:

– This is the problem with this whole lousy relationship: it's Thursday so it's The Circle; tomorrow, don't tell me, a *dinner* party, some bunch of media whores.

– Your friends are media whores, too.

– I'm not saying that. I'm just saying the whole thing's deeply unsatisfuckingfactory, but you're not willing to admit that.

– Because it isn't. Think of something better.

– Good simple people.

– For God's sake, Patrick.

– No, for fucking God's sake *you*.

I kill the radio. We're silent the rest of the way and I feel a little remorse but don't have the *cojones* to apologise or make amends.

We park in an NCP on Brewer Street. The Circle is a converted townhouse on Wardour. It's still our place, our club. In the old days at The Circle, everyone screwed everyone else. A quantity of bacteria finding itself in The Circle could travel through the bodies of the whole of media London in less than three weeks: from novelist's nostril, to TV producer's lung, to columnist's mouth, to foreign correspondent's anus, to actress's snatch, to agent's foreskin, back to novelist's nostril: what goes around comes around. Now we're older, grown up together, it takes a little longer. It's all got more complicated, what with wives, even some kids, slowing down the carousel, but The Circle is right: closed, no way out, swallowing its own tail all day and all night.

The leaving party we're attending is in the private room on the first floor. I must have been there two hundred times, but each separate visit is indistinguishable from another. In fact, each visit to the private room is indistinguishable from any visit to The Circle in general: walk in, get caught by someone I don't like, miss all the people I do like, get drunk, end up with people I'm not sure whether I like or not, take some drugs, find that I like everybody in the whole fucking world, black out, go home. There is a difference between eras: in the old days I used to try to get laid. Recently, I just try to imagine who I would like to lay and leave it there.

We're standing at reception while the vicious little martinet looks us up on the guest list. She's new, otherwise I'd give her a hard time. I am known here. It is known. Susie's craning over the desk, I'm gently massaging her broadening mobile buttocks, partly because there's nothing else to do, partly in assessment.

– Who's leaving again?

– For the two hundredth time, Sarah Pyman.

– Have I met her?

– Of course you've met her, you've met her a thousand times. We spent a weekend with her in Kent.

– Oh yeah, short blonde, huge arse.

– You think everybody's got a huge arse.

– Everybody *has* got a huge arse.

– Get off.

She wriggles away from me and jabs at the guest list.

– Look, there we are, Fisher and guest.

Displeased that she can't politely ask us to leave, the receptionist reluctantly gives us Teletubbies stickers (Teletubbies – *so* last millennium they're nearly *this* millennium) on which our names are written and sends us through to the party. The private room is, in fact, two rooms. The first is a lounge with semicircular banquettes enclosing circular tables and a pay bar. The second, entered through a short corridor, is a small dance room where they put the buffet table and where eventually young women in black miniskirts will dance to Fat Boy Slim with a Silk Cut in one hand and a vodka and tonic in the other while young men in black-framed spectacles dance more mutedly in front of them and attempt to brush their crotches against them while talking loudly about recent developments in their media careers.

We start in the lounge, Susie with her work personality in play, which is slightly bitchy, 'feisty', of course, but still tinged with motherliness. She's like an over-excited, recently divorced aunt who's turned up at her niece's wedding dressed too young and hanging out with the kids who want to get rid of her. I'm slightly out of tonight's thing, as it's all people from *The T——*, so as she works the room I have to hover around, and rock slightly on my heels and jingle the ice in my drink and smile and raise my eyebrows and exhale through my nose in sympathetic sniggers. I wonder which one she's screwing: could be any of them.

They're playing Daft Punk, then Beck, then Lo Fidelity All Stars, which sounds like music chosen by a woman to keep the men happy, and somehow touching because of it. Then we get to sit down. She's zhuzhed up on to one of the banquettes, whereas I'm left marginalised on one of the low pouffes and feel my trousers riding up to reveal white hairless shin, and it's a hassle to reach to put my glass on the table and I can't quite get started with anyone, always on the periphery of every conversation, occasionally

75

attempting to join in by crashing a fag from someone or laughing a little bit too hard. I end up getting my phone out and pretending to check my text messages while actually having a game of Tetris, which is a game about fitting in.

This doesn't work for long. I go to the toilets and take half an e, wash my face then take the balance. It might be too much, but I need to feel loved. I go back into the lounge and scan the room again for likely Susie screwers. Hundreds of them.

I see that there's now a free space next to Susie on the banquette. She is talking to her boss, Georgia Fenwick (née Tracy Fenwick), and looking worried.

– Georgia, can't this wait till tomorrow?

– No, Sooz, it can't, this is serious, we need a plan.

– All right, ladies. Good party, I'm toasted *already*.

They look at me, both frowning a little, somewhere else. They're either talking about work or bad sex. Georgia's hair is almost black, in a long bob that drops like a scroll down past her shoulders. Her lips are very red on her small round face. She doesn't look forty, apart from her hands, which are venous and knuckly. She continues:

– We've just got back a reader survey, and your numbers have nosed.

They're talking about work then.

– What numbers?

– Sooz, mind if I sit here?

– Georgia, mind if he listens?

– Of course not, it's just work stuff. Anyway, numbers, all of them. All of your numbers – 'is a part of the paper I always turn to', 'always find column interesting', 'Susie Fisher is a columnist I can relate to', 'is the best part of that section' – all of them.

Susie lights a cigarette in a fluster. Georgia continues to talk. She is single, once divorced, I think. I would like to have sexual intercourse with her. She looks as if she'd be

76

grubby and insistent and servile to the point of shameful-
ness. Forty, after all, and single. She's a Geordie, but by cracky
she's scrubbed out every trace. I bet she yells a lot and sticks
her fingers up your wazoo.

– But it's just one survey. It's probably a blip.

– Listen, Sooz, I'd say they were a blip as well, if the
numbers hadn't dipped so steeply. It's fucking carnage, and
Threlfall . . .

– And Threlfall what?

– He's antsy.

I laugh into my hand. She actually said that. Susie has
talked to me about Georgia. She used to be a journalist, but
is now in 'editorial management', which means nothing
to me, but obviously means you end up talking horseshit
American; 'antsy', I ask you. Maybe saying words management people say makes you feel as if you yourself are management. Susie was incensed recently that they fired the
political sketch writer because 'he'd stopped adding value'.
The T—— was no longer the paper, the rag; it was 'the
brand'.

What. Ever.

Susie is shaking her head, pursing her lips.

– But, Georgia, I don't understand it, it's not as if I've
changed much.

– You may not think that, but the readers . . .

Georgia now produces three or four pages of the survey
from her boxy purple handbag. Brought especially. She
smooths the pages on the table. The Zippo comes out and
she starts gulping on a fresh diesel-flavoured Marlboro. Her
'I'm going to tell you exactly how bad it is' cigarette going
down right on top of her 'you're in the shit' cigarette. Gay
men think she's *just so amazing*, straight men avoid her when
she's drunk.

– Here we go. 'Not as funny as it used to be': sixty-eight
per cent. 'Self-indulgent': seventy-one per cent.

– But it's always been self-indulgent, that's the whole point.

– Exactly. But Threlfall reckons that if they're enjoying it then they don't care that it's self-indulgent, so the percentages stay low. But when they start to hate it for other reasons, everything that could be a negative comment they stick the boot in – the numbers skyrocket. Nosedive.

– Hate it? Who hates it?

– What?

– You just said 'when they start to hate it'.

– Did I? Sorry: shorthand. Like it less.

– So what are you saying?

Susie seems panicked. They surely wouldn't fire her on the basis of one survey? No, but Georgia is being so crisp and businesslike, pretending to be efficiently concerned, really all a-squirm with glee. No, this couldn't wait for tomorrow. Positively bursting with the news.

– What we're saying is that we think you're going to have to change the column.

– We? Who's we?

– Threlfall, marketing and Snyder.

I know that Martin Threlfall is the editor, but I don't know who Snyder is. Now is not the time to ask. I am actually becoming indignant on Susie's behalf. Does this mean that I love her? Does it even mean that I *like* her?

– But it is what it is; what can I change? To change the column I'd have to change me.

– To be straight with you, Sooz, I think that's bullshit. You can change it, unless you're telling me that you can't bear to compromise your fucking *integrity*. It's a chick column, hellooo.

Susie's now swallowing lumpy anger, but doesn't want to show it. She wants to match Georgia *mano a mano*, keep everything firm and professional.

– Change in what way?

– Listen, the way Snyder . . . the way Threlfall puts it, and I think this is kind of neat, the simple fact is, happiness writes white.

– Meaning . . .

– Meaning, basically, it's all getting dull and suburban, the interior deco gick and so on. Twenty-fives to forties want a bit of suffering, a bit of self-loathing psychosis to make them feel better about themselves. Other people's happiness is just so *depressing*.

Why is she saying all this in front of me? Is it some sex strategy? Why is Susie letting her say all these things in front of me? Is it some sex strategy?

– I'll think about it.

– If I were you I'd think quickly.

– I said I'll think about it.

Susie stubs out her cigarette with aggression. Georgia stuffs paper back into her handbag, wriggles merrily on the banquette. Yes, other people's suffering can be tremendous fun.

– Also, it would be good if we had your column at two tomorrow.

– Two?

– Snyder wants a look at it before it goes in.

She hasn't been pre-edited for five years. I remember her saying that it's in some way important.

– I'll think about it. Come on, Paddy, we're going.

In the car, she's driving and furious.

– Can you believe this? Fucking marketing never wrote a word of journalism in their lives.

– Nor have you.

– Piss – off – Patrick.

– Who's Snyder?

– Some hotshot nonentity – worked on some lads' mag

79

then did something at some fucking tabloids, skewed them young male or something. They don't get it, do they? They just don't get it. Everything has to be the same, nothing's allowed to move on. Who *are* these people?

– Same everywhere, it's the same everywhere, honey.

– *Honey?*

– Sorry, I dropped an e.

– Oh great, I've basically been fired and you'll be tearing up paper and giggling to yourself.

– Nononononono, I'll listen, I'll listen.

– Unbelievable. What am I going to do?

– So fuck them, man. Just leave, just resign and fuck it, babe.

– *BABE?*

– Sorry, sorry. Leave, work on the book. We could live on what I earn.

– If we lived in the Sudan.

– Why not? You said you'd like to live abroad.

– Right, let's pack up and move to the Sahara, we're ideally suited. You could do rep in Khartoum and I'll carry jugs on my head.

– Why not? Fuck the London suburbs. What kind of life is this anyway? The whole of life boiling down to half an acre in Hampshire and a kid at Newcastle University. Why not Africa?

– What the hell are you talking about, Patrick?

– Just maybe changing our lives so they stop resembling the TV programmes we don't like anyway.

– I don't even understand that.

– Just leave, you can figure something out.

– I'm not going anywhere. That's the last thing. That's the last thing.

She looks cool now. She's kicked off her shoes, she's sitting right up by the steering wheel, clanking her rings against it, staring through the windscreen at the firefly taillights of

Euston Road. No music now, just two people in the brown
light of the London evening. Amidst the muted swishing
noises of heavy traffic in the dry warmth of the car, the two
of us together in a car going home together to our home
together after all this time. I kind of fall in love with her all
over again.

– You look amazing.
– Well, that's ecstasy for you.
– I'm really going to go for it tonight.
– Don't say that, Paddy.
– Why not?
– Look, you're putting too much importance on it.
– But I'm going to try. If you'll help me.
– OK.

She's so elsewhere.

– Let's go for it then, the Fish.
– Yes yes, the Moon.

Later in bed she's been trying – kneading stroking nibbling
slurping fluttering yanking battering moulding trepanning
ululating – but I'm the consistency of a flat bicycle tyre.

– I'm so sorry.
– Oh, don't apologise.

But there is maybe for the first time some impatience in
her tone.

– Whose fault is it?
– Nobody's. It's just a phase, like the doctor says.

She relinquishes her intricate hold on my glistening softy
and lights a cigarette.

I am temporarily transfixed by a mole on her shoulder.
Three hairs sprout from it. I detumesce at the speed of a
partially inflated balloon. Indeed the effect is so marked I'm
surprised my dingus doesn't fly around the room trailing
an extended raspberry.

81

– Maybe you're gay.

– That's too easy.

– Well, maybe we should try something different.

– Yeah, let's try anal, that's going to work.

Mussel into Cheerio won't go. Besides she was never interested in buggery – 'a place for everything and everything in its place' – and I was with her. I've found almost every part of a woman's body arousing – the ears, the friendly 'H' behind the knees, the Achilles tendon, the teeth, even the mind every so often – but I've never been able to eroticise the anus.

So what else could something different mean? Whenever I've floated the idea of a threesome she just thought I was joking. I was so not joking it wasn't even not unfunny, but I let it pass. The one I didn't mention, the old favourite, the ejaculation in the face, was wildly ambitious in the current circumstances. And I had always been faintly disturbed by my desire to turn my girlfriend's face into an action painting anyway. It was all right in the stringy, pulsing moment, but afterwards I felt like such a naughty little boy, spilling everything like that all over the place, you little devil.

– I can't think of anything.

– I could dress up.

– I'd feel silly.

– I could dress up as a schoolgirl or something.

There is a moment of wild-eyed speculation in my heart. Too great, too horrible, too super, too crass, too fab, too ineffably sad, please yes. But I hear myself saying:

– No, it's cheating. And where would it lead?

– Who cares?

But I won't have it. Anyway, she might turn out to be that lunking, spotty-foreheaded girl with the brace clogged with old bread. She stubs out her half-smoked cigarette and snuggles up, strokes my neck with the back of her knuckle and says softly:

– What are you thinking?
– I'm thinking about our life together.
– You big soft twat.

I play with her hair. She gently shakes me off.
– I suppose you could try a French chambermaid.
– Why is that better than a schoolgirl?
– It's more tacky, I'd question my motives less.
– Ooh la la.
– I wish I could just do it normally.
– You'll be fine. You need time.

I'm supine, hands behind my head now. She's nuzzling my ribs, her chubby white arm across my chest. This is love, I suppose, as nervous fathers declaim from pulpits at weddings: Love is patient, love is kind. Love is being prepared to dress up in fishnet stockings and a frilly pinny to summon a hard-on from its boyfriend. The duster as well, *ohh, mon dieu*. But I can tell it wouldn't be enough. Oh lord, I do not ask to be multi-orgasmic, but quasi-orgasmic would be nice once in a while.

I hear the hum of the ring, embedded in my sweater drawer today, hard and smooth, at the moment pitch dark, just ready to burst with light. And at this precise moment – something about the half-hearted movement of her hand, a twinge of impatience in her breathing – I know that she's seeing someone else.
– What are *you* thinking?
– I don't know really. Nothing.
– Oh sure.
– No, no, Patrick, not now.

She rolls off me, moves to her edge of the bed, a region of absolutely elsewhere.

Two a.m. I wake. She's not next to me. I get up, walk downstairs towards the murmur of the TV. No lights on. She's curled on the sofa in a T-shirt. The screen gives off its flickering aquatic glow.

   – Hey.

   – Hi.

   – What you watching?

   – Basketball.

I watch for a minute. The sound is muted, the crowd like distant seagulls, the commentators' quiet shouting. It seems disproportionate: the men are too big, the court is too small, the ball is too big, the goal is too small. Much waving and faking and crouching and bouncing. Everywhere I am, all this strenuous futility.

   – Who's winning?

   – It's looking like a Lakers blowout.

   – What does that mean?

   – They're up by fourteen and we're still in the second. The Sixers are lacking intensity on the D.

   – I hate it when that happens.

Two mostly naked people alone late at night not really knowing what to say after all this time. It makes me feel like a grown-up.

   – Tea?

   – No, I'm fine.

   – Shall we have a long important conversation about the state of our relationship?

   – I'd rather not.

No, I see why she wouldn't.

   – I will have tea.

   – Who are you screwing?

She shakes her head, keeps watching the TV.

   – Just please will you fuck off.

7

Mary's on the phone, using a tone of voice with which I'm familiar, but from a long time ago.

– It's hopeful, that's all I've got to say.

– So what did they think?

– I don't know exactly, but the girl phoned and they want you to meet Ray Borg.

– Why him?

– He's in it. He's the other lead, playing the American.

– You're kidding me.

– No, really. I don't know what the meeting is exactly, but I'd treat it like a job interview.

– How many others are still in it?

– She didn't say. At least two or three, I think.

– What do you know about Borg?

– Nothing, basically nothing. I don't know his agent, either. I'm not even sure that he has one. I've heard rumours that he's difficult, that's it.

Borg is good, flat-out good. In fact it might be the case that I want to be him. He does good work in good movies, never a hint of sell-out, no TV, good, strange theatre. He's just a damn good actor.

– So how should I behave?

– I don't know, Patrick. Enthusiastic, interested. Other than that, be yourself.

– Have we got a script?

– No script, but they've got the money. I know they're making it, I asked around.

– What about for me?

– Not much, but Fryman is really hot. It's his first feature but he got the money really quickly. There are lots of genuinely big people watching him.

– Holy shit, I can't believe it.

– See. I still trust you. If only you could be the same.

– I trust you, Mary, maybe too much.

– That's actually a coded insult.

– Look, it's OK, really. When do I meet him?

– Next week. Let's meet before, talk it over, do some other things maybe.

– Look, Mary, I can't do it.

I put the phone down, but in a way she'd understand, slowly, the pause signifying doubt and longing; she's heard it before.

I look up Borg on the internet: IMDB, Amazon. The world is in agreement: man he's good.

Susie's in Paris for the weekend, notionally with two of her girlfriends. The mystery of what women say to each other. Every time I listen to her talking on the phone it's the daily stuff: jobs, parents, single friends, *Sleb*-based speculation. But what about when I'm not listening? Insurrection, betrayal, desire, the other man, the life-changing joy of illicit hard sex, *of course* size matters, of course it matters, girth, girth, girth, girth . . . – it kills me that I'll never know.

It's midnight, I'm standing naked by the window in the sitting room, my hollowed body silver in the streetlight. The road is still, the cars vigilant and somehow inane.

Fear the stillness.

This is the insomniac's masturbation hour, but despite the slow squeegeeing action I am applying to my clutch of genitals, nothing stirs. The non-sleeper is unduly proud of his affliction, but not at the time that he's not sleeping. At this time he's ashamed and sore all over, bored and singing softly to himself any old thing that enters his mind. I move to the bookshelves and cock my head, shuffle along, my feet dusty and sticky on the wood floor. I'm looking for poetry, but not the type of poetry that's ever been written. I'm looking for poems of frictionless joy that have the lulling powers of valium. The type of poems Keats tried to write but kept messing up with actual things and places and dryads and small birds and vases. I move back to the window, press my head against its coolness, press harder, feel the unwilling flex, test it just a little more. A fancy cat moves in dressage gait down the middle of the road, tail held in a high question mark. *Does anyone want my little pussy ass?*, it seems to ask of no one in particular.

Twigs bat at the window with surprising vehemence and make me start.

Fear not the stillness, Patrick, fear the faint peripheral stirrings.

My inner music continues: '*Non più andrai, farfallone amoroso*' perhaps. It all sounds the same reorchestrated for whispering drone. Maybe it's 'The Macarena'. Whatever.

I walk to the bathroom, my feet unpeeling themselves with each step as if I'm walking on fresh paint. The bathroom is tiled and cool, but with a thick pile rug next to the bath. I stand on the rug, wiggle my toes in its synthetic lushness. I am trying to get in tune with my bodily sensations. I turn the shower on, the water batters the plastic. I step into the bath and breathe deeply, letting my strained hand hang loose by my side, soaping my ribbed stomach, lifting my face into the tepid downpour.

* * *

87

It's 1984, I'm on the school bus home. In fact, it's not my school bus. It drops me about two miles from home, and I have to get another, or maybe travel a stop on the Underground, but that's not important, because it's Naomi Miller's school bus, and she's the reason I'm on it. I sit on the upper deck no more than two rows from the back. I know that she tends to sit in the middle of this deck, usually with Rachel Levitz and that fat Spanish girl who clacks gum and laughs through her nose like a cartoon horse. I adopt a mask of brooding indifference. It is difficult for a fourteen-year-old boy to brood indifferently, particularly when he's six foot tall, as thin as the wind and suppurating with difference. I feel as if I'm collapsed into the bus seat like a snapped heron. Gangly. Gawky. Angular. Glandular. Geeky. All ankles and knees. A gawp. But nonetheless in love, so excruciatingly in love. The deck fills with its usual collection of hormonal typhoons in polyester blazers, stuffed Adidas bags as shiny and smooth as aubergines hung over shoulders or banging against scrawny calves. The talk is loud and indistinct, catchphrases from the comedy shows, nicknames kids are trying to make stick, bits of pop song. I am above all this. I float above it magisterially. I am thinking. I am thinking deeply. About thoughtful things. Thoughtful things that are also somehow sexy and of particular interest to girls called Naomi with plucked eyebrows, freckles and clean, clean mouths. Before I see her, I sense her, walking down the bus towards me smelling of jasmine, apple blossom, ozone and lychee. Although I don't know what any of these things smell like, they sound about right to me. She goes to her usual place, a few rows ahead, on the opposite side. But today she's alone and steals a crafty-eyed glance at me, nervously flicks back her shambles of curly black hair before she sits down. I watch her profile, which seems to me to be turned away from the window, almost as if she were trying to catch me in her peripheral vision. I feel a recklessness grip my heart. I walk up the centre of the bus, lower myself gently beside her, trying to breathe naturally, hoping she can't hear the massed drummers of Burundi hammering at oilcans in my rib cage, and say:

– Naomi. Hi, I'm Moon. As in 'fly me to the'.

She turns to me. I won't write down how I feel, because I can't.

– But we can't fly, can we?

I am confident in spite of myself. The weight and awkwardness, the growing pains and the knobbly wrists, red sticky-out ears, all sense of them gone.

– We can if we want to badly enough.

The roof of the bus lifts off, and I leap into the air, catching her by the hand, pulling her with me into the windy sky. The other children don't see us, their concerns so irredeemably earthbound. She gasps and yells in excitement as I lead off, arm raised like Superman, look back at her, see her hair streaming behind her, her feet kicking at the air as we ascend and wheel away over west London. First the moment of being up there occupies all the senses. I barely notice what I'm doing, luxuriate in the sensation of soaring, her cool palm resettling, gripping tighter. But then we become used to the feeling, and take our time admiring the view. We rise on the thermals, London a tight-packed toytown below us; silent cars and buses stop/go through the narrow streets, rows of houses jumble untidily together like on a Monopoly board late in the game, children run through small green parks. They think they're so quick, but we know better what quickness means. Another flip of the legs, we dive towards the river. Naomi pulls sharply on my hand, I turn round and look to where her small brown finger points. Swans in strict formation fly below. One honks, is answered by another honk, making her laugh. She holds my hand tight; I let it go. She shrieks and starts to paddle desperately at the air. Then the shock that she isn't falling makes her squeal; she makes a dolphin kick and surges through the air towards me, quick and distinct against the slow teal river, the brown and grey of the city streets. I kick off in response, keeping just out of reach. We play tag in the sky, skating around in the air like water-boatmen, zigzagging here and there as we please. We are downriver now, agile and frictionless, zooming, making invisible infinity signs around the towers of Battersea Power Station. I sway out of reach, swoop down, skim the river's surface.

If I were a swan, my wingtips would dip into the water, under this bridge, over the next. I can feel her close behind me. I bank and twist and turn, but keep the river below me, keep heading east, out towards reaches of the city that are as foreign to me as Zanzibar. Her cries become more pleading; my desire to stay out of contact is diminishing anyway. I let her catch up, move into a vertical climb, slowing as I near the apex, then hover like a hummingbird high above the city, St Paul's to my right, Naomi suddenly in front of me, rising slowly until her face is in front of mine, and all of London recedes. All I know now is her wet, thick-lashed eyes and how I feel when they close and what happens inside my chest when she makes a nervous gulp and moves her soft mouth towards mine –

I become conscious that the shower has run cold. This is no good at all. My right hand has created a huge cumulus of lather around my crotch, there is no sensation, it feels as if I'm slowly folding eggs into a giant meringue.

The problem is that Naomi was love, and actually had nothing whatsoever to do with sex. She was pure and ethereal, newly hatched, unspoiled by bodily desire. I never touched her, never even spoke to her, too perfect for me. I used to dread her ending up with some sporty blowhard who might brag about his progress with her after rugby practice and make me seethe with sadness and regret. When I found out ten years later that she was an air hostess living in Dubai with a tennis professional, that was somehow all right. There was a lightness and ease implied by her new existence – twilight in the desert, her in visor and whites drinking iced tea on pastel-coloured furniture, her brown legs crossed, a superwhite tennis shoe bobbing as she watches a match, the balls looping and popping in effortless arcs around the crisp geometry of the court. This wasn't a bad place for Naomi to end up, less tethered by gravity than most, far away, out of England's clutches.

All this slow ruminative activity and I'm now effectively a mound of bubbles. I rinse and step out of the shower, knees a little weak from the heat and the dreams. What to do? I wrap my lower half in a thick white towel and lie on the pile rug. I almost fill the whole floor area, right foot on the door, the other leg crooked, foot pressed against the sink's cool pedestal, head jammed into the corner where the bath meets the wall, hands laced over my chest. It feels comforting to be braced in this way. People should spend more time in canoes or in coffins.

I haven't tried this since I was fifteen, but what with all this time to kill and as there's no one around for a while and a million other reasons related mainly to fear in some way, I will try to bring myself to orgasm with my own mouth. The first step I assume (although I am improvising, there being no manual currently in print) is to get oneself comfortable. I shuffle down the carpet and let my legs hang over the cool rim of the bath, thus granting my head and body a wider range of motion. I roll my shoulders and press my hands into the carpet scrunching the thick pile between my fingers. This is far more fun than I anticipated. I do it again, putting a little buffer of pleasure between now and the fast-arriving moment of truth.

I am thinking about two girls. I call them . . . actually, I don't call them anything; it's important that they remain anonymous. I am walking into my agent's office in the early morning and there is a new receptionist, a black girl, and she is typing away assiduously, the words on the computer screen reflected in her large-framed glasses. She is wearing a crisp white blouse unbuttoned just far enough so that the soft rise of her breasts are visible and the tiny scalloping around the cups of her snow-white bra. She is black like blue-black ink, not one of your honey-coloured, whitey-wannabe-type black chicks. On the surface she is efficient and suburban, what with the straightened hair

and the starched blouse and the tight grey skirt, but underneath all this there bangs a juju heart. I can't help it, I
really can't, but as I approach she does indeed start to suck
her pencil. Something about this is working, I don't know
why. She stands up as I walk over towards her, moves
round in front of the desk and claws her pink-nailed hand
around my cock and balls, says 'hi' in a voice like bur-
nished gold. Unconvincingly, but also somehow inevitably,
a button pops on her blouse and the breasts are further
revealed, pushing from their lacy housings like dark chocolate sponge rising from a baking tin. We kiss, she pushes
me back on to the reception sofa, tries to get astride me,
has to push up her skirt so it is around her waist, revealing
the muscular arch of her legs and – well, I'll be – orange
panties (whatever, I have to go with it), and just as she
kneels between my legs and starts to unzip me, looking
me in the eye, full slow motion, no smile, a look of something approaching anger on her face, in walks the ash-
blonde with the turquoise eyes dressed in full sweats
(carrying a basket of fruit – why? who knows? who *cares*?)
marl grey, alternately clingy and baggy – and a look of
cutey-pie surprise on her adorable ultra-Scandinavian face.
And little cotton socks too, why not . . . ?

Nothing doing. Can't reach, everything still floppy and
stretchy, my mouth making fish-like lunges at bait that isn't
there. I get up, wrap myself in a towel and go downstairs.
In my wallet the little card that Fineman gave me: *Las Vegas
Escorts*. I dial and try to figure out what voice to adopt when
you're booking a prostitute. The woman who answers is
cheery and businesslike.

– Have you registered on the website? Great, we'll check
your preferences and try to get as close as possible. We can
get someone to you in an hour, pay by credit card, and it
is customary to tip.

I watch TV and pace around and look out of the window,

change my clothes a couple of times. I settle on a white T-shirt and jeans, everything's as normal as it could be. The nerves don't do anything for my level of desire, in fact I consider cancellation, but the buzzer goes.

– Who is it?

Who could it possibly be?

– 'Allo, it's Marinara from Vegas.

I let her through. I didn't realize she would be so small. She is mixed race, in fact conceivably a blend of Nubian and Swede. She shakes my hand, lots of eye contact, very chirpy, and I offer her a seat on the sofa. Of course, I want to talk. She tells me fine but I'm on a meter, hundred and twenty pounds per half-hour. I never imagined that she'd be so *real*. The idea of a prostitute and the actual thing don't have much in common. The idea has no will, no body weight, no characteristics that make her an individual. Marinara is undoubtedly a fully rounded human being.

– So you make a reasonable living?

– Not too bad. Are you sure you want to talk about this, love?

– Yes.

– Sorry about the cozzie. 'Cos you was a rush job we got as close as we could.

It actually looks like a souped-up PE kit, which is fine by me. She wears so much make-up that her face is an archetype or caricature of femininity, the hair a strange brittle texture. We sit on the sofa, me looking straight ahead with my hands trapped between my legs. She strokes my hair. It occurs to me that she is not a whore but a nurse.

– So how long have you been in the business?

– Five years.

She is kissing my neck now. I shake her off and stand up.

– I'm sorry, I don't think I'm ready.

– OK, don't worry.

– Would you like a drink?

– Have you got a Diet Coke?

– I'll have a look.

In the kitchen I take a couple of deep breaths. There is no way I can go through with this. I don't have the necessary equipment, not just physically but in every other way. What is it? I think I can't cope with the fact that she'd be faking it. I get her a Diet Coke and go back to her. She is retouching her eye make-up.

– Marinara, interesting name. Nautical, is it?

– No. It's Italian.

I hand her the drink, an act which has a curious intimacy for some reason.

– Marinara. I'm not sure I can go through with this.

– Why not?

– It's a long story.

– Oh.

– Does it bother you?

– No, not really. It happens every day. First-timers usually. First-night nerves, probbly, innit?

– I find that reassuring.

She sits on my knee and I feel her fat tongue in my ear. She whispers:

– I could frig myself off?

– That's very considerate of you but, no, I don't think it would help.

– It's worked before, I frig myself off and it gets 'em going a bit.

– No, don't frig yourself off. Don't do anything. I'm sorry.

– Nuffin' to apologise for.

– I think you're right.

She looks at me smiling and blinking. She may be compassionate, but she doesn't give a damn either. Of course there's no reason why she should get involved with her patients.

94

– Do you want to settle up right now?

– Whatever you like.

I sign a receipt, give her a thirty-pound tip in cash.

– Do you have to work all night?

– Eight till four.

– God, it must be pretty lonely out there.

She stands, sounds almost a little annoyed.

– Don't overdo it, love. I get by.

– Of course, sorry, I didn't mean to patronise you.

– Don't worry, sweetie. Call again, when you've got the nerve.

I offer my hand, which she shakes limply. She leaves and I watch her from the sitting-room window as she walks down the path. I hear her faint laughter as she talks into her mobile. She gets into a little red sports car and drives away and instantly I want her back.

8

Mary was clear: lunch with Ray Borg is as much an audition as the meeting with Fryman. Borg has sway. We meet at the bar in a sushi restaurant. He walks in five minutes late, shorter than I imagined, wiry, the thin blond hair shoulder-length.

– I'm Ray Borg.

– I know. I'm Patrick Moon.

– I didn't know.

He ignores my extended hand. I feel uncomfortable towering over him, sit on the edge of a barstool. A couple of people seem to recognise him. A girl next to me bends over to sip from her straw, looking at him out of the corner of her eyes, momentarily oblivious to her boyfriend. I understand the magnetism of moderate, street-credible fame, in as much as I feel it too, but you can't explain it, the need to stare and drink it in as if you might decipher some arcane meaning in a face, or be granted some finer understanding of life. Borg narrows an eye in search of a barman. He wears a fading black T-shirt, old jeans and slides. I am nervous, because he after all is Ray Borg, and I am merely Patrick Moon.

– I just want to say I loved you in *Let the Dawn Break*.

– I was the only good thing in it.

– I'd agree.

– I just want to say I've never seen you in anything.

He lights an American Spirit, rolling it between his spaced-out teeth.

– That's OK, there's nothing to see.

– I never watch movies anyway.

His sake arrives. He necks the first cup and, after refilling, takes a more savouring gulp of the second.

– Fryman said you did an interesting audition.

– I couldn't tell. He didn't seem to respond that well.

– He liked you.

– Really? I don't know what I think of him.

– At least he's interested in the work and not the money.

– I wasn't really aware of him before we met.

– He's talented.

– He seemed self-confident.

– He's an egomaniac. But have you met a director who isn't?

I have to admit I haven't. Borg is rotating on his stool. He looks as if he'd rather be elsewhere. He nearly looks at me.

– Who's your agent?

– Mary Learmont.

– She any good?

– I don't know. I haven't done that much lately. She seems to do all right for other people. Maybe I'm no good.

Borg finally trains his characterless watery blue eyes on me.

– Never say anything like that. Never. You're the artist, she's the drone.

– Really, she's a friend.

– Does she become less of a friend when you're not working?

– We speak less, but I think she feels the same.

– Let's eat.

I scan the menu but nothing's quite right. Borg's mobile rings, he talks quietly in what sounds like code, setting up some meeting, stares into the middle distance through a haze of cigarette smoke. I order a vodka and soda, go to the toilet, snap off a third of an e, take the two-thirds. When I come back, Borg has another bottle of sake in front of him.

– I love this drink.

I order sashimi, he nothing.

– Has he shown you a script?

– No, I don't know why.

– Trust him on the work. The work's the only thing, Patrick.

We talk about his career. He didn't go to drama school, travelled until he was twenty-five, mainly in the US, Central and South America, started going to open auditions on the fringe of the fringe. He worked in the theatre, turned down TV.

– I don't do TV. I won't do it. It's not proper work. It's bastardized, anodyne, lowest common denominator.

My sashimi arrives – salmon, yellowtail, tuna, squid – wet and obscene. I mix some wasabi in the soy dish, dip a piece of salmon and bring it up to my mouth. It is sea-perfumed and slimy, womanly. I force myself to eat it, it slips down whole.

– The money though.

– Fuck money. The only thing money solves is money problems. Fame is a sickness. The work is all there is.

I am nodding a lot, agreeing in principle while actually profoundly conflicted about whether or not I want to be on TV. There is only one motivation for being on television, and that's the desire to be on television. It's not even nuanced, or freighted, or related to something else. It's the purest emotion we've got left, and I should know, because I've had it since I was *in utero*. It's why everyone's in such a bad mood at the moment: there just isn't enough band-width to accommodate the ardent desire of six billion people to be on television. But for me, it can't be just any old TV. No ads, soaps, cop/doc/legals, comedy-dramas, sitcoms or kiddyshit. Which leaves –

Borg looks at my barely eaten food, then back at me with his pale, bored eyes.

– Come on, let's carry this on elsewhere. I've got to go meet someone.

We walk east, out of Soho, through Holborn into Clerken-well.

I'm attuned to the nuances of London neighbourhoods, still won't go south of the river, feel bogus out of zone one. So reassuring that so much of the city is still unknown after thirty-three years, it goes on for ever. My manor is WC1, EC1, W1, WC2: even this tight-packed district is fundamentally unknowable. I like saying 'I'm a London-er', and wear the city's anointments with pride: dry skin, black snot, hair always in need of a wash, the fed-up look.

We walk slowly. He tells me about how he likes to work.

– Fast, slick, spontaneous. The important thing, Patrick, is that we do this together. We're on screen a lot together. We've got to be the centre of this. I'll follow you, you follow me.

We walk down St John Street, surrounded by references to everything that's gone before, not just here in London or England, but ever, anywhere: a new Moroccan restau-rant with a mural of the Atlas mountains; an Italian espresso bar called Bellini, a Venetian *madonna col bambino* hanging behind the counter; a French bistro called Pigalle, where they have mock-distressed the typography on the windows, BIERES – NOS VINS – CAFÉ; a pub called The Sessions House, which serves twelve English 'real ales', Vietnamese seafood bouillabaisse or andouillette sausage and hash browns.

– It's collaborative. There's no room for ego or self on these small projects.

We turn down a side street and are shortly in a more gothic place, tenements looming on either side of a badly laid road, the light suddenly inky. We cross a small patch of scrubland, fenced on three sides, more tenements beyond. It is littered with cans, needles, the remnants of spent bonfires, cracked black wood like pterodactyl nests. Down some steps to a stretch of canal, the banks over-grown with marsh grass, bulrushes and nettles. The water is stock still, silvery oil swirls traced on to its brown sur-face, three or four slender barges hugged to the bank. Borg steps on to the prow of one painted deep-green, blue-black and grey, NO NAME etched in white block capitals onto its hull.

– This is me.

The vessel tips when we get on board. He opens the door to the cabin; it is unlocked. I follow him through a tiny room, with a narrow mattress stacked with scripts, into the living area, maybe eight feet by four, stinking of damp and camphor. He turns on the stereo, muted ambient electronica fills the space. He gets a bottle of vodka from the fridge, pours two shots. The liquid is slightly viscous, a pale straw colour.

– Does this thing move?

– It does, but I leave it here.

– So why not just get a flat?

– Property is bullshit. Something to talk about while your life sifts away.

The room is dark; he reaches for a light switch. The bulb is dull yellow and just makes the room more shadowy.

– I'm reducing everything to essentials.

– In reaction to something?

He frowns, lights a cigarette.

– No, not in reaction to something.

I feel uncomfortable; we are close enough for me to lean over and kiss him. His eyes are scribbled with lines. He chews gum, knobbly movements around his jaw.

There is a knock on the door. He gets up, quick and slinky, walks hunched through to the back of the boat. A brackish draught of air fills the boat. There is a murmuring from the door. Borg returns with a small velvet pouch roped around the top.

– I think I'd better go.

He looks confused, even a little panicked.

– Er, who's auditioning who here?

– Oh, I'm sorry.

– Too right. Stay a while, Patrick.

– OK, I will.

He sits down, peers into his bag.

– So why do you do this?

– I've never thought of doing anything else. I'd do it for free. Doing good work is the only way I could ever be happy.

– That's the right answer.

He nods, waves the bag at me.

– Shall we?

– Sure.

He gives me the bag, gestures at me to skin up.

– Patrick, so much of this is bullshit.

– Yes, yes.

– Can you believe that there are actors who do *commercials*?

– The lowest of the low.

He watches me finish the joint, make the roach, tie and shake it. I roll it in my fingers for a moment then torch it.

Nice skunky weed. I pass it to him. I've done a good job, a lovely even burn; the air is suddenly sweet and rich. Borg takes a long draw, holds the smoke in his lungs for a while then breathes out, his face a slit-eyed comedy mask.

– You're going to be fine, Patrick. I can taste it.

9

The sex therapist who is about to arrive is not my idea. She was recommended to Susie by a friend on one of the women's mags: Janey Drew, The Doctress of Desire. Janey's always telling people to experiment with something new – lesbianism, anal sex, chocolate sauce, zippered masks, fisting – as if sex were a consumer choice rather than a compulsion. However, despite all the expertise, her own sex life had been in the doldrums until she employed the therapist.

– She's marvellous! Sorted Keith and me out in a tick. Back at it like Bengalis, darling!

Apparently Keith and Janey now employ pornography before the act, blindfolds during. To me this seems to be a dramatisation of various aspects of the problem rather than its solution, but what's the use of complaining, it was all arranged before I could intervene.

It's Saturday morning, as we wait for her arrival. Inevitably Susie is on the sofa, Little Mermaid posture, reading *Sleb*, surrounded by bales of newspapers, playing with her toes. I keep pacing between the kitchen and sitting room pretending I'm restless because I'm waiting for the call from Gideon. Of course, what I am hoping is that

103

an upturn in my career will coincide with a rediscovery of sexual potency, and therapists will be superfluous. Deep down, in my id or my yang, the two notions of performance are inextricably connected. When permitted to express my art, my cock will judder to attention like a night-watchman caught napping on his rifle, and loving will be easy again.

– Sit down, Patrick, for God's sake, man. You're not about to be executed.

– But if I sit down it'll be even worse because I'll just start jiggling my knees.

– Read the papers.

No way, I might learn something.

– What are we going to say to her?

– I don't know. Wait till we find out what she asks us.

– We don't have to be honest, do we?

– Of course we do. That's the whole point. Look, she does this for a living. She'll have come across far worse cases than us.

– Who? What could be worse than nothing?

– I don't know. Premature ejaculation?

– I dream of premature ejaculation.

– Vaginismus then.

– What's that?

She doesn't look up. Absorbed presumably in some column about some column that some columnist wrote about some column.

– Oh, Janey was telling me. It's a condition whereby the muscles spasm. Closes it up completely. If you're lucky it happens pre-insertion, because then you just can't get in. But if it happens post-insertion, then the shit really hits the fan.

– Yeah?

She looks up now, making her hand into a claw.

– Squeezes the blood right out of you. You're stuck together in hospital till they give you amyl nitrate.

– I dream of having the blood squeezed out of me.

– You already have, haven't you?

– Thank you, Susie Fisher.

– Put some music on or something.

How does one create the correct mood for the arrival of
a sex therapist? Death metal, which I don't have? Donna
Summer, which I also don't have? *Tristan und Isolde*, with
the seven-orgasm duet in Act II, which I wish at this
moment I didn't have? I cower in the presence of all this
excess sex. How nice to remove all strings of mucal fluid,
all robotic twitching, all slight soreness from life. Let me
keep the cuddles and the hugs, delegate all the procreation
to the geneticists, let the proles and Janey Drew keep on
copulating if they must. I put on a recording of the
Brandenburg Concertos. Only chess grand masters could
find this sexual in any way.

– What's this?

– What do you think?

– I don't have a clue.

– Guess.

– Oh I don't know. Bach.

Her triumphal air-punch would annoy me too much.

– No. It's Scarlatti.

– It sounds like a knitting machine. Or the fucking Horse
of the Year Show.

– I find it so relaxing when you ask me to put music on,
then criticise me when I do.

– Keep your shirt on.

– There is sexual tension in the air.

– That I doubt very much.

– Thanks for that.

– Stop feeling sorry for yourself and do something.

– I'm listening to Bach.

– Aaah. Not Scarlatti then.

I retire to the bedroom, knocked out in an early round

with a 1-2-3 combination – breadbasket, kidneys, jaw. I pick up *Ulysses*. Every day I transfer it from the rucksack to the bedside table. I dip in. Some time soon something will happen that I will either care about or notice. I turn it over and read the blurb. After how many re-readings of the jacket copy, introduction and notes on the text can one safely claim to have read the whole thing? I feel I'm getting near. Who would notice anyway? The closest that people I know have got to reading *Ulysses* is watching *Jason and the Argonauts*. Susie would notice. She knows too much. She must be stopped.

The buzzer goes. I hear a flutter of newsprint, she runs into the bedroom, kisses me on the forehead, whispers sorry and runs down to let Ms Panetta into our lives.

She is a swaying giantess. Like all truly enormous women she has developed a way of dressing that makes her look square rather than round. Apart from when sitting down, when she looks like Buddha in the 'before' pictures: before he slimmed down to his 300-pound fighting weight. She takes the weight off her feet without being asked to, knees like bowling balls in their shiny black housings. Her leggings are splitting down the inner seam and a thick hair coils out of one of the apertures like the mainspring of the world's most unpleasant watch movement. A sex teacher. People who can, do. People who can't, teach. People who can't teach, sit on my sofa open-palming Jaffa Cakes into their mouths. I have been instructed to call her 'Bobby', I presume in fact spelled Bobbi, or maybe Bobbii – 'OK, I'm not that cute, but my *name's* cute.' All this would be fine, I would be doing just groovy, if Bobbi wasn't currently talking about my penis.

– Right, Patrick's thingy . . .

She might have noted that I have made no reference to her genital area, despite its prominence (it is the rhino in the room), but this has proved no impediment to her rigorous analysis of mine. As if to prove she's not really a slob at all her dark, thick hairdo has a three-hundred-quid look. Layered, subtly tinted, conditioned to the point of liquidity, and as her bestest friend says to her, 'Oh but, Bobbi, your hair is so *gorgeous*,' the subtext actually more of a subtitle, scrolling below: 'it's just the rest of you that sucks.'

Susie and I are sitting on the sofa under the window, uncomfortably, I might even say touchingly together but apart. Bobbi is making a deep, wide dent in our sofa, facing us across a low glass coffee table groaning with elevenses, Janey's tip to keep her interested. Bobbi has taken down some hard facts on a tatty, disorganised-looking pad. This makes me suspicious. Rigour doesn't look as if it's Bobbi's strong suit, and I need more than well-meaning muddle and airy generalities.

One thing about hard facts is that they are easy to be truthful about: we've been together eight years, lived together for four; I'm an actor, she's a journalist; I had five sexual partners before we got together, Susie had twenty-three. (*That* still hurts. I know she was seeing some other guy for a couple of years before we met, she's two years younger than me, so, let's see, that makes twenty-one sexual partners in about three years, as I also know when she lost her virginity. What made it so much fun back then? Did she do stuff we don't do? Well, obviously she must have. Was she known as the university bike? Did men say about her the things I've heard them say about other women: 'You've got to fuck Susie, she fucks like a tiger', or 'Susie gives the best head in town, she paints it like fucking Picasso', or 'Fuck that filthy slut Susie Fisher and you won't walk right for a fortnight', 'She likes to fuck hard', 'I fucked her ragged all night', 'I fucked her spastic all weekend', 'I fucked her to a standstill all week', 'I fucked her to within an inch of her life', 'Have you done that bitch Susie Fisher yet? She's a real *fuck.*') But, the facts and their comforting certainty now out of the way, I sense we're moving towards more treacherous areas: genuine feelings, unspoken notions, things it's impossible to be honest about.

But more for the moment on my thingy:

– You see, Susie, love, Patrick's – what do you like to call it, darling?

– Love truncheon.

– Patrick's – love truncheon? Are you sure, sweetie?

– It's just what I call it. We are still the masters of irony, aren't we?

– That finest of distinctions between irony and lies.

– Thanks for that, Susie.

– Anyway, loves, whatever it's called, Patrick's love truncheon is a sensitive flower. It needs care and attention, affection and kindliness if it's going to stay blooming. Because, you know, they say the body's biggest erogenous zone is the mind, but I think it's most important to know that every bit of you is cherished.

I would not want to cherish any bit of Bobbi. More pubic sprigs are visible in the stretching openings in her leggings. 'LET ME OUT' they seem to spell out in dense mediaeval Arabic.

– Right.

– Now, what was your sex life like before the recent ups and downs?

– Disastrous.

– I was going to say average.

– Average for a nursing home, Patrick.

– Great, so we're in agreement, then.

Bobbi tries to move forward on the sofa, eyes trained on the biscuits. In order to progress to the edge of the cushion she has to heave herself from side to side. This manoeuvre arduously completed, I draw the plate of Jaffa Cakes three

108

inches towards me with my fingertips, putting it just out of reach of her desperate lunge. Her hands are like those of a gigantic ape baby: dimpled, a deep crease where they meet the arm, but from pinky to wristbone a nimbus of black hair.

– Now, Susie, love, when you say disastrous – give me a Jaffa Cake would you sweetie? Thanks my love. When you say disastrous, what do you – what do you *mean*?

A discus of sugar is scarfed in one and starts its journey to an outpost somewhere in the western districts of her left thigh. I speculate that once there it will ironically resemble what she *should* be eating: i.e. cottage cheese. With a hair growing out of it.

Susie produces a crisply folded sheet of A4. I try to read it over her arm. She holds it up to her face and it becomes backlit by the watery London sunlight, but I can see the list spooling seemingly endlessly towards her lap. I can also make out the word 'disgusting', which does not augur well.

She starts to read, stressing whichever word in the sentence makes it sound as if she were reading out a shopping list:

– For I would say about three years there's been no passion, no intensity, the frequency has been very low. I rarely had an orgasm, I got the impression Patrick found me disgusting, we could never talk about it afterwards, he never initiated sex, oral sex was a no-no – I mean he wouldn't do it to me. We would both adopt avoidance strategies; when we did get round to it, it was routine and repetitive . . .

She tails off, suddenly looks terribly upset, actually holds her mouth tight shut, downturned a little as if she might burst into tears. I panic, want to hold her, stare at the seagrass instead.

– Like I say, average.

Bobbi goes all quiet and husky, like a grief counsellor.

– And Patrick, darling, do you recognise the picture Susie is painting here?

– *Guernica*, isn't it?

Susie regroups, folds the list up tight, scores at the edges with her perfect fingernails. Bobbi tries to lean forward indulgently, but is prevented by whichever laws of physics govern colliding spheres, tips/rolls back softly, tosses the impeccable hair.

– OK, loves, let's start from the basics. Do you both like to fuck? I mean, you have actually both had times when you both enjoyed fucking?

She has those uncertain vowel sounds, the sound of an accent cleaving towards standard English now standard English doesn't exist – elongated dead sounds, circumventing the dreaded flat 'u' with an 'err', what a bit of lerk, what tremendous fern, fancy a quick ferk, oh you silly cernt: all vowel sounds blurring, merging or smudgy in the estuarial marshlight.

– Doesn't everybody?

I don't want to talk, Bobbi, not to you, I'm sorry. I need to talk to the world's cleverest, kindest person and you're not her. Susie, you were once, but you're not any more. Oh really, damn sex for once. Damn its all ubiquity and longevity and complexity, the fact it's now compulsory, the advertisers swathing the billboards with six-packs and perfect racks and buns of steel and the insolent gawps of post-coitus, all that bed-head and dummy-fucking and the humourlessness of the whole fucking culture. I want to change the subject. Love and the fading of love, that's the theme I want explored. And what about the rediscovery of love? Love and its redemptive power. Can that make an appearance at some time?

– No, Patrick. You see some people don't need sex. And you know what? That's fine if that's where you end up.

Some people can be very cuddly and lovely with each other, but not actually fuck.

– 'Fuck' – is this the new euphemism for 'making love'?

– I could use any term you like, sweetie. My customers tend to prefer that I don't beat about the bush.

And what a bush it is. You could beat *within* it.

– I think ideally, don't you think, Susie, we'd rather find out if we could breathe some life back into everything before tying a knot in it.

I look at her and in some bizarre piece of learnt behaviour reach my hand out towards hers. She takes it non-committally.

– Yes, I guess so. I mean definitely, I think.

And on this note of hesitant hope, we surrender to this stranger. It is clear, as she jams an entire chocolate Home-wheat into her mouth, that she knows something about appetite. There are crumbs in her hair and a dewiness in her eyes as she says:

– Now, let's talk about your fantasies.

Later, I'm sitting on a bench in Highbury Fields, watching the lovers pass by, bickering or mute, swinging big square shopping bags filled with lamps, cushions, linen, tea towels, mugs. I feel like telling them that all those mutually agreed purchases will one day make them feel sad, whatever happens. My mobile rings.

– Patrick, it's Mary.

– Yes, I know it is.

– You've got it.

– You're lying.

– No really. You've got it.

– You're lying.

– No I'm not. They start principal photography in six weeks.

111

– Fuck me.

– Did you really say that?

I cut her off, conscious that I'm now standing up. I think about calling Susie, but curiously, I want to keep the news secret for a while. I smuggle an e into my mouth and re-seat myself. My phone goes again. It's Borg:

– Let the party begin.

10

Borg has invited himself over again. He's my new best friend. I find it undesirable to be separated from him. He's funny and strange, tells me good rude stories about famous actors and their perversions. X likes boys, Y likes girls, N likes lying under a glass coffee table while a motorcycle messenger craps on it. Bobbi is seemingly part of a global operation.

Borg's also a theorist. Currently he's on all fours rooting through the video collection stored under the TV, theorising.

– The world, Patrick, it's a terrible place. More and more fame-crazy fuck-ups, all of them more and more desperate to get the love they didn't get at home from some audience or some media outlet. It won't be too long before the entire population consists of starlets and moguls. Doctors gone, teachers gone – just a vast landscape of underloved adolescents trying to get an agent. Now – porn porn porn porn, where's the fucking porn?

– I haven't got any.

– Don't be silly, man, where is it?

– I don't have any. I don't like it.

He's delving deep in the cupboard, throwing tapes behind him. It's as if he's tunnelling for freedom.

– Oh, give me a break. What's this? *Brief Encounter*, *ET*, *It's a* Godforsaken *Wonderful Life*? Where's the fun in that?

– They're sort of horrible and degrading, aren't they? Besides, I never know how to get hold of one.

He swivels round, looking affronted.

– What?

– Pornography. It's degrading.

Borg takes a deep breath.

– Patrick, why do you watch films?

– Entertainment?

– Right, because they provide entertainment. Pleasure, in other words.

– Yes.

– In which case, pornography is the highest form of art.

– I'm not with you.

– Direct cause of orgasm in the viewer. How much more pleasure do you want?

– Well . . .

He holds up a copy of *The Bicycle Thieves* and looks at it with disgust or loathing.

– Come on, you must have something.

– I think I've got a Russ Meyer.

– Oh, put it on, put it on.

He throws himself on the sofa while I try to find the tape.

– So much to learn about the noble craft, Pad. Got any booze?

– It's not even brunch time, Ray.

– Well, what else you going to do? You've got a movie job in the bag, it's freezing out and your chick's at the office.

– Vodka?

– Vodka and soda would be good. And a pill if you've got.

So we each drop a pill, drink warm Stoli and settle down to watch *Faster Pussy Cat Kill Kill*.

– Your pad?

– Her pad. Our pad.

– Girlfriend, of course, not wife, right?

– Maybe wife one day.

– No no no no, Patrick. You're not getting married.

He sniffs, turns his head, taps his ash deliberately into the Stoli lid.

– I'm not sure. It might be unavoidable.

– No, no, Patrick, you are sure, you just don't know it yet. You're a rational person and rational people don't get married any more.

He turns towards me, his face so close that I can see the irregularity in the grain of his eyebrows, stray bristles on his chin, the red fretting in the corners of the eyes.

– Marriage: the two big thoughts. One: if everything goes to plan, the plan you make on the day you get married, you'll never fuck anyone else again. Intolerable. Two: you know you *will* end up fucking someone else some day and that wrecks your plan. Intolerable.

He looks at me, challenging me to disagree.

– You with me?

– No.

He stands, hitches his old jeans and starts to walk the floor, one hand occupied with the joint, the other gripping the vodka bottle by the throat.

– OK – ninety per cent of men are unfaithful at some point in a marriage. What does that say? That ninety per cent of men are evil? Or that ten per cent of men are idiots? Take the ten per cent, you could just say they're lying, but that's too easy. Let's say some of that ten per cent are religious in some way, which I take it you're not, and that's why they don't screw around. Some others may be straight-down-the-line normal men who don't screw around; let's be generous and say five per cent. OK – but you think they aren't in some way fucked by Thought One? That it doesn't prey on them, every woman they meet? So

115

even if Number Two doesn't get you, Number One'll get you every time.

He looks at me, eyes intent, swigs some vodka.

– You with me yet?

– No.

– All right, more. What happens when the divorce rate is higher than one in two?

– You tell me.

– Getting married doesn't make any sense. It's acting irrationally, because we know it's more than fifty-fifty that it'll collapse. You can't do it. If we abandon reason we're no better than *animals*, you're no longer *human*. You want that?

– I was going to say what about love, but I don't want to now.

He takes a big sharp draw on his spliff.

– No, love's important, but it's different from marriage. Marriage is about sex, not love, Pad. You love your friends, right? You don't need to go to a contract on it, though, because there's no sex. Men wanted to keep women from screwing around so they got legal on them, gave them a contract, so they could oppress the jaysus out of them.

– You're a feminist, Ray, I knew it.

– I'm a humanist, Paddy. Men, women – no difference to me.

– What about children?

– Yes, children – another reason for the contract. But in case you haven't noticed, children aren't the product of love, they're the product of sex.

– So what's instead?

– Nothing.

– Open marriages?

– They last five minutes.

– Why?

He smiles at me now, as if what he is saying is self-evidently true.

116

– Because we're savages, we want to have our poom poom and eat it. 'I want to fuck around, but I'd hate it if you did.'

– Savages but not animals.

– That's exactly the distinction.

– So what's the alternative?

He turns to watch a moment of FPKK. Varla is in her Porsche about to run a guy over. Go-go girls are cool and powerful.

– Take it as it comes. Every man for himself. Only collide.

He's doing the audition now. He is auditioning for a central role in my mind.

– I need more than that.

– Marriage was invented by men to stop women fucking around. It's anti-nature, Patrick, it's *unnatural*. So do like the fish and the frogs and the spiders and the flies. Stumble into women, fuck them, don't fuck them; whatever happens happens. Only one rule: to thine own self be true. Only collide.

– Right.

Borg looks at the movie for a few seconds, then at the TV.

– Think about it.

– I will do.

– Damn right.

We half-watch the movie, the violent, grotesque, dirigible women. We can't concentrate, rubbing ourselves, scratching ourselves. I've got headspin and maybe so has Ray because he says out of nowhere he has to leave and stumbles down the stairs mumbling:

– This film is too frightening.

He leaves me alone, drunk and absurd and I hope Susie never sees me like this.

* * *

117

Much later, I'm in front of the computer, kind of sober, gazing at a slowly blinking cursor. Bobbi has asked Susie and me to write down our sexual fantasies. We are not permitted to share them with each other in any way. They must be given to Bobbi prior to our next session and (presumably after she has used them to heave and slop herself to climax) she will use them as a basis for finding an 'erotic meeting place – somewhere you can both go where you feel safe but excited, comfortable but thrilled.' I have got this far in distilling my usual scenario:

> *Two chicks, pref. one black one blonde, office environment, sort of* competing *over my cock – playfully, but definitely competing. They are both wearing tennis gear. One (the black girl?) is wearing spectacles.*

Jesus, enough. For a start the word 'spectacles' has no place in a sexual fantasy. Anyway, my current sexual fantasy is to direct enough blood to my penis that it becomes parallel with the floor. Once this is achieved, I'll start thinking gingerly about fun.

Susie thinks there's still enough Catholicism in me to screw with my sexuality. I don't agree. I have guilt, but it's more to do with death. Ask a Catholic and they'll tell you that at one point in their lives they thought that they were an incarnation of the devil. Ask a Catholic who their favourite painter is and they'll say Hieronymus Bosch. They can *really relate* to his characters. Particularly the severed guy hanging out of the demon-fish's throat. Literally, you see, consumed by guilt. Now, of course, I realize that death follows *everyone* around, with increasing abandon and frequency, and that it's usually nobody's fault and we get over it eventually.

I stopped believing in Catholicism before I even had a chance to start believing it. It was the dramatic structure that did it for me. OK, comedy is tragedy plus time, but is Good Friday to Easter Sunday *enough* time? Every Easter at mass I would mentally append a stage direction in the liturgy: 'and with one leap he was free.' Nobody buys that crap any more. Once I'd determined that the story was little more than rickety action/adventure material, everything else collapsed with it.

The Seven Deadly Sins, for instance. It didn't take long for them to lose their force as instruments of moral terrorism. When I was nine, I realised I was committing every one on an hourly basis. I had self-loathing night sweats whenever I boasted about my new shoes, coveted someone else's pencil or thought about Sarah Hennessey's knees. When I got to the stage where I was averaging a deadly sin a minute, I figured that either I was a psychopath or the sins weren't that deadly after all. No, I've decoupled sex and guilt. If only I could do the same with sex and fear.

I can't make any progress with my fantasy, so I check my e-mails. One from my RADA alter ego Donachie head-lined 'Larging it in LA', saying he's coming back to London for a while to do some 'meetings'. I invite him over for dinner, of course, hoping to contract a mild dose of his success disease, or at least to experience the burning sensation. Then one from Hillary:

From: Hillary Kelly
To: pmoon109@hotmail.com
Subject: 'A Modest Proposal'

Dearest Patrick
This may seem a little previous, but I have 'a modest proposal', which I think and hope may be of some particular interest to you.
I am in the process of writing a play which will be the culmination of all these many years that I have spent

119

watching plays and thinking heavily and often about the theatre and all its multifarious aspects. It is entitled at the moment as very much a provisional title 'The Love Game'.

What it hopes to take on is the several issues surrounding love in our society, particularly various types of love about people who have never met, the possibility of love at first sight and other romantic notions and perhaps some exploration of the more brooding types of emotion – such as obsession, perhaps.

I don't want to give away too much of the 'plot' or 'structure' at this present juncture. It is about an actor is maybe suffice to say thus far.

I know that you have recently not found it as easy as you should to exercise your considerable craft. I would wish that this might be the vehicle that brings you back to 'centre stage' as it were! In any event, would you consider doing me the infinite kindness of provisionally agreeing to read it?

I think I can attract some fiscal interest as it were from some of the many people I know in the various realms of the theatre all over the country.

Obviously, it would be for me some kind of extraordinary honour if you are in agreement with my 'modest proposal'.

I feel that a luncheon might be the best forum within which to explore and develop the notions suggested herein – what about you?

I await your response with relish and no little anticipation! All regards and respect.
Here's to that lunch!
Hillary

Why does her prose seem translated from the Russian? By someone who has learnt English from a man who speaks only Russian? Some of the clauses unsettle: 'Such as obsession perhaps'? Why is the 'perhaps' bit more frightening than the 'obsession' bit? I write back, attempting to tread the fine line between outright rejection and encouraging her, feeling somewhat grand when I point out that I actually have a job in the movies at the moment.

Then, back to the homework. Maybe the white girl should wear spectacles. I wonder what squash gear looks like. What's on the frigging television?

I go downstairs. Even all these days later, I espy a tiny coiled remnant of Bobbi on our white sofa. Her parting shot, yelled in the hallway so that anyone in N1 could hear, continues to resonate:

– Anyway, Susie love, in the meantime, as I say, if you are going to try love-making, remember the basics: take your time and don't neglect the plums!

I remove the last scintilla of Bobbi from my house with the extra long nozzle of the Hoover, but I can't get her out of my mind. She squats in there like a bullfrog, ribbiting about my dong and my plums as I try to watch some teen drama. Girls are all so beautiful now and so everywhere, breasts so perfect and they start learning how to fellate like top-of-the-line geishas before they learn where babies come from. Like Borg says:

– All the unimportant stuff – lyric poetry, opera, the standard of the public discourse – is getting worse, but the important things – infant mortality, life expectancy, general prosperity, the sexual technique of sixteen-year-old girls – the world just keeps on exceeding expectations, Pad.

11

I'm uncorking a bottle of wine. The corkscrew is like a metal sculpture of a one-legged woman. I turn her trapezoid head round and round; her arms rise up. I push them down and she sucks the cork up into her body. I sniff the cork, a chrome pigtail peeking through it. It smells rubbery. Mary is here, flicking through *Sleb*.

– Have you noticed all these people getting pregnant?

– It's disgusting.

Borg is also here, in our house, one of us now.

– That's a bit harsh, Ray.

– I would have thought by now the reasons for not having babies were obvious.

– Expensive, I suppose.

He ignores me, gets on with saying what he needs to say.

– Firstly, in life ninety-eight per cent of the people you meet are wankers, idiots, cretins, egotists, moral cripples, neurotics, manic depressives and losers. So you've got a two in a hundred chance yours is going to turn out OK.

I go to pour him some wine. He holds his glass up to the light. We can both see the milky vestiges of a lipstick mark on the rim. I half fill the glass.

– Think about it. Chances are you'll have a child you

think is repulsive and stupid. What's more, chances are they'll think you're repulsive and stupid as well. Think of the odds. In any parent–child relationship there's a two per cent chance that the kid's all right and a two per cent chance that the dad's all right and a two per cent chance that the mother's all right. So effectively a nought per cent chance that any of them will like each other. *Ergo, id est, quod erat demonstrandum, et cetera* – families: forget it. For evidence of this, look around the room.

– I *like* my parents.

Mary is dolled up, she is actually *molto fuccabile* tonight, the wear and tear concealed under several strata of gunk and a turtle neck. She wanted to meet Borg, was maybe half thinking of trying to seduce Borg. She is on a dining chair, leaning forward, elbows on knees, stockinged feet clawing at the seagrass mat. She is wearing a black skirt, slit most of the way up the leg. Seated as she is, it falls open prettily. There is a thin triangle of gauzy thigh and then a strip of black stocking top. I study this interesting geometry and listen to the sound of the wine gulping into her glass. She looks at me from under her brow, checking me out checking her out. She's really good for forty-five. She moves her hand over the glass.

– Enough.

There is a moment's silence filled with the arrhythmical sawing of a Bach Partita. It's probably good background music if you're chopping up a body. Borg wants to be heard:

– Nobody *likes* their parents. But, anyway, I'm talking to Patrick. And I haven't finished.

He quaffs a quarter-pint of wine in one, lights a cigarette, cupping his hand unnecessarily around the lighter flame, as if he's standing on a blustery heath.

– Secondly, the fontanelle. That little bit on top of a baby's head, before the plates of the scalp have joined? It's like the paper over the top of a coffee jar – thock – you'd put your thumb straight through it.

– You're just being disgusting now.

– And finally, we're running out of sperm. The sperm count's plummeting. Really. Watery non-viable sperm every-where. It's nature's way of telling us not to bother. Spend your money on something else. The kid era's over here: leave it to Africans.

Susie comes in from the kitchen, the tips of her hair damp with sweat, smoking hard.

– Totally under control.

I taste the wine, but I don't like it. It's over-flavoured, buttery, nutty, creamy, almost like white chocolate. I want a vodka and soda. Maybe some *water*.

The buzzer goes, Susie heads towards it.

– I'll go.

She wipes her eyes with the back of her reddened hands and goes into the hallway. Floury, flustered, apron, fat ankles, bustling to get the door – *hausfrau*. I moved the ring to my sock drawer a couple of hours ago. I feel it winking at me blackly. I make a stiffish v and t. There is a sense of limp chamois leather in my undershorts. Borg is lolled deep into the sofa, still in his vagrant couture but washed and scrubbed for some reason. I'm looking forward to the moment, Borg, Donachie, me all together in one room, a group of promising young English actors. We hear Donachie in the hallway, the sound of him squeezing the breath out of Susie, and I turn my eyes towards where he will enter the room. He makes an entrance, arms outspread, accom-panied by a bracing wind of transatlantic energy.

– Heyy, Moony, I'm back.

I try not to appear too excited, but I am. Whatever you say about Donachie, you can't deny that he illuminates a room. He's dressed in authentic Manhattan Neutral: black crewneck sweater, charcoal flat-fronted wool trousers, black thick-soled boots. His naturally endomorphic English frame has become totally Americanised: the sweater is taut over

124

his bench-pressed pecs. He is cut, man. I'm smiling hard and hugging him, genuinely happy. This is what it feels like. Donachie gives me a frat-boy bear hug and thumps my back vigorously. He is short, five seven, actor sized; his face is against my neck.

– Tim, you tart.

– Paddy, you old lesbian.

I'm still beaming, as is Mary, obviously wowed, as is Susie, as she always is. I ask Donachie if he wants a drink and feel proud to be his friend. Amongst the general din of greeting, Donachie's girlfriend has followed Susie into the room. I see her and hear a comedy noise in my soul, a metallic twang, the sound of a train hitting a wall or a cymbal crash or a cartoon spring springing. She is beautiful, utterly beautiful. She is taking off her padded ski jacket and bobbing from side to side, grinning. She too is in Manhattan Neutral, but Manhattan Neutral Sport, a tight sheeny black blouse, black low-slung capri pants, little Prada sneakers. She is fair-haired, probably bottle-enhanced, but done well. It's in *pigtails*. She is tiny, but with tits. There is an inch of hard belly between her shirt and the top of her pants. I move my head over to kiss her. She smells of fruit tea and cigarette smoke and her skin, still cool from outside, feels soft and pliable as I linger for a nanosecond too long over it.

– Hi, I'm Beth. Cool *apartment*.

A sing-song American accent, that tricked-up, cheery sincerity they can muster at will. I'm panicking for some reason, because she is without doubt the most beautiful woman I've ever met. Maybe not woman, she can't be more than twenty-three. Twenty-*three*. *Twenty-three*. I notice Susie looking at me. She gives a little whistle, which makes me laugh, and everyone settles round the dinner table while Susie goes to get the soup. Borg has noticed Beth, and he and I swap wide-eyed glances of appreciation, which is good because it means he's probably going to try to be charming. Susie bustles back in holding the soup tureen out in front of her as if she's about to empty the contents onto a fire.

Beth sits down, so juicy and fresh. This girl is amazing, Tim knows it, deliberately sitting nowhere near her, emphasising the ease he feels, the power of ownership.

Donachie has always fucked slightly below his ability. One position on this is that it's because he's insecure, and still demands unconditional love, the kind that only a mother or a girlfriend who's much uglier than you can give. But now he's punching his weight, and knowing it. The Big Beast with the life force, getting famous, the looks and the talent spilling from his being, back in the city after a successful time in America, young, amazing, and now he's oinking this little precious.

The soup is served but not eaten because everyone's tuning into the drink and Tim's prodigal vibe. He dominates the table. The English women are quiet, which isn't like either Mary or Susie, particularly when they're leathering the white wine, but what with our guest jangly and raw from the NY flight, so juiced and so full of it, the fucks, the fights, the dollar frenzy, the mojo, the moxie of Gotham, the 'Snowcone', the 'Motherboard', 'whatever', 'totally' and so on and so forth. Borg is quiet for the moment too, but wry and smiley, particularly as he's sitting opposite Beth – oh, he is suddenly *so* wry and smiley. She has small neat Scandinavian features, which makes all of us from the Northern European gene pool (me half Irish, half Welsh, Donachie a Scot, Mary a Norman, Borg pure pillaging Viking, Susie's legs thickened by childhood holidays tramping Cumbrian fells), all made hardy from the thousands of years that our ancestors spent squatting on the edge of the ice sheet grubbing a living from the hard earth. Different now, but still damn tough, tougher than ever in some ways.

Presumably the girls are hoping Beth's some airhead, but no, she keeps them quiet because she's funny and hyper-smart and works for Malaba Films – only as some minion but, as we know, when it happens it happens so quick. I hope we can talk about my career quite soon.

The two of them met in LA where she sees new plays and reads new books and passes them up the line for go/no go. Beth is originally from Madison, Wisconsin. Nobody knows where this is, so I get an atlas from a cupboard and she kneels on her dining chair, ankles crossed, squeaky bubble butt wriggling around, making jokes about her home state, the rising intonation making questions out of statements, statements out of questions.

– Cheddar, Miller Light, Joe McCarthy, America's Dairyland? Basically a German statelet? Check this out, my mother's maiden name is [pause for effect, her eyes look ceiling-wards, her face remains lowered, fingers of both hands splayed and still] *Eichmann*?

Hold on a second, so the Holocaust's funny now? What a relief. Donachie adds his bit, which is obviously rehearsed, or at least often repeated, and he says it over a suppressed giggle.

– Wisconsin, from an Indian word meaning 'place of the beaver'.

He is conscious that this breaks three ways. For Beth it's just his little joke, to Mary and Susie it's a reminder, if one is needed, of his protean masculinity, and to me it says, 'Look at me now, Pad.' Beth gets up and rummages in her coat, and I simply can't stop staring at her ass. Internally, I use the American-English formulation because all the English-English formulations have been stolen and clapped out by cheap comedy – arse, bum, bottom, sit-upon, rear end, backside. None of them is remotely adequate – in relation to an ass of such global quality, at any rate.

– Mind if I smoke?

127

– 'Course not, love, I'll join you.

This is Susie, characteristically trying to make the early connection, sounding to me like a friendly spinster aunt all of a sudden. She is wearing a T-shirt upon which is printed the phrase: 'Vaginas are Way Cool'. Why is my girlfriend mothering my friend's girlfriend? Well, she is *twenty-three*, for God's sake.

– How's the States?

– Fuck, I love LA?

He's only been away six months, but he too has caught the rising intonation, which laid over his RADA RP should sound phoney, but he can pull it off.

– The weather, it's a cliché, but I just love it?

– And you know what else?

This is Beth: Madison, WI, is presumably even further from the light than London, so she's used to relating her big California upsides.

– The people are so *nice*; like it's such a myth that everybody's a shark. I think the sun makes people goofy?

Oh, tell me more about Los Angeles, I'm riveted. Donachie takes a cigarette from Beth; they start doing a double act.

– And the women are awesome – all the racial intermingling, man – it's the future of people.

– Mariah Carey.

– Jennifer Lopez.

– Alex Rodriguez.

– Derek Jeter.

– Ricky Marteeeeen.

– Tiger Woods – cablanasian, man, how cool is that?

He lights the cigarette slowly, and exhales as if he were smoking a Romeo y Julieta. He looks into the middle-distance, considering awesome American people, smoke oozing from his mouth in slow baroque curls. A cooze connoisseur, a tobacco savant, a eugenic prophet with the looks and this delicious little screw. And did I mention the talent?

– Donachie says that some day soon *everyone* will be the same colour, like *latte*-coloured?

I look at Beth and want to take her upstairs and fuck her now right now right NOW, it's all I can think about, her clothes falling away from her like liquid, the supple little limbs pulling me in. I perform a couple of drastic calculations about how to separate her from the group and do it tonight, right now, on the table, under duress even, but then feel melancholy reason return, and a spongy sensation in my groin, and picture myself binking her over the head with a big pink foam hammer. I get up to change the CD.

– Something a bit more fucking lively, Patrick.

I can't think what note to strike, but with a rush of relief I catch sight of Susie's *Otis Redding's Greatest Hits*. That is perfect: safe, inoffensive, still retaining some credibility because Atlantic not Motown, listenable but not *too* obvious. However, just in case, I skip *Dock of the Bay*, which is the first track and *is* too obvious, and return to the table. Susie's talking quickly, pinging on her cigarette every five seconds. Beth is turned towards her, politely asking the questions.

– Yeah, it's been eight years.

– Are you thinking of getting married?

– Oh, we've talked about it, but the timing never seems quite right, somehow.

I notice that we only discuss the possibility of getting married when we're in company, and always use this sound-bite to describe our position. I also notice that this bit of news management has been arrived at without ever having been discussed, and consider the fact interesting and in some way significant, but I have more pressing concerns.

– I don't think we want to talk about our wedding all night.

Particularly as this wedding's never going to happen, I think, shocking myself by how close I am to saying it out loud.

129

– It wasn't all night, Paddy, I was *asked* about it.

– It's dull. It's like other people's dreams or other people's children, for God's sake.

– Or other people's lives.

– Or other people, period.

This is Borg, but Susie addresses me:

– Christ, I'm sorry, what shall we talk about that's so fascinating for all of us?

– I'm not saying that, I'm just saying that people probably don't want to hear about our maybe wedding all night.

– Sorry, Paddy, let's talk about something trivial.

– Why don't we all talk about me?

Donachie hates conflict, of this sort anyway, so he makes the joke to head it off. I go to the bathroom, briefly checking myself out in the mirror. I'm crinkling a little around the eyes, but that can work, and the jug ears have charm – character charm, not juve-lead charm, as we know – and she won't be able to tell that I may not have the talent either, unless Donachie's already told her. I open the medicine cabinet and take down the clear plastic pill phial that contains my ecstasy supply before I decant it to the Altoids tin. I snip off half a pill with my front teeth and wash it down with water from the tap. Susie was never big on e, but was quite cokey once. She stopped because it gave her big downers, which made her eat, which made her fat, which made her want to do more coke, which started the cycle again. Susie on coke was unsettling anyway, tending as it does to accentuate rather than alter, she was 'feisty' to the power of n, where n is a very 'feisty' number. I try not to do coke, as it makes everyone so loud and boorish, and when I think of it I think of my own voice, brayingly amplified, and open mouths, slippery-looking teeth, too-pink tongues and gums, that feeling that everything's suddenly making sense, coalescing around your world view. Like alcohol, though in some ways alcohol makes me feel worse, more regretful the next day. But who doesn't drink? And I'll do coke if anyone's got any, obviously.

I sploosh my face with the coldest water I can stand. Time to raise the film maybe, but I'm nervous in case Beth says she knows Fryman is a talent-free fuck and Donachie tells us his agent turned down the lead months ago because the money was 'like, so pitiful?'

I go into the bedroom and check the ring, tuck it further out of sight, start to feel a little loose in my setting. Donachie's in the doorway when I turn round;

– It's great to see you, Pad.

– And you, Tim.

– How's the work?

– Good. Good. Just got a movie, actually.

A quick shadow of distress passes over his face.

– Movie?

– Yeah. Little independent thing. I thought I'd told you.

– No, you didn't. That's great.

– What about you?

He has to snap himself out of some anguished reverie.

– Oh great. Up for this Broadway thing. Lots of stuff in the pipeline.

– Ah, I'd like to do a bit of theatre again. Proper acting, right?

I enjoy for a moment this victory in the actor's scissor-paper-stone match (movies cut theatre, cover theatre, blunt theatre), then I move us on.

– Sweet chick.

No response. Wow, he's really disturbed about this movie I'm in. He looks at me with a kind of desperation.

– What? Yeah, she's lovely. Anyway, as I say, it's great to see you again, mate.

He moves swiftly off to the bathroom. I say under my breath:

– God exists.

131

I go back downstairs and Beth is talking to the table. Borg is wearing a fixed grin, hunched forward, winding a napkin round his hands. He's almost certainly picturing what it would be like to be fellated by her. Do beautiful girls know that this happens? She must sense the hot breath all the time and ignore it. Borg is nodding now, eyes widening, grin slashed across his face. *She's on her knees looking up at him, lips now reddened with the alcohol, sliding, cheeks hollowed.*

– We're always looking for English talent to attach to things? But a particular type of thing? More Irish, or romantic-comedy-type things? The American idea that England's full of charming, hapless, upper-class people or rude mechanicals, preferably Celtic? Or costume-y stuff, classic adaptations and so on?

Beth's breasts are like breasts only more so: more gravity-defying, more archetypal, more *perfect*. I consider that Borg is probably mentally preparing to ejaculate in their vicinity, if he's got any sense. Susie throws a half-smoked cigarette into the soup tureen and stands to clear the table. Nobody managed more than a mouthful, what with so much going on. I didn't even ladle any into my bowl.

– Aaaachoooo!!

This is Borg, silent while he mentally made a pig of him-self over Beth, the sneeze putting an exclamation mark on his exertions. The ecstasy may be fazing in, just a gentle buzz. I start to become strangely appreciative of the British film industry.

– Literate. Literate films. Merchant Ivory.

– Life is so terribly terribly pretty yet so terribly terribly sad.

Borg leans forward across the table, still winding his napkin.

– You know what I love about Americans? It's still all so new to them that they haven't worked out what to do with it.

I try to stop a diatribe, bored by the prospect of a Europe v. America conversation. It's a mismatch anyway, has been for a century or so.

– Borg, that's boring.

He looks on the verge of saying something, but stops himself with another mighty slug of wine.

– Oh fuck it, let's talk about property prices or kids' TV or something.

Donachie has returned to the table, managing a smile again, recomposed. I don't know what he must have been through in that bathroom, but he's a trouper.

– So, Donachie, what did you miss about England?

– Nothing. *Sleb* and *Bagpuss* reruns.

And everyone is relieved, Susie, even Borg, because when you come down to it a dinner party's no place to talk about baby brains or cultural ascendancies or acting careers or cancelled wedding plans, and the evening continues without incident.

In bed later, Susie moves towards me and starts trying to arouse me, stroking my back, kissing my neck, moving her cool hand round to stroke my narrow long-muscled legs, but I draw them up, throttling my cock and balls between my thighs to keep her away.

Do it now right when she least expects it when I'm in one of my grumpy moods and imagine her burbling pride: 'you wouldn't believe he bought the ring six weeks before but didn't have the nerve but I don't care', and we fuck on the bedroom floor and on the bathroom floor and on the landing for good measure and the film will be an astonishing success, and work will crash towards me, life will be simple and good because it's all about the right girl and she's right here in front of me and always has been and always will be and I could never hurt her, or rather I'll always do what's in her best interests, and imagine the children and I hope they're like her because if so they'll be perfect if only she wasn't screwing someone else.

I close my eyes and think about Donachie in his West End hotel, Beth breezing round their suite in T-shirt and panties, him considering her lionishly, distractedly massaging himself to erection under the cool, thousand-threadcount sheets. Susie holds still for a moment, warm against me, and then without a sigh or a word, rolls over into her other world.

I feel dangerously on the verge of something.

12

Next day:

– Listen, it's obvious. You can't stand her, she disgusts you, you've got to get out.

Borg and I are the firmest of firm friends. I really fervently hope I'm not hanging out with him because he's famous. We're on the South Bank, the place Londoners go when they're feeling filmic. I wonder if before films people went to filmic places when they were feeling filmic? Or in the early days of cinema did people hang off clock faces on high buildings, get chased by dyspraxic cops and kick villains up the backside when they were feeling filmic?

– I've seen it so many times before: you're blowing it.

– Listen, it's OK for me.

Borg looks at me, his eyes streaming. He moves to the railing, watches the Thames. What does he see in rivers, what does the wind tell him? He doesn't seem to have much affinity with nature – there's no opportunity to enforce his will. We both stare downriver, he turns to me, full of gestures.

– Right, fast forward, picture the scene forty years hence. You're in some nursing home in Bexhill, incontinent, dribbling, alone, your kids have got their own concerns, the family thing will be dead in any case, Susie's on machines at the cancer ward, you'll be watching golf on the tele-screen every so often, tipping your head back and bellowing, 'What the fuck did I do with it all?'

– You just missed out forty years.

– Too painful to relate, but, OK, I'll give you a taste. Think of that phase when her looks finally go for ever, and the ovulation stops and she has to start developing *interests* or, God forbid, a *personality* now the primary purpose is gone, and you're having this empty, afternoon hotel room affair with a woman you don't fancy *that* much, but at least she's not your fucking *wife*, because *she's* started wearing clothes that are too young for her and getting tipsy at dinner parties and giggling and dancing badly to the 'old songs' and joining a fucking reading circle and pawing at her sagging, pouchy face in the mirror six hours a day and smelling of dust and moisturiser and bitching about the TV stars' thighs and how everyone who isn't eighteen stone is anorexic and how the kids worry her and the fact she wants a winter coat and the godforfuckingsaken carpet in the hall needs replacing.

He has worked himself up into a minor frenzy. It's interesting: all this passion makes him seem weak.

– You'll never get it, Ray. I'm not like you. I need a home and a girl.

– Home, I like that. You live with a woman you no longer love in a flat with no porn. If that's home, then what's the value of home?

– You're over-simplifying.

– And you said she's screwing someone else.

– I don't know she is, I just think that she may be.

– Well, find out.

– I don't get it, Ray; why do you give a damn?

– Because people on the outside see things more clearly.

– I don't get why you're so bent on this.

– I'm not bent on it; it's just so obvious to the outside

136

observer it makes me mad you can't see it.

He's told me a little, always in asides. His father is a failed painter who lives in Denmark and drinks. His mother has retired to France and grows herbs and bakes her own bread. He has a brother in California who lives on a beach, surfs, screws, works in a bar. The family atomised utterly. He never talks about them, visits his father once a year, his mother the same. As for what makes him tick, who knows? I think it might be some form of neurosis. What I do know is that increasingly he lacks affiliations, a sense of allegiance to anyone, anything, anyplace. This is what makes him dangerous, because I may be going the same way.

– You've got to find out if she's screwing someone else.

– I don't think I want to.

– Of course you do.

– I'm not sure I'd be able to cope with it.

– It seems to me that we're getting near the heart of the problem. You're a pussy.

– So how do I find out anyway?

– Ask her. Hire someone. Espionage. Anything.

Maybe it's Borg who needs a home and a girl. Now religion's gone and families are going and if money just gets rid of money problems, maybe girls are the last thing left. But which girl for Borg? Which girl generally?

Later at home, she's lying on her back on the sofa, smoking softly, her feet wriggling around.

– What are you thinking?

– Hmm?

– What are you thinking?

I'm standing, arms folded, leaning against the wall. The TV's on, of course: without it the place feels that much lonelier.

– Oh nothing. *Last night was just so good, I haven't fucked like that in years or ever, maybe, Jesus, this is what it's supposed to feel like, and he's so huge it's just a different kind of thing altogether, maybe I should try to cool it with all the noises and all the clinging but five times, that's just insane, my legs ache my jaw aches my ass aches my* stomach *aches, for God's sake, I'm a wreck but I've got to see him again soon all of me just needs him so much.*

– Are you sure?

– Christ, Patrick, why are you so paranoid?

– I'm just curious.

– Well, stop it, it's abusive.

– What is?

– Asking me what I'm thinking. It's invasive and disgusting. It's what wife-beaters do. It's a white-trash tactic and I'm not having it.

She stubs out her cigarette and folds her arms, looks upset. I try to make my tone more conciliatory.

– I was just curious.

– No you weren't. It's some hideous male primal ownership rubbish and I don't like it, so just back off.

– If it's genetic I can't control it.

– I didn't say it was genetic – and that's bullshit anyway. You can control whatever you like.

– Apart from what I'm thinking. My mind takes me places without me asking it.

– I don't want to know, so let's drop it.

– You don't want to know?

– I know too much already.

What is she thinking?

– When are we seeing the leviathan again?

– Next week.

– Can I crib your homework?

– Please, Patrick, drop it just tonight.

Just tonight, Susie. Espionage it must be.

13

Susie's office is on Old Street, above a tobacconist. This is the only place on earth, other than certain types of government property, where I am strictly not allowed.

I walk up the narrow staircase, the paint grimy at hand level, the carpet worn through to the webbing on the knuckles of the steps. There are four locks on the door to Susie's office, there are four unmarked keys on her spare key ring.

Intelligence test. If there are four unmarked locks and four unmarked keys, what is the maximum number of times Benny the Baboon must try the keys before he is guaranteed to open the door?

What if Benny the Baboon is in fact an underemployed actor called Patrick Moon who forgets that if you try a key once and it doesn't fit the lock, the chances of it fitting the third time round are negligible. But all keys look the same to someone who's never used them before. Try staying in someone else's house for the weekend to prove the truth of this:

– *It's really straightforward. The silver Chubb's the top lock on the outer door, the Yale with the chunk out of the middle is for the mortice, the other Chubb is the lower lock on the inner door, the Allen key opens the French windows and the funny little one with*

the pointy end is for Terry's pornography casket in the garage. If
you go out, you can leave the back door on the latch.

Nod pleasantly, don't write any of this down and prepare your-
self to spend the weekend sleeping on the freezer, three copies of
Hustler *for a pillow, another for a lullaby, wondering what the*
hell 'mortice' means.

But, after securing what would be a straight fail in my
primate IQ test, the last deadlock clunks open, with a noise
as heavy and promising as a jewellery box lid.

The room is a womb. It is tiny, painted crimson, a minia-
ture, superstuffed blue sofa in the corner, a thick sheepskin
rug on the floor. Her I-Mac looks wildly anachronistic sitting on the old roll-top desk we bought for her five years
ago in Hackney. There is an artful mess. Books, magazines,
newspapers in precarious heaps on every surface. Remove
one from any pile and it will collapse like a Jenga tower.
There is a picture of me in a heavy silver frame on the
desk. Me years ago, smoking, looking out over the Grand
Canal from the terrace at the Gritti Palace. There is also one
of her mother in the breakfast room of the house in Surrey,
cigarette in one hand, goblet of white wine in the other,
keeping her lips tight closed over her higgledy-piggledy
teeth, French lacy underwear printed on her apron.

I open the top drawer of the desk. Silk Cut Ultra Mild, a
plastic jar of Quality Street, old cheque books, some CDs –
Suzanne Vega, Janis Joplin, Joni Mitchell, Alanis: fallopian
tunes.

In the next drawer there is a manuscript, *The Golden Age*,
which I remember was a working title of her second book.
It looks as if it's been printed off recently. I flick through it
for a second; it's full of cackling girlfriends, warm-hearted
gay intimates, cigarettes, vodka, menu-satire, semen flying
around all over the place, as if the London air was thick
with it, as if it whizzes by your face morning noon and night.
Look, Susie, you should know by now, this is demonstrably

untrue. You have a credibility problem and a triviality problem. Let's have some books about what's important – like – I don't know, betrayal, for instance.

Anyway, the room – so far so reassuring; a reconfirmation of my idea of Susie. I start to feel guilty. I like this room, the idea of it. A space that's hers and only hers. I remember how proud she was when she first got it, how it made her feel adult and sneakily glamorous, her own office, her own phoneline – 'call me at the office' – how much she liked the sound of that. Not just the work thing: how wise to have an inviolable place where you can't be watched, or listened to.

The phone rings, diverts straight to the answer machine.

– Hi, it's just Martin, sweetie. Now I think of it, Moira said you were away until Monday. Anyway, give me a call, you fabulous bitch. We need to talk.

Martin Threlfall, the editor of *The T———*. I don't like his tone, the knowingness, the implication that there is a version of her I don't know very well. I'm aware she has a 'professional persona', with a distinct vocabulary, subtly re-emphasised character traits, specific unsharable memories, work-specific gossip that is untranslatable to an outsider. I tolerate it, though, because people need acting to get them through the day. And who's to say that the way she is with her work friends isn't the way she really is? Or if it's even desirable to be honest most of the time? Or that anyone is entitled to discover the parts of someone that they don't choose to disclose? What the hell, for instance, does she really know about me?

In the second drawer down there is a fancy blue cardboard box with a gift tag.

Dearest Sook
Better than the real thing!?
Mummy

I open the box. A vibrator set into a blue velveteen mould, *Slave Deluxe* stencilled into the lid of the box. I take it out and wonder at the super-sized realism. It is sculpted from heavy black latex, each vein and ridge perfectly rendered. Balls the size of nectarines crowd its thick base. It must be nearly a foot long. I flick a switch. It starts to hum. I clasp it and the warm buzz permeates my hand and forearm. I flick the switch again and it oscillates more markedly, the noise becoming more of a whine. The last notch on the switch and it wobbles frantically. I lay it on the table and it seems to take on a life of its own, spasming like some hideous sausage-beast in its death throes, the noise now like a chainsaw heard in the distance, or a fat bumblebee in late summer, indolent and lascivious.

So what? She uses a fat black vibrator. What I want to know is, what is she *thinking about* when she uses a fat black vibrator? *Who* is she thinking about?

I put it back in the box, fire up her computer. It's programmed to sing Dee Lite's 'Groove is in the Heart' as it warms up. The human mind is rarely so innocently employed as when it is changing the settings on a computer. Why this impulse to leave an individual imprint on everything? It occurs to me that it is especially true of computers: set your preferences. So many ways in which they reveal character. So, what does the computer say about Susie? Is any of it a reflection on me? And why all this effort when she must have believed that no one would ever see this computer?

Sound of Music wallpaper, Julie Andrews wheeling across an Austrian meadow, ecstatic, cruciform. Susie's folders are arranged in an orderly phalanx, colour co-ordinated – a row: blue green red blue green blue red, a column: blue green red and so on, the script underneath each one cryptic abbreviations all in lower case – clms, ints, feats, prsl, emls, corr, gage – all of them I notice, not exceeding the edges of the folders they caption. The intended impression: a fanatically tidy mind but with a semi-ironic kitsch bent (Julie) and a funky soul (Dee Lite). One possible interpretation: an anal sadist struggling with the conflict between control and letting go, and aging without grace in addition. The rest of the room is eloquent of her desire to coddle herself, surround herself with comforts both sensual and psychological (and 'erotic', if we factor in *Slave Deluxe*). She is an orally fixated (the chocolate and lollies) narcissist (the gallery of byline pictures), a princess who couldn't sleep because of a pea under the mattress, a flibbertigibbet a will o' the wisp a clown.

'prsl', I imagine, is her terse rendering of 'personal' and it is inevitably where I begin, with a heavy, heavy heart.

Half an hour later I'm rootling around in the guts of the machine red in snout and hoof.

An hour after that I escape to the street, the true story of Susie's erotic life wadded into my jeans pocket, the livid imagery from it playing and replaying on all screens of the porno multiplex which has just had its grand opening in my mind.

14

I have some final tasks to attend to. Borg, Fryman and I are spending a weekend in New York to meet our American money-man. A month after that we start rehearsals, then the shoot in Scotland. My feeling is that the time is absolutely ripe for a completely fresh start. In order to do this, I have to act. Act in the sense of actually doing something, rather than merely pretending.

This is more difficult than I imagined. It's been a long time since I made a decision. In fact, it seems that decisions have had a habit of taking me. Something I never understood made me an actor, something mysterious and chemical connected me with a girl, something equally mysterious gradually moved us away from each other. I guess it seemed easier to drift with whatever wind was behind me. Not now, no time.

OK, new resolutions, I'm nearly ready, but to overcome the last vestiges of doubt, I make myself revisit the decisive texts:

> Bobbi
> This is a kind of 'standard' fantasy I return to quite often.
> I've found it difficult to recreate exactly because some of

the elements change a lot from occasion to occasion. I actually found it cathartic writing this down, so I hope it's helpful to some degree.

I'm at home, cooking, something elaborate, totally absorbed in it, music playing, the world shut out. I'm dressed casually, just in running shorts and a T-shirt, bare feet. I'm always very hot and bothered, all the rings on the hob going, the oven on, things bubbling and simmering. It's cold outside, so there's thick condensation on the windows. The flat is hot, the way it can only be in the depths of winter. I don't know why this is important. Then I am taken by surprise – I'm grabbed from behind and I don't even have time to cry out, and there's this cold, tough hand over my mouth, one of my arms bent behind me as I'm pushed over the counter. I hear the creak of leather, and get frog-marched to the bedroom. I can feel the scale of his body behind me. He's very big, makes me feel so light and my feet barely touch the floor. I'm stumbling but, as I say, lightly. He throws me face down on the bed, tells me to stay still. I hear the unbuckling of a belt and feel his hand pull at the waistband of my shorts and hear them ripping. My mouth is so dry I can't swallow, my heartbeat sounds as if it was filling the room, but it's a feeling I like a lot. Then he pulls my hips up off the bed, the thickness and strength of his arm making me feel like a little girl. Always at this point I want to see his face so badly, I need to look into his eyes, but he won't let me. Then this feeling, it's not rough or violent, in fact it's almost tender, I imagine it like a giant engulfing, my face buried in the bed, a delicious engulfing, I wish I could explain how it feels, I feel sorry that he'll never know what it feels like, a kind of swallowing, or a hugging something with your guts or your whole body, there's no way to communicate it. And after a while as he starts to fuck me harder, so huge and hard, the feeling is just this side of pain; the fineness of the distinction heightens the

145

intensity. I don't know where this comes from, whether it's what I'm thinking in the fantasy or it's my commentary on it, but I'm thinking something like 'the sheer fuckness of the fuck'. And then when he finally tosses me over and tells me to put it in my mouth it barely fits. I look up into his eyes and he comes almost instantly in my mouth (you'll have to forgive me the next bit, but it is what I think about) he comes so hard that I gag, then it's over my cheeks and chin, in my hair, and I want his fucking black balls in my mouth, his whole body, my tongue up his ass, and for him to fuck me again anywhere and everywhere – in the ass, in my mouth, in my cunt simultaneously. All the time he doesn't say a word. And then as I curl up in the space for me between thighs and neck and reach for his cock again and feel it thicken and twitch, I hear the soft padding and the small creak of the door as the other man comes into the room and starts to put his fingers in my mouth . . .

Here I lower the curtain on Act II, the first protagonist's unlikely early recovery, the new arrival's brief yet memorable cameo, and the passive yet nonetheless compelling development of Susie's central role. As for Act III – to be truthful, I never really saw the point of The Third Man, and the action didn't so much develop as repeat itself in a somewhat predictable fashion. I couldn't finish it.

And, anyway, eventually I found what I was looking for elsewhere.

Dearest Martin

As I said last night, we must stop seeing each other. You're married; I'm in a long-term relationship. These two statements were true three months ago, and they're still true now. I don't expect you to get a divorce. I'm not currently thinking of leaving Patrick. It may sound brutal and practical, but the existing conditions prevent this relationship from working.

More than this, I think it's actually been a terrible mistake, jeopardising professional relationships as well as personal. You have been so kind and affectionate and loving, but it's going nowhere. I still love you, of course, but this is my final word. Please understand this. I'll call you.

Susie

Which was worse, the action or the thought, the betrayal of the imagination or the betrayal of the body? Neither – it's the 'I love you' that's the worst, because writing that is a betrayal of both. That's why it's over.

She gets home at six-thirty and I'm waiting, scratching myself with nerves and fear and relief, the ring now in my trouser pocket niggling my thigh. I reach in and it's like an unpicked scab and luxurious and compelling because of that, and when she comes in she's surprised to see me and big, boxy cardboard bags swing from her wrists and I say I need to talk to you and she says wait a minute, disappears upstairs and after five minutes' bumping and clanging calls me up and I go into the bedroom and she's standing there in a French chambermaid's outfit even down to the big bow in her hair and she says in a lousy Clouseau accent, 'Allo! Allo!' and I'm pulled up short for a moment. It was never meant to be like this, the collision of tragedy and farce in one moment, and I reach into my pocket and spin the ring in my awkward fingers and feel a great clenched fist opening within my chest and everything's going to be absolutely all right.

15

Borg books himself into Club, I'm in Coach, woozy on the comet tail of a long weekend of post-break-up narcotics, wrapped in a blanket, quivering in the cabin half-light, when we hit an air pocket and dive three thousand feet in ten seconds and I become aware that we're in a paper-thin tube of steel up beyond the air and there's nothing below but ten miles of empty space and then water which from this height is harder than granite. Everybody on board shrieks like Beatlemaniacs. We regain equilibrium, but my heart is still banging and sputtering.

I'm sorry Susie, it's over.

After some more heart-stopping hurly-burly, when the plane starts making noises like a train – tackety ra tickety ree – the captain apologises in an urbane bored-sounding growl and we resume our journey. I flick through the movies – I could do that, I could do that, I could do that –

The intensity of her reaction.

MARY MOTHER OF JESUS!! I've still got at least four tabs of e in the Altoids tin! I remember being told that the narc dogs at Kennedy can sniff an aspirin up a Turkish whore's grumble from ninety feet, so all the drugs have to go NOW. I repair to the toilet, feeling as if I'm being photographed:

by Interpol, Global Airline Control and my mother. I fumble the tin open. I take a piss and flush one of the tablets out along with the urine, which, in my newly arrived-at state of heightened consciousness, I picture forming a jagged saffron-coloured icicle on impact with outside. I bolt the other three, praying that they'll take the edge off my newly aroused fear of flying and my even more newly aroused fear of being sucked into the sub-zero void and impaled on a dagger of my own waste.

The violence of her reaction.

I return to my seat and twitch like James Brown all the way to America. My neighbour puts it down to air-pocket aftershock and is sympathetic. I get his minibag of salted peanuts. Still flying well after we've landed, I remember I went out with this girl once and then I broke her heart, but that was in another country and besides, Jesus, in America now, so much to see and do.

I was astonished, and I must say in some way gratified. I never thought I could be so powerful.

It's ten p.m. and misty, as the cab pitches and rolls down the Van Wyck, me three-e awake, Borg crashed, soused with Club Class Merlot, armagnac, tokay, malmsey and sack. The first sight of the skyline is über-mythical. It looks as if dense chunks of the cosmos have fallen to earth, some of the starlit, fogbound buildings receding into blue or green or silver nebulae, red giants winking and pulsing from unseen pinnacles.

– Borg, Borg wake up, the skyline.

He stirs, jaw slapping, breath Mephistophelean.

– Look, Ray, it's like Valhalla.

– Or Oz.

He collapses back into sleep despite the fact that the cab driver is playing salsa/soca at ninety decibels. All the windows are open and he continually rubs his face with his pudgy brown mitt. His neck is shaved and fat, the thick rolls of flesh making it look like a trussed lamb joint. He has an aristocratic slave name, Orlando Luis Garciaparra. I lean through the gap and shout in his ear, tiny on his great head:

– Can we take this down a bit?

– Feefteen fockin hour, man, I bin in this cab.

I don't force it – *chico no bailes en casa del trompo.*

We're booked in at the Groom on Park and 50th. Borg sees himself to his room, I dump my case and spin out through the chrome-lined revolving door and into the cathedral serenity of late-night Park Avenue. The drugs buzz fatly in my gums, and I can't but feel as I walk towards Met Life, separated from but close to the atmosphere of twentieth-century myth, post-war NYC, Bogie, Cary Grant, Salinger, the great movies, monochrome but luminously so: the images of beautiful, fabulously dressed people dancing, the giant Ellington glitterball, unfiltered cigarettes that do no harm and make you look like a god, vodka Gibsons, Sinatra in his 55th-floor suite looking out towards the Hudson, it's a long way from Hoboken to New York City, another highball, another blonde, silk socks padding across the midnight-blue carpet, the rumbling money mills of deep downtown keeping it all viable for the time being, printing electronic billions onto the ether.

She bit, spat, scratched like a weasel.

But what it reduces to is buying a torn *New York Times*, sitting in a Starbuck's and staring restlessly into the newspaper's lapidary tedium for an hour before retiring to my Swiss-efficient corporate hotel room and watching relays of ads interspersed with glossy snippets of talkshows and sports highlights, teases on what's just coming up, reminders of what's a little further off, another minutely orchestrated ultra-burnished sliver of content, and then just ads half an hour long for ab machines, rotisseries, protective crystals. I eventually fall asleep with a sexline number on my lips.

But everything's going to be just fine.

Calmer now, woken by an instantly forgotten dream, I decide to take my time over the morning. We are lunching with Stephen Buha, our producer, at one-thirty. There is a balcony outside my room. Park Avenue is eighteen stories below, traffic and people, mid-paced and familiar-seeming. It's not yet nine a.m. but the air is viscous and dusty. The heat is collecting in the city, redoubled by the absorbent steel and concrete, reflective glass. I get back on the bed, stretching out into the cool half. I think of Susie, our bodies heating the bed until the warmth radiated out to surround us, then in the morning how I liked to stretch out into her side and feel the warmth receding, her slow fading. It's afternoon in England. When I picture her it's from behind, her walking, head slightly bowed, but purposeful, I hope.

I can still feel the spit on my cheek.

I call Borg.

– The question is, Ray, what do we do till lunchtime?

Through a thick soup of jetlag, hangover and bad personal hygiene he answers:

– Sleep.

No sleep for me, I've murdered sleep.

Out on the boiling dusty street, I start to walk, buy some Aviators for eight bucks from some oil-black guy barely weighing down a calypso shirt who talks the universal foreign language – nanananana dollar nanananana dollar nanananana dollar.

My plan is to walk all morning: it collapses within half an hour. I'm footsore, chafed. Chilly beads of sweat appear intermittently in surprising locations – down my ribs, the

151

backs of my knees, inner ankle. I stop by a deli, and drink a quart of water in thirty seconds sitting at a bee-strafed bench. I think of calling Susie. Then an odd swoop of realisation – *she's not there*. Another swoop of realisation – *really, really it's all OK*.

It is all too fucking much – the heat, the foot-swelling, ball-shrinking, eye-melting heat. So I decide to sit till lunch, drinking iced coffee, which ironically is the colour of me, zoning in and out of the Midtown sirens – scandalised dowager, Wagner tubas, triceratops rampant, querulous hoopoe – and watching the girls of the world over the top of my paper.

We're meeting Buha in a restaurant called Blood. It's situated in a hollowed-out warehouse a block from the river just south of Canal. Gideon, Borg and I are seated. We order Bloody Marys. Stephen Buha is late, but that's all right because he's the money guy. Gideon runs us through a list of things Buha's produced, exec-produced and co-exec-produced. It's all second-tier blockbuster, straight-to-tape rom-com, a couple of pseudo-arty cop flicks. I try to think of nice things to say about at least a couple of them. *Dead on Arrival* had a good title sequence, *Streets* was short.

Blood does offal stylishly, unusual cuts of the animal, raw shit. The brick walls are painted industrial white, the ceiling is thirty feet high, but even in all this space you can feel the air crackle as he lumbers towards us. He has a SoCal tan over a whisky flush, black wavy collar-length hair that tufts from beneath his Brooklyn Dodgers baseball cap. He clinks and creaks in his heavy leather jacket, trousers and square-toed motorcycle boots. Fryman greets him with an awkward semi-hug, which Buha seems to decline. He dumps a pile of books, files, a Palm pilot, an

A4 sized Filofax and half a dozen videotapes on the medical-lab steel table. He's wearing a mobile phone earpiece and, unburdened, wrenches the mouthpiece on its black wire closer to his lips. He's talking hard, staring ardently over my shoulder.

– I *hate* Arizona, find somewhere sunnier, fresher, non-fucking film industrialised, think the Samarkand, Uzbekistan, I don't know, fuckin' *Bosnia*. Keep me away from the admen and ten-dollar-a-day backpackers. Use your imagination: if I'd wanted a tourist video I'd have asked for one. No, that's it – and to you, too.

He disengages his earpiece, which is clotted with amber wax, and surveys the restaurant.

– Why am I here?

– This is Patrick and Ray, from the movie.

He looks briefly fuddled, starts to address me, jabbing his finger in a staccato rhythm.

– I try to tell people, I try to tell them, but they just won't listen. This business, it moves, it turns on originality – the new thing, what's the new thing, the look, the way of seeing, the idea – that's the big thing, the idea. Can we get some fucking water?

– It's here in the –

– That's what they *say*: originality. But it's not true, never was – maybe for ten minutes in the seventies. We're moving through this new paradox – OK, you with me? It used to be you could make a movie for adults, for grown-ups, for intelligent people like you and me, but not now. You know why? Fucking gangster movies, the heist the broad the coke, the money the girl the gun – every film, the money the girl the gun the drugs, every film that *matters*, I mean – where's the money? We need a gun – Where's the girl? I need the money – And where's the money? I need a gun. And how do I get the money? The drugs. And who are the injuns? The cops. That's the switcheroo. And the cowboys?

They're the thieves and murderers, the new heroes – that's the switcheroo. The white European female, lashed to a tree – which means *raped* by the way, if you hadn't noticed, pounded in the ass by the redskin savages – she's still there, she's still lashed to a tree, but now the tree's a pimp, or a mob boss, or a *really* evil gangster rather than the *good* evil gangsters in the rest of the show, and the *really* evil gangster's screwing her blind, and we can't take that, it sticks in the throat, so we want the good evil gangster to take him out and give the girl what she's always wanted, hard and gentle in a motel bedroom on a spread of money and drugs. It doesn't matter, find me the money and I'll find you the right gun, the .45, the semi-automatic, the twelve-bore, the Glock, the whatever. That's the new paradox. Are you with me?

Why look at me, why look at me?

– Paradigm?

– Paradox, *exactly*. And this is what I do: I spend my life following the trail – the girl the money the drugs the gun. You know what the perfect name, the subtitle for every novel ever written should be? You.

He points at me.

– I . . .

– *The Way We Live Now*. You know what the perfect name for every film ever made should be?

He jerks his head at Borg.

– *The Way* –

– *Beautiful Women, Heavily Armed Men, With Drugs*. That's it – right there. And do you know, now we no longer make films for grown-ups, for intelligent adults like you and me, you know what? They're *better*. We like them more. Why? Because we don't want to be adults when we see a movie, we want to be little children again, kings of the castle, with the biggest gun the most money and all the drugs and the most beautiful girl – and that's what we deliver, for all these

154

people who have no lives of their own but sure know what they could do with a big enough gun, a stack of money and a beautiful girl with a torn dress and these big cocksucking lips. Vice versa with the chicks by the way if you follow. Right?

– I . . .

– Good. Now why am I here?

A waiter is standing at Buha's mighty hidebound elbow looking amazed. I don't know why but I feel that eventually his repeated questioning might be designed to invite some form of response.

– What about *Four Weddings*?

– Excuse me?

– *Four Weddings and a Funeral*. There aren't any drugs or guns in that, are there?

– You haven't been listening; people just won't listen. *Four Weddings and a Funeral* isn't a *movie*. It isn't a *movie*. It's a . . . it's a fucking *commercial*, that's it right there, it's a commercial, I don't know, for queers and gimps and jolly old fellows and the Merrie Old fucking England Tourist Authority. But most of all you know what it is?

Nobody seems willing to hazard a guess.

– I'll tell you: it's a commercial for American foreign policy. Through the instrument of Andi McDowell, America can save the world – from poverty, from history, from fat assed, no-tits English chicks. That's it, it's a commercial for American full-spectrum dominance. And I fucking loved it, two hundred million dollars.

The three of us nod slowly in unison. The waiter remains alert.

– Are we ready to order, sir?

Without looking at the menu, he barks:

– Sirloin, blue, frites, bottle of Oregon pinot noir.

And then, more slowly, as if saying something of archetypal profundity:

155

– What we need in this business, boys, is some clear thinking.

He sits back, fingering his grubby earpiece, gently nodding his head.

Nobody can speak, our minds vaporised by his furnace-like onslaught.

– I'll have the same.

– Me too.

– I'll just have a green salad.

The waiter stabs at his booklet and disappears, leaving us in the awkward position of actually having to say something. Buha looks around the table, beckons us with eager hands.

– Come on, come on, talk to me.

– I . . .

– Ideas are everything to me: big, bold ideas. Star Wars. Nine parts. I love that. Nine parts.

Buha is looking at me, small thick-lashed eyes squinting in disbelief.

– Hey, what movies do you like?

– Err, Scorsese obviously, Truffaut, John Woo, err, Almodovar.

– OK, faggot or Democrat or both. That's OK, got that straight. What about you?

Borg has retained some suavity.

– I've always liked *Streets*, in fact that's definitely my favourite cop movie, I'd say.

Buha nods, says quietly:

– I made that movie. It broke my heart. I love it.

I make a bid:

– And, of course, I really liked *Dead on Arrival*.

Someone kicks me hard in the shin.

– They butchered it. They wrecked that piece of shit. Fucked it to pieces.

Gideon tries to move us on.

– So, we start shooting next month.

Buha shrugs and starts to look bored. He scrolls through the address book on his PDA.

– Yes, yes, I know, I know.

He looks at me with what could be resignation.

– Peter?

– Paradigm.

– What?

– Nothing.

His voice becomes low and charged with regret. He leans over, squeaking leather, herbal-fresh breath.

– You know what makes me so sad? These people, they're trying to sell me an idea, and they aren't giving me an *idea*, they're giving me some concept, some bullshit concept I don't and can't understand. It's fucking horrible. But that's OK, because ideas are horrible at the moment. We're at the end of something, do you follow?

The strains of Colonel Bogey peep from deep within his person.

– That's my cell.

The waiter returns with two bottles of wine and Borg and I start to drink them while Buha shouts at someone about some money he's got tied up in some film project he's involved in. When the steak comes it looks as if it's just been sawn out of a cow. I feel that it might have bristles on its underside. I don't eat while Buha talks hard into the middle distance. I dwindle away to nothing. Fryman is expressionless, looking with exaggerated quizzicality at the soft drinks menu. Buha, still on the phone, is now in a mild bovine rage when suddenly he gets up from the table and strides across the restaurant, talking all the while about money, actresses, time and violence. We watch him standing outside the restaurant, contorted with disbelieving anger at something related to motion pictures. I turn to Gideon:

– This is going well, isn't it?

Borg continues to watch the crazy display, the pawing of the ground, the snorting.

– This guy is my absolute god.

16

Gideon's schmoozing some more money-people, so he gave us five hundred bucks to get wretched. It is an offer that Borg intends to honour. We're sitting on swivelling bar stools in a Chelsea lounge. I'm triple-soaped, over-cologned and sucking vodka soda through two straws. Borg's on pints of Sam Adams with Baileys and Coke chasers. I've kept the clothing pared back and clinical: white T, smart navy cargo pants and some new all-terrain sneakers I bought that afternoon, because who knows what terrain lies ahead? Borg is in a wool crewneck sweater and beaten-up jeans, but manages to look cool. He's effectively a black guy, looks cool in anything. The bar is almost entirely without light, the walls floor to ceiling with broken mirrors. There are three customers in addition to us, and they're all sitting around a coffee table on low black sofas – office girls smoking heavily and jig-gling to the old-school hip-hop that's being played way too loud. Borg is watching them. There are revolving blue police lights up in the ceiling, which make the girls look flickery and pornographic.

– The one in the red fucks anything.

– How can you tell?

– Fat, ugly bitch in this city *has* to fuck anything to stay alive.

– I like the one with the long hair.

– She's frigid.

– Yeah?

– A girl like that can fuck anyone she wants, so she freezes. This cock, that cock, those cocks, *these* cocks. Too fucking much.

– What about the black one?

– I'm not yet prepared to make a judgement.

The girls have started to pay us some attention, glances held overlong, walks to the toilet infused with extra poise and wiggle. I'm not ready, so I ask for more drinks. The barman's body is panelled with muscle, narrow lines of facial hair etch his jawline. Queer in England, anything here.

– Why's the place so empty?

– It doesn't pick up till later?

The sleeves of his T-shirt grasp his biceps like a bandage, his arms are braided with thick veins. You feel that the glasses he fills could crumble to powder in his hands. I am mesmerised by the sheer superfluousness of it all, the American hyper-abundance, over-engineering.

He goes off to empty the glasswasher machine, polishes the spirits bottles displayed behind him, throws ashtrays out along the bar, makes sure they're all clean. It's good watching him being professional in this small way, unobserved but doing the right thing.

– Women are like animals, Patrick. It's primal; they want us to seek them out. They pretend to run scared, go to ground, but once you've got the scent of her in your nostrils, you'll run her down and tear her limb from limb.

– The one in the black's the one I like.

– Picture her wide-eyed, panting, haunches quivering.

She's waiting till her heart-rate dips below one eight five. Then you're in. It'll be like splitting fresh baked bread.

Four hours later and we're sitting amongst the office girls. The place is thronged with people much younger than me. They're playing dance hall. In this concrete black box the bass line inhabits your gut and won't stop kicking – *mi wanna bikky wit you I am da bikky bikky man.* Borg has been deep-mining the beautiful frigid girl for two hours. He's leaning in, his foot on the low table. Every half-hour or so his arrangement becomes more advantageous. She has stayed very straight-backed, but on both occasions she's been to the toilet she has returned to the seat next to him, maybe even a little closer. I'm alternating between Gracie, the fat, ugly one and the black girl who is either called Taeesha or sneezed when I asked her name.
– I love your *ACC*ent.
Gracie is deeply amused every time she says this.
– I'm from the Shetland Islands.
– English, right?
– Well . . .
– I love that guy? That English guy?
– Which guy?
– You know, that English guy in the movies?
– Which English guy?
– The guy who's always like this English guy in the movies?
– Which guy?
– He's like always playing the English guy? And he's in like some English movies? But also I guess normal movies also?
– Which fucking guy?
Taeesha never addresses me directly, just turns to Gracie when she wants to communicate something.

161

– Gracie, do you mean the young guy or the old guy?

– Kinda middle-aged guy? With that accent? I *think* he's English.

– Are there any other clues you can give me?

– He's like a fat typa guy, sorta unconventional-looking guy? Hot. You know I hate all these pretty little boys like Johnny *Depp* and Brad *Pitt* and, you know, *Leo* frickin' Di *Barf*io.

I notice with grief that Borg has his hand on top of the beauty's thigh. Her eyes have become a little more intense, her head angled towards his. The blue police lights continue to revolve, the music is louder now and the bar is thronged with the promise of sex.

– Can you remember any films he has been in?

– *Films?* I love the way you say that. *Films?*

Gracie has an English face, a great benign oval, her features too small for the wide expanse of skin they lumpily inhabit. You'd see this face at the bus stops of inner city Leeds, the dole offices of Carlisle, battered-wives' shelters anywhere. In America, goddammit, and this is where I end up.

– Movies then, which movies?

– I got one now!! Remember that movie with Meg Ryan or *some* bitch? He's like trying to get into the US but they won't let him because he's English or something? He can't get a visa?

– Gracie, I think that movie was called *Green Card*.

– Yeah, that's it! The big distinctive-looking guy?

Gracie sure is distinctive-looking.

– Gerard Depardieu.

– That's the guy! That's the guy! I love that guy.

– You know what, Gracie, it's funny you should mention Gerard Depardieu because he's from the Shetland Islands too. Same place as me.

– You're kidding! Do you *know* him?

– No no no: it's a very big place.

Another vodka and soda, I'll have another one, and a vodka straight up to chase it down.

The music is cranked up to sonic boom, everybody dips and pulses and shimmies and moves a little closer, and Gracie begins to look at me with some fondness and I feel as if I want to go home, not knowing exactly what I mean, and the dance hall keeps on booming: *SEE here's the man with a plan who can – and SEE he's the man that de others cyan't stand – and SEE here's the man that da yer woman tinks grand – and SEE de bikky bikky bikky bikky man.*

Borg may be kissing her now, his face looks muscular with effort, or maybe he's still talking. I notice her foot resting on the low table is oscillating violently, his hand on her haunch, pulling her in.

Later – difficulty – I lean over – try to kiss Taeesha – move hand round her big hard ass – feel her hand hard on my sternum – must try fuck – she lurches back – I stumble towards her again – she scratches at me – long red nails swipe my slack face – one last lunge – just one fuck – she stamps my foot – you filthy bastard – I will not eat your swine wherever you go you desecrate destroy and pillage I will not read your white words or listen to your white lies and watch you on top of your self-created tower of filth and ruin and torture. To which I reply 'Steady on', and she lifts her hand to her elaborate spidery fringe and staggers as she walks away. I stand on a piece of broken glass but don't fall, just sway and stumble – WHOOAA! – and catch a dark glimpse of Borg and his girl. He's pushing her off. The crowd now sashays and spins and grinds as one – as one apart from me and I sit in a kind of inner silence amidst the noise and stare into the police lights until it's time to go.

* * *

Things moved quickly for a while, but they're starting to slow again. I'm standing with Borg in a room the size of a confessional box. The room is curtained off from the rest of the bar. There are three other people in here, one of whom is holding a key up to my nose. The end of the key is piled with coarse yellow cocaine. My nose is already twitching like a vivisectionist's least favourite rabbit.

– Go on, friend, just one more.

The man is mid-twenties in a basketball shirt, and there's a black-faced Movado watch gripping his fat wrist.

– I can't, I don't think I can, I'm wasted.

My heart feels as if it's bursting out of my chest, the nerves around my mouth pulsing and tugging.

– One more, friend.

I put my finger over one nostril, bow to the key, close my eyes and inhale with manic force. When I look at the key again it's totally cleansed of coke.

Borg does likewise.

After a moment's mature reflection, we walk back into the bar. It is called Snowy's, but Snowy isn't the owner, it's a description of the prevailing atmospheric conditions.

It's decorated like an English motorway café: Formica tables, grimy salmon and black tiles, bad watercolours on the wall of archetypal mountain/lake scenes. I don't know how long we've been here, it could be three hours, it could be seventeen. It's totally windowless. People come and go in no particular rhythm. Borg and I are the only white guys. We are developing a rep as the generous foreigners. Generous to the point of insanity. I'm probably $400 down on the evening and liberally spreading the booty around. I think this could be the reason we're getting coke hand-delivered directly to our faces, but I can't be sure.

Twenty minutes later, there is a small commotion. People are queuing at the back of the club.

– Titty bar time.

– What?

– Midnight the titty bar opens. You've got to see the chicks. Hungry, too many kids, drugs to buy: it all makes for great theatre.

We walk straight through, sit down and Borg is instantly surrounded with scrawny crack moms.

I leave him, his head bobbing amongst splayed and jack-knifed limbs, greyhound ribcages, whippet haunches, the clefts spliced with spandex. I am sitting in the toilet on the attendant's chair while he arranges the cologne bottles on the tiled sink surround. He is handsome, short dreads, a magnificent profile. I want his attention, approbation:

– God I love New York.

– You're English, right?

– Yes.

– What you doing over here?

– God knows.

– You working?

– Kind of.

– What do you do?

– I'm an actor.

– Yeah, so am I, brother.

He continues to polish the cologne bottles, his hands deft and sad.

– Then maybe one day you'll end up like me.

– Or you like me.

I lift my head, he looks at me in the mirror, his brow and eyes moving in and out of shadow as he cleans the taps.

– Maybe like you.

And I start to laugh, stand and hug him, which action he endures with a certain frozen nobility.

And, unexpectedly, a strange happiness grips me. My perceptions are raw, I grind my teeth and somehow the accumulations of the years are chiselled away and in the toilet of a strip club under a bridge somewhere in New York City holding on to a complete stranger for dear life, I have a moment of clarity:

Yes, I'm an actor, and finally I am free.

part two

1

Free indeed. Gone the girl, the money, the drugs, but free certainly.

There are no compromises in the ex-council flat in Holborn, no obligations to anyone in the coffee shops of Soho, no need to get back for anything, nothing to do, no one to call, no old friends, no history, no regrets.

The flat is a cell. Freshly painted white and equipped with the basics, four rooms: one has a bed, one has a TV, one has a bath, one has a gas ring. Sleep, watch, bathe, eat.

No money means no money worries. I subsist, keep it sweet and on doctor's advice I run at dawn.

Fineman again:

– Do you ever do any exercise?

– No point.

– Why not?

– I'm not fat.

He sat back on his squeaky chair.

– Do you ever think that there might be additional benefits to exercise other than outward appearance?

– Absolutely not.

The leaflet he gave me is called 'Love Begins in The Heart!'. It is my bible. Pastel illustrations of wholemeal loaves, fresh fruit and vegetables, a photograph of 'A Healthy Heart', plump, red and muscular, next to 'An Unhealthy Heart', shrivelled and marbled with fat. More illustrations: smiling generic men in tracksuits doing star jumps, squat thrusts and wind sprints. There is a diagram that seeks to draw a direct parallel between physical jerks and sexual prowess: a cross section of a man's body. Tiny little arrows whizz around it, apparently pumped directly from the lungs, through the pristine heart down to a vividly distended phallus.

No drugs, no cigarettes, aerobic exercise, a good diet, early to bed, early to rise, work hard, make a net contribution to human happiness, have sexual relations with squadrons of actresses, die a contented man. It's really that simple. At first it was tough: I clambered down the wet morning streets like a short-circuiting cyborg, my limbs seemingly attached to the wrong sockets, bad mechanics, rusted up, joints clicking and clacking. But now – after four weeks of daily effort– every morning it's the West End, Hyde Park, Green Park, St James's, Westminster, Covent Garden and then home – as easy as dreaming. One leg in front of the other, a sense of inevitability. One leg in front of the other to stop me falling on my face, that's all it is, each stride a narrowly averted fall, arms swinging freely, the mind in white-out, pure oxygen, anonymous to the dark-clothed workers making their way to offices, the crazy dawn runner.

I see Borg once a week, we drink till late, my one night on the vodka. I tell him I am happy with my new situation, he refuses to take credit, and seems upset when I leave him. Two hours' sleep, then more running, to burn off the poison. The past is a collection of chemicals that build up in your body: burn them all off.

No contact with Susie. She could get me if she wanted to, but so far nothing. Yes, I've had moments of doubt, flashbacks to her shocking contortions of pain and grief, but they've passed quickly. Living with someone is unthinkable for now: bumping into her in the corridors, her mess every-where, having to accommodate her social arrangements, aesthetics, media choices. Such a relief to be free of all that. Hell isn't other people: it's other people's laundry, other people's preferences in TV.

Also, the habit now broken, I have this notion that there is some other way of operating. Not 'only collide', but, I don't know, maybe 'never connect'. This doesn't mean being bad to people, but not getting so close you start to affect them. Why this frantic global need to get involved? Why not set each other free by staying out of each other's busi-ness? Or only so far that you get from them what you absolutely need?

Home, showered, I wait with confidence. The doorbell rings, my Thursday morning appointment, because I finally gave into Fineman on another issue as well:

– *So you've come around.*

– *It looks that way, doctor.*

– *I'm very pleased.*

– *There are just a couple of things I need to get cleared up.*

There is a new picture on his desk. Alongside his velvet-swathed family a small silver-framed photograph of a blonde woman with hair blown across her face on what looks the rear deck of a yacht, or maybe the porch of some tropical beach house. The sea behind is turquoise, a pale band of haze at the horizon, then a perfect air-blue sky. Fineman has a tan, his beard is glossy and rich.

– *How does it actually work?*

I've only just let her in but already she's massaging me firmly, mouth and tongue swarming over my ear. She has laid the ground with an interesting claim:

– I'm just the best at this.

She's rubbing through my boxers, tugging, stroking. It's good, it's insistent, but it's gentle. She is wielding all the

171

power, which is odd because she's assured me that she is for some unspecified period of time my slave. So, revolution, the slaves are in the senate house – but I'm not in the least bit worried, it's all working out beautifully so far.

Her hand is now inside my underwear, performing an intricate reiki massage of my bwana. Mostly I can just feel the heat of her hand, occasionally she makes a feathery contact. The tongue is still in my ear, seemingly seeking contact with the pulpy base of my libido. It hasn't started yet and it's already the best I've ever had. Yes, I look forward with relish and anticipation to my continuing involvement. And now it appears as if it's starting.

– Right, so the physiological mechanism involves the release of nitric oxide in the corpus cavernosum, here.

Fineman taps the penis poster on the back of his door with his bulbous Mont Blanc.

– The nitric oxide then sets off an enzyme which causes increased levels of this stuff called cyclic guanosine monophosphate.

– It sounds like the ingredients list on a can of Coke.

– So this stuff – let's call it CGMP, everybody else does – produces what is called 'smooth muscle relaxation' in the corpus cavernosum, allowing a considerable inflow of blood. Bingo, if you're normal you get an erection. Are you with me?

– Just one little thing. You're telling me that being turned on increases the production of nitric oxide in the penis?

– Yes.

– It's all so impossibly romantic.

– Isn't it just?

He rejigs his specs on his nose. He's having fun, I think.

– So the drug produces nitric oxide?

– Yes, kind of. What the drug does, it enhances the effect of the nitrous oxide by preventing the production of this other stuff – let's call it PDE5 – which is normally responsible for degradation of CGMP.

– CGMP being the substance causing 'smooth relaxation'.

– Right. So when sexual stimulation causes the release of nitric oxide, the drug inhibits the PDE5, letting the CGMP flow. Bingo, smooth relaxation – you get an erection.

– Any particular type? On a scale of one to ten?

– Ten. A good, hard, true erection with enhanced sensitivity that's guaranteed to go the distance.

Through some elegant sleight of hand, my underwear has vanished and my balls are now snug and secure in her cupped warm hand. Her tongue is heavy, wet and warm, deep in my groin, then a surprising and welcome development, she takes a swig of steaming cocoa prepared especially for the purpose and part of me is enclosed in the delicious hot rockpool of her mouth. Can she retract her teeth? It's incredible, the intensity of the friction, but no scraping or nipping of any sort, not even a sense of cartilage or tendon, just all wet mouth, flesh, inner cheek, lips, tongue.

Also, she is dextrous, possessed of scintillating hand–mouth co-ordination. One hand is gently wetly circulating round, the other moves with slimy confidence; her tongue is recharged with cocoa-heat and slathering, careful as yet to avoid full engulfment.

– Enhanced sensitivity?

– Generally speaking, that's been the experience. It's not necessarily that dramatic, but a pleasant boon all the same.

– Why isn't everyone on it?

– I think most Americans are.

– They always seem to get there first.

– They feel some sense of entitlement. I think they call it 'the pursuit of happiness'.

*   *   *

– Patrick.

I look down, she stares into my eyes for what feels like hours or nanoseconds, the hands still active around the whole sopping arrangement, then without blinking the lips move over the fat strawberry, the hands subtly increase their speed of rotation and firmness of grip. That's not to say anything's too fast or too firm, no no: everything is moving along just perfectly, everybody involved is delighted with the progress that's being made. And 'Don't neglect the plums' seems to be inscribed into her soul. My plums may not ever recover from the love and attention they are receiving: I fear they may become spoiled. What's that sound? What's that sound, that comb and paper sound? Oh I see, she's providing musical accompaniment, she's humming some insistent and repetitive tune in a loud filthy way, and it is the sweetest music ever tipped from heaven. Maybe it's *'Non più andrai, farfallone amoroso'*. Maybe it's 'The Macarena'. Whatever. The tempo is andante shading into allegro, there is an occasional sloppy percussiveness, the sound of some bit of me being beautifully consumed. I add appreciative audience noises, my vocabulary somewhat limited, a strange collision of appeals to most of the Holy Trinity and remorseless bad language. A hideous moment of shock for a moment, she takes her mouth away, returns with a couple of ice cubes pouched in her cheeks and, I believe, something mentholated. I convulse, wondering whether this is, in fact, fun or a little too elaborate, then five seconds later, the mouth moves away again and after a messy gulp of cocoa it makes its return and everything becomes crystal clear. Some of me feels as if it's disappearing into my torso, some of me feels exactly the opposite . . .

– *So, it seems to me, then, that the drug doesn't work on the cause of the problem – say, just to take two at random, neurosis and low self-esteem.*

– No. It goes straight to the mechanics. Then, once the mechanics are improved, the confidence improves. It's a virtuous circle, based in good biochemistry. Better than any therapy.

– I would hope so. So is it like you take one and there it is?

– No. You have to be aroused for it to work. They haven't figured out how to actually provoke the arousal, but who cares? It works.

– But there must be some side effects.

– Headache is the main one.

– 'Not now, honey, I haven't got a headache.'

– Then I've had a few patients who had some bone pain, a couple of accidental falls, a couple with a marked increase in sputum and one who became prone to abnormal ejaculations.

– In what way abnormal?

– Don't focus on the negatives. The chicks dig it too.

He looks at his yacht-blonde, a blur of love forming in his eyes.

– Can you overdose?

– Just stick to what I give you and you'll be fine.

. . . the tune she's humming is an octave higher, my being a fizzing pile of burnt-out synapses, screeching ganglions. There is now a slowing, a freshly surprising lunge, and I am disappearing into her, her exquisite training keeping the rhythm despite my dreadful bucking, I feel something like a wave of grief building in the core of my being and try to speak but can only say 'gghheeeaaaiirrr' at the top of my voice and feel something hard, something soft, something somewhere in between. She knows exactly what to do and after an infinite moment of writhing whiteout I eventually dare to glance down and she's looking me in the eye, gently swatting her lips with it, and blowing tiny bubbles, as if she's the one who's had all the fun.

– Hhhaaooouahhhh.

– Hello.

– Ghhhuuaogh.

Her actions wind down, the teeth finally come back from wherever she hid them, raking my suddenly shamefaced balls and being gently sunk into my leg. All of me throbs for a long moment. Surveying the scorched earth of my body, I think I may have a little bone pain. It is possible my sputum levels have increased. My ejaculation was utterly abnormal.

I can handle it.

– So how much do you want?
– You sound like my dealer.
– How much do you want?
– I'll say what I normally say to my dealer.
– Which is?
– How much have you got?

Ten minutes later, when my conscious mind is finally ready to reassert itself, I say as she walks in from the bathroom retouching her lipstick:
– How much did you say?
– Hundred quid.
– There's a hundred and fifty, and it's nowhere near enough.
– Very generous.
– Marinara, that was exquisite.
– Fanks.
I watch her as she brushes her hair vigorously.
– Acksherly, I was finkin' of changing me name.
– Don't tell me – *quattro stagioni*.
– No, don't be stupid.
– Come on then.
– 'Putanesca'. Nice, innit?

– I think it's perfect. Now if you'll you excuse me, I have to make a phone call.

– *Can I speak to Dr Fineman, please?*
– *I'm afraid he's with a patient at the moment.*
– *Could you leave him a very brief message?*
– *Is this personal or professional?*
– *It's both.*
– *OK, sir, fire away.*
– *'I love you', from Patrick Moon.*

2

Today the first of our three days of rehearsal. At a studio in Southwark we gather: Fryman, Fryman's emaciated line producer Carver, Borg, Minna Howard and me.

– My God, is this really Patrick?

Carver holds me by the hands, looks me up and down.

– What happened? You find Jesus or something?

I laugh, take my pages, rejoice in the powerful clouds of breath that I make in the cold air. Borg looks hungry and loose-limbed, Gideon crackles with energy, as soon as he's out of his lotus position:

– Just remember, people: be fast, understate everything; the words will do the work when you need them to.

The set-up of *The House of the Mind*: I wake up with no memory in a house with two people, my doctor and nurse. They tell me I have a terminal disease and that they are just trying to make me feel comfortable for my last few days on earth. They make me sumptuous meals and play me my favourite music. They feed me drugs that make me happy, or sleepy, or energetic, depending on the time of day. The script is elliptical, but is charged with a certain minatory power.

We rehearse one or two scenes. I stop halfway down a page.

– Why only twenty pages, Gideon?

– The rest to come.

– What exactly would you say the film's about?

– Don't worry about that, Patrick. Trust me.

– Not even an inkling?

– The idea is that, like your character, you're kept in the dark. Keep reading.

Fryman stalks around us as we work. I am nerveless, clear-voiced, have no doubt. Borg is so good, no time for banter, our exchanges crisp and rhythmical.

Then Minna, the love interest. In real life smaller than is imaginable, but possibly even more ravishing than she is on screen. She is hesitant and her voice breaks up or tails away mid-sentence. This doesn't matter, because she is Minna Howard, England's finest, loveliest young dramatic actress. Everybody, of course, raises their game, becomes forty per cent sweeter in the presence of this beautiful young woman. It is ridiculous but I realise that I am already in love with her. I know this because I have an overwhelming craving to be pressed up tight against her for a very long period of time – the opposite in fact of my stated policy of 'never connect'. The conscious mind's an eight-stone weakling, instinct's a nine-hundred-pound gorilla.

She spends her down-time on her mobile phone, walking in circles or cross-legged in the corner, facing the wall, rocking backwards and forwards, her tone dull and insistent.

– Actresses, Patrick. Always so exquisite and mad.

Borg has me in his confidence over our lunch of mineral water and cigarettes.

– The sex is world historical. All that delicacy, all that damage, all yours for the night.

179

– I don't know how to tell you this. I've never slept with an actress.

– Really? Well, it's not to be missed. They warm up slow, but once the neuroses are coughed out then it's carnage.

– Right.

– Thrash around like mackerel in a bucket.

– I'm sure that's right.

– The post-sex can be problematic. Who wants a week of self-loathing after you did your damnedest to have a good time?

– Not me, Ray.

– But all in all, well worth it.

Delicacy and damage is right. She's tiny, the bones so slender and fragile. We rehearse a scene where I have to hold her chin, tip her head so she looks me in the eye.

– Look at me, Anna.

No response.

– Look at me.

And I put my hand under her chin to lift it. The bone feels as thin as the stem of a wine glass. Her eyes look through you as if you're not there at all. This close up, she begs to be kissed. I hold her face until Fryman says stop. She pulls away, out of the scene as quickly as she was into it. Back to her corner. She has a book called *He's Out There Somewhere*, which she reads fitfully, flicking through the pages backwards and forwards, never settling for more than a moment, as if she's looking for the one paragraph, one sentence that will make everything clear. God, he might even be in here, you know?

I walk back to Borg as Fryman and Carver confer.

– Shit, when she cracks it'll be spastic. Epileptic love, Pad.

But as I say, I must hold back for now. All you have to do is step back a little, give yourself room and you realize you can survive on so little. Sleep, eat, watch, run, bathe.

In three days' time, we fly to Scotland to start shooting.

Even better, even further away: all that newness, infinite air and space, a new little society cut off from history where I can concentrate on doing what I do, let everything else fall as it may.

3

Our first morning in Scotland. We are a compact yet disparate crew as we gather around for breakfast.

Gideon – slick, authoritative, serious-faced. I notice that everyone tries to stay close to him. It may be sycophancy: more likely people want to feed off his mood. He is so young yet so self-possessed.

  – Everybody's going to be great, right? Just listen to me and don't fuck with the energy. What we need is four solid weeks of pure forward energy.

Carver – multitasking gracefully. Her hair is freshly cropped. She gives Gideon a bowl of mushed fruit and a mug of warm soy milk. She chews a crust, studies her clipboard, talks quietly on her cellphone, circles the table constantly, watches the weather through the thick warped windows. She tousles my hair as she walks by and whispers:

  – You're going to be great.

Tomasz Viragh – a slender white-haired Hungarian lighting cameraman, his face deep-scored by millions of bad European cigarettes. He wears a black cashmere turtleneck and

182

reads a week-old Libération, obviously working his way through a Samuel Beckett fixation. His cigarette smells of burning rubber and he will speak only to Carver, and then in guttural French. He is important, because he is the only person here who actually knows how to make a feature film. In fact, Carver tells me that without him the money wouldn't have come through. Gideon doesn't speak to him.

Tomasz's people – I guess a focus puller and a grip of some sort. Also Hungarian, or as far as I can tell. They play three-card brag cross-legged on the floor, seemingly comfortable in their status as minions. They inspire confidence.

Phil and Eddie – the sound guys. Phil is a bald Cockney lummox, Eddie a muscular Yorkshire dandy: tight polo shirt, tight jeans housing a remarkable power bulge. Phil has *The Sun*, Eddie has *The Mail*. One will occasionally make a cryptic comment to the other about booms.

Hair, Make-Up and Wardrobe – mimsy, overdressed, each with a copy of *Sleb*, they nibble toast, leave the crusts and drink tea that smells like air freshener.

Art and Props – two tidy-looking sisters who pore over a long list of items with an air of deep seriousness.

Venetia – she described herself as 'Assistant Producer'. She has 'miscellaneous trivial crap' written all over her. She sounds like the Duchess of Kent's voice coach, dresses like she's from the Liverpool slums.

Then the talent: Minna Howard, Ray Borg and me.

Ray – a model of coolness and reassurance, my pal. It feels good to know him.

Minna – this morning she has the sleeves of her sweater pulled over her hands, sits cross-legged on a stool listening to everyone and smiling thinly. You feel like if you touch her she'll bruise. Carver tells me we have a big love scene at some point. Aren't we already having it?

Me – I'm comfortable with it all, a professional actor, a free man.

We are living and shooting in Barrie Lodge, a black granite Gothic manor house, forty miles from the Aberdeenshire coast. It may be the perfect place in which to go mad. It was previously occupied by some McTrooser of That Ilk who has moved to a bungalow in Arbroath. The house is condemned, but the land is up for sale: 3000 acres, salmon river, innumerable sheep, an angus herd, eighteen bedrooms, a grand ballroom. Black clouds scud over and around us like spirits of much ill-portent or rumours of war. The landscape is russet, grey-green, bruise. The whole place feels at the limits of human habitation.

It doesn't get dark till 11 p.m. There is a constantly shifting metallic light: zinc, lead, silver, bronze towards evening; no noise except the wind. We are all metropolitans, dusted with car emissions, pathologically incapable of being moved or surprised, but this place has already effected some changes. I have observed numerous unusual incidents: was that a healthy flush I saw on Borg's cheeks? Did I catch Fryman simply standing still on the front lawn, cocking his head, listening to the silence, breathing in the air, quaffing it down, with its barely detectable whiff of the sea? Even the techies are ravished by the space and air. Make-Up and Wardrobe have bought themselves matching pristine mahogany-coloured walking boots, hiked almost to the end of the drive, came back and professed the Highlands good.

And Minna is responding too. It is good to see her still sweet and breakable as sugar glass, but she is talkative now – to me at least. Maybe she senses that there is no threat.

Tomorrow we start shooting, but tonight she and I sit by the fire in the library. She is just out of the bath, her toes, finger-pads and earlobes translucent, baby pink all over, wrapped in a thick blue robe. Borg and some of the crew are playing poker elsewhere. Fryman has taken his customary early night. We read. I am still inching my way through *Ulysses* – page 51 now, and I don't remember a word of it. She sidles through an old *Sleb*.

I clear my throat on the verge of opening a conversation, but my mouth fills with silence.

In fact, maybe I don't want to say anything – the status quo is just fine. I'm having a quiet evening with a young movie star and we're simply enjoying one another's presence. Yes, it is becoming increasingly clear, she is very beautiful, but in some way it's more that she's *watchable*. My eyes hurt with the effort of keeping her within my field of vision and pretending to read at the same time. There is a restlessness about her, she hums and harrumphs, twists her hair. She drops her magazine and goes to sit on the hearth, drying the tips of her black hair with the heat of the fire, the skin of her neck illuminated in flickers of soft orange, and now she lifts her foot and rests it on my lap. I don't know whether to sing or weep. I merely smile benignly at her and stare at my book.

– I hate that magazine.

I barely overcome my desire to cram her foot in my mouth. I scan my frozen mind for something to say.

– Yes.

– Every picture of me, they always get me when I'm looking terrible.

– That's impossible.

185

Too much too soon. She shifts, withdraws her foot. I groan inwardly at the plain cosmic injustice, but am somewhat solaced by her promising feline stretch.

– I'm going to go away somewhere, you know, when I've done this.

– I know the feeling.

– They think I'm this bad person, but I'm not.

– They don't think you're bad.

– Then why do they hate me so much?

She is drinking whisky from a mug that she holds as if it contains hot cocoa.

– They don't know any better.

– Well, fuck them all.

– I agree.

– They make me fed up with everything.

– What does that mean?

– Oh, I don't really know. It's just that sometimes I wish people would go away.

– I'll leave now if you like.

She looks alarmed, reaches her hand out to my knee.

– Oh no, not you.

They say she has a drug problem, many and various boyfriends. *Sleb* loves her, addicted as it is to light and shade, ups and downs, the more Alpine in profile the better. The weekly photographs, her with her eyes red-rimmed and a shiny pale skin very late outside nightclubs, never ever smiling.

The hand leaves as suddenly as it arrived.

– This is my last job for a while.

– What are you going to do?

– I'm going to Spain with my friend Alice. We're going to live in some little fishing village. Or France, somewhere in the middle maybe. Or maybe Thailand. What do you think?

She looks at me as if she really wants my opinion. My

opinion is that she should go with me rather than with this terrible Alice person, but I need to stall:

– About what?

– I mean stopping work and leaving.

– I don't know. It depends what you want.

She slumps over her whisky mug and looks irritable.

– I'm going to bed.

– You don't have to.

– I want to go now. I'm fed up; I'm half drunk again. I'm sorry to go on all the time.

– Really, don't worry, that's what I'm here for.

She bends over to kiss me goodnight, little hot hand splayed against my cheek, lips against mine, thigh forward between the folds of the robe, soft pale globes gently kissing together as I try not to look. She rolls her eyes for no reason I can determine, and pads off to bed, the smooth humps of her ass just discernible beneath the heavy velvet robe, oh Jesus.

I gaze into the fire. London is so far away, a pile of rubble built on a boneyard, fishbones, skeletons of stevedores and hookers frozen deep in the black clay, everything in the entire city clapped out, ossified, grimy, covered with a film of vaporised oil.

Now that she's gone, there's no reason for me to be here. I put the guard on the fire, turn out the lights. The talent all have rooms in the house, thin temporary beds in the otherwise stripped-bare bedrooms. Mine is at the top of the main staircase, not more than ten yards from hers. Just for half a second, I think of knocking, but don't.

4

_____

Next morning I'm up at six. I run out into the damp morning air, down the drive onto the narrow road, across it, down to a wooded stream, along the stream for half an hour or so until the stream rises up to a narrow valley strewn with boulders. I rest against one of them, look around. There's nothing to see. What I mean is, no pictures of beautiful women on no billboards, no pictures of beautiful girls in no magazines, no beautiful girls on no TV. None of the Picasso-esque juxtapositions – knees jack-knifed over ass, eyes on end peering through a tangle of ankle and elbow – to make you angry and full of grief. They haven't yet learnt how to skywrite porn, but soon, I guess. Until then, this place is out of reach, I was right, the perfect spot to start afresh. I find myself watching three deer crossing the stream. They look towards me and freeze for a moment before springing up the opposite hillside. Low clouds speed across a backdrop of high cloud, a foreground of brown suede hills. A complex of Minna-related feelings surfaces – venerate, befriend, cuddle, then what? I have had the fore- sight to fill my Altoids tin with friendly blue diamonds but the pleasing prickliness in the balls I sense is all natural.

I start to run back to the house, following the stream.

Easy, easy – one leg in front of the other. My first call is at eight-thirty, I'm fine for time. I'm nervous, happy, excited. I never expected this, truly I thought I was done, and now here I am with Ray Borg and Minna Howard notionally an equal. It was tough to find out that the world won't allow you to do the only thing you've ever liked doing. I told myself I was getting over it; of course I wasn't. All I really want is to do well in this, to do it properly, with honesty, commitment and passion. My father always says that he understands why I persevere, because when it's good it's the best thing on earth.

My father has been an actor for forty years. He made a crucial decision when I was small: when offered a role in a soap opera he took it. The following year they made him a permanent character. You know him: Martin George, the once Jack-the-Lad now well-to-do car-dealer torn between his love of the local community and his desire to rise above his roots. You will remember his reconciliation with his on-screen father: front-page news in the early 1980s. Now he's in it maybe four or five times a month in some secondary storyline. They keep him on because he's a link back to the show's heritage for older viewers, part of the reassurance that keeps people tuning in year after year.

Before the soap, Dad was a stage actor, apparently a good one, and spent most of his time in rep travelling the country. He met my mother in a touring production of *As You Like It* and they married a year later. I came along a year after that, a mistake. Freedom gone, stability now an absolute priority, they both found themselves in the wrong career. Mum stopped working entirely. They lived in a housing-trust flat in Pimlico, poor and trapped. What he says now is that he regrets nothing. Parents have to say that about the big things, though, otherwise they may have to make the assessment that their lives have been a failure. And in one analysis he is Martin George, modestly wealthy, famous, liked and admired across the country. I get the sense that he in some way blames me for having to give up the life he loved in order to do what has turned out to be little different from an office job. If he doesn't blame me, then he is well aware that I am the reason it happened. Is there a difference? When I left home, they completed the illusion of bourgeois normality by moving out of the Marylebone flat where I was brought up. They went to a big, ugly house in the north London suburbs: black and white mock-Tudor gables, a bushy conifer by the front door and a conservatory. They live in half of it, get someone else to do the garden. Dad stands by the French windows all weekend watching the squirrels on the lawn, smoking his little cigars, regretting nothing.

I make a promise to myself that this won't happen to me now. It's only worth doing if you love it, there's no valid motivation but the fact that you know you can't be happy doing anything else.

I sprint back down the path to the house. There is movement, purpose, energy about the place and I'm part of it.

The opening scene. I wake up in a bedroom, to find Minna asleep on the chair in night clothes. She wakes as I stir. My first line: 'Where am I?' Her response: 'Where are you? You're at home.' Then the long conversation that establishes I've lost my memory. I get the waking up wrong approximately fifteen times. Fryman keeps telling me I look like an actor acting out someone waking up.

– I don't get it, you'll have to help me out.

– Say that a different way.

– I don't understand.

– That's it. That's it, that's what I want. I want you to do it as if you don't understand.

I do it that way, not understanding, and everyone agrees it's perfect, but Fryman doesn't seem so sure.

We do another short scene from later in the script, just Minna and me in the bedroom. The idea is that her character wants me to do some word association to trigger my memory.

– Your mother.

– Is dead.

– Your father.

– He was, he was . . . I don't know.

– Your wife.

– You're my wife.

– No, that's wrong, I'm not your wife. Your wife is someone else.

– You're my wife.

– No. That's wrong. Yesterday. Where were you yesterday?

– I don't remember.

– Of course you don't, of course you don't.

Minna comes alive when the camera rolls. Instantly, she takes on this brightness and energy. I feed off it and we do the scene in two takes.

It's difficult for me at first, acting in a vacuum. I'm used to scenes, narrative, reaction. Here it's just fragments of script then stopping, silence; the inevitable conference between Carver and Fryman as I lie back and look at the ceiling; either 'that's good, that's a take' or, more usually, 'one more time'. I think I'm doing OK; nobody says otherwise, at least. Minna spends the down-time in silence, looking out of the window or into space. She's two people: alive for the camera, half-dead the rest of the time.

Once we wrap, Fryman disappears to his office to watch the dailies with Carver. I am sitting on one of the heavy white wrought-iron chairs on the rear terrace with Minna, talking over cigarettes and white wine as the evening moves

in slowly. She chugs a full glass back in one, pours herself another. I say:
– This is perfect.
– Is it?
– What else would you do?
– Who knows?
– You're so good it's embarrassing.
She shakes her head, irritated or embarrassed.
– Sorry, Minna.
We watch birds arcing high overhead. I lay my hand on her cool forearm and don't dare to breathe. I study her profile. I lament quietly the way the eyes are already cross-hatched at the corner, the laugh lines deepening and the tiny pouch of soft, white flesh suspended from her otherwise perfect chin. I narrow my eyes to get soft focus. That's better.

She looks at me, notes my narrowed eyes, stands and walks onto the lawn. She bends over every so often to pick a flower. I take one of her cigarettes, smoke it without conviction, listen to the doves, crows, geese, watch her graze through the meadow.

She returns to the terrace, a bunch of ill-favoured meadow flowers in her hand.
– What are they?
She looks at them, drops them onto the table.
– I don't know. I don't know anything about that kind of thing.
– You make a convincing country girl.
– I hate the country.
She pours herself more wine, emptying the bottle, shaking out the dregs, then resting the top of the bottle on the lip of her glass, rotating it so the very last drop slides in.
– I hate the city most of the time as well.
– That doesn't leave much.
– I decided last night. Alice and me are going to go to

Spain. I told you. I think I was meant to be on the run all the time.

She drains her glass, lights a cigarette.

– Tell me what you mean.

She becomes more animated. She has a strange inner mechanism, one that speeds up, slows down, stops and starts at times that are not of her choosing.

– When I was small, I always wanted to stay at my friends' houses. Just for one night, then move to the next one. I used to imagine I was an orphan, or escaping from something. I liked being in temporary beds, up in the attic, or in the back room somewhere. Strange books, the smell of someone else's house, that bit when you wake up and you don't know where you are.

– I remember that feeling.

– You know what I think? You know that kind of embarrassed feeling when your friend's mum asked you what you wanted for breakfast, and you always just said something like, 'Oh, I don't mind'? I loved that feeling. Whatever she said: 'What do you want to do today?' 'Oh, I don't mind.' 'Do you want to watch the telly?' 'Oh, I really don't mind.' You'd never say that at home. You always knew exactly what you wanted at home, or they told you you had to. I was so much happier not minding. That's stupid, isn't it?

She turns to me, wanting me to tell her she's stupid, or challenging me to say she isn't. I'm still bad at talking to girls, so frightened of making mistakes.

– I don't think it's stupid at all. What was home like?

This is probably bad small talk: I expect her either to back off or produce a litany of dysfunction, psychological disorders and insoluble grudges, and things will become unpleasant, sex will get very distant.

– Oh nothing. Boring. Parents at each other a lot, I suppose, constantly bickering. Nothing really horrible, but they were just so rude to each other all the time. I just thought

193

that was normal. A swing in the back garden, TV on all the time, awkward Christmas mornings, friends that never quite came off, fishfingers, beans and oven chips every night. Nothing to hate or even dislike too much. I can't work it out.

She looks sad. I want to know everything, but it feels like it might be a long haul. Intimacy is the price men pay for sex, sex the price women pay for intimacy: Oscar Wilde. Firstly, what would he know? Secondly, it's a mournful thought, but only when reflected upon after the transaction has been made. Before that point, things are too serious for witty poignant observations. She looks at me, twisting a lock of hair.

– Do you get the thing about wanting to move around?

– No, not really, I don't think. The opposite. I used to think that I always wanted one place, one girl to share it with. I think maybe I was born to be suburban. Now I don't know. I don't know what to replace that idea with.

– I hate the suburbs too.

– I'd got that far.

She draws her hair behind her head, snaps it into a bobble, joggles the resultant ponytail. Her jawbone has the faintest trail of soft hair up by the perfect tiny ears. It feels exciting and intimate to see it.

– I've got this feeling if I have a little girl, we'll live in hotels all the time, and I'll never raise my voice, and she won't have to do anything she doesn't want to do, especially at Christmas, and we'll never have a TV so she'll turn out to be the opposite of me.

– Oh, but you're not so bad.

This feels like it was a risk, my tone too tender, but she just shakes her head, impatient. I had forgotten that beautiful, talented people are inured to flattery as much as they need it. It passes through them like the air they breathe, essential but unnoticed.

– Listen, though, I was thinking: if everyone just learnt how to be better parents, imagine how much better everything would be.

– But isn't that just asking people to become better people?

She scowls, tips her head back, suspends the empty glass over her mouth. A teardrop of wine creeps towards her lips. She dabs at it with her tongue, looks dissatisfied.

– I need a drink.

I go back into the house to find more wine for her, but none for me. Whatever happens now the night won't end soon.

I'm sober, she's a mess. I'm helping her into her bed, she looks up at me and smiles stickily.

– Hello, Patrick, how are you?

I try to shake her arm from round my neck, but she pulls me closer, her mouth reaching towards mine. Three hours of her unhappiness, the root of which is hard to determine, the solution to which is obviously unavailable. The wine has bad effects, the last hour I was almost bored at the relentlessness of her dissastisfaction, her eyes were raw and vague, her lips scabbed with tannin.

– No no, Minna. That's not right.

– Oh come on, Patrick, please: it's cold in here.

– No, really.

I untangle myself as she moans in frustration, and bundle her tightly into the bed.

– Please, Patrick.

– No, really, it would be a big mistake.

She complains again, but very soon, after I stroke her hair and turn off the bedside light, I sense that she's sleeping. I remain sitting by the bed, deriving perhaps an undeserved sense of righteousness from my act of restraint.

The house ticks, creaks, snaps as it settles down for the night. Minna is only fitfully asleep. She can't get comfortable in her dreams, lets out small groans of discomfort or anguish. I watch her closely and can't resist the urge to touch her again, just brushing her pulsing temples with the back of my hand. Yes, she is beautiful, and maybe this intensifies my feelings, but I make a resolution that whatever else happens I will try my hardest to protect her. From Borg, from Fryman, from whatever else might threaten her. She seems to represent a chance at some form of recovery.

I close the door behind me. The world must know that I just turned down sexual intercourse with Minna Howard, but I resist the urge to yell it from the balcony, and turn in and enjoy the sleeplessness of the just.

5

It hasn't taken long, but there is the first suggestion of dissent amongst the crew. Viragh, our Beckettian DP, who it transpires speaks only French and Hungarian, is unhappy. I come out of make-up to find him toe to toe with Fryman. Viragh stands with arms folded, looking at the ceiling:

– Tomasz, I don't like it. It has to look real, like a real morning.

Tomasz speaks quietly without moving his gaze from the rafters.

– Goulash croissant danube periphérique.

– No, you asshole, real. It looks too artificial, too much like a film, too glossy.

– Budapest chantilly ferenc puskas cote de beaune.

They eventually reach an accommodation, which involves us waiting around for another hour while the crew move the lights. Tomasz is not happy about this. He understandably resents being called 'a self-indulgent Transylvanian motherfucker' by Fryman: even if the precise meaning didn't cut through, the general sense was extremely apparent.

He retaliates by smoking Gauloises two at a time and mumbling at everyone in Franco-Magyar.

We do the scene, then move through to the hallway for the next. But Fryman can't resist:

– All these European fuckos are gonna be unemployed in a year.

Tomasz turns on his heel and stalks back to his bedroom.

– Moholy-Nagy camembert sir georg solti con con con!

We lose most of a day, which makes Carver crazy, and Fryman promises to think of something.

Next morning he appears to have thought of something. He has called a meeting for cast and crew in the house's grand ballroom. It's first thing Sunday, but could be any day. The calendar has no meaning on set, all the external rhythms of time are gone. Carver has issued instructions that we are to turn up in shorts, T-shirts and bare feet. We file in, all twenty or so of us, fractious and uncertain. Carver instructs us to sit round in a circle. She says, without much conviction:

– Make yourselves peaceful and, er, void your minds of all emotion.

The room is stripped, a vast parquet floor, heavy flock wallpaper. The electrical fittings have been pulled out leaving sprigs of wire twisting from the walls.

Fryman joins the group as we settle, carrying with him a branch.

– This is the rainstick.

Before he sits down he up-ends it and it makes a noise like rain, or at least like movie rain. We're all settled into our positions and Carver speaks again.

– Today I want us to talk about how we're feeling. How's the shoot going, what do we think of the beautiful location, what about all our new friends? Or maybe someone has some ideas they'd like to contribute to the group. What will happen is, Gideon will pass the stick to his left, the person will close their eyes then make their observation to the group. We will respect that statement with a moment's silence and then the stick is passed on. At any point, turn the stick upside down, and we shall hear the sound of refreshing rain, er, cleansing our psychic palates.

I look at Borg. He has his eyes closed, ankles crossed, hands resting on his naked hairless knees. I look at Minna, she smiles at me and I feel a sunburst in my breast.

Fryman starts the process.

– I think that we are blessed to be in a company of such gifted and diverse people and to be working on such an exciting and fresh piece of work. I think it is important to remember that all views are respected on the set, and that no view on how anything should work isn't open to challenge. For me, movies are about new ideas colliding with new ideas to make new ideas. Let's all embrace the specialness of that.

He holds the silence for a moment, then cleanses our collective psychic palate.

Whssshhhhhhhh.

The stick goes to Carver, who holds it as if it were about to spit venom at her.

– This is going to be a great movie. I think that it's important that we are all brave enough to accept that there are so many ways to enrich our experiences, maybe even if we think that we already know like how the best way to do something is, and so on.

Her silence is as unconvincing as her speech. She passes the stick to Hair, remembers she hasn't cleansed everyone's id, tries to grab it back, then shoos it away, saying:

– Whatever.

I am mildly alert by this point, as the stick is now only three people away from Tomasz, who has adopted an expression of Augustan haughtiness.

Hair is brief and somewhat haircentric:

– This movie is such a blast. I was really worried I hadn't quite got the look right on Minna yesterday, and I was freaked out all morning, but then Carver said it looked awesome. So I really think that with the help of all your strength the hair in the movie will be just great.

Hair turns the stick as solemnly as Hair can.

Whssshhhhhhhh.

Our minds tingle with minty freshness. Make-Up now:

– I know I'm not the most important person on the movie, so sometimes people don't think my feelings are validated? But I'd just like to say that I think this movie could be great if everyone was just mutually supportive a little more? For instance, giving praise and encouragement when it's deserved, like Carver did about Minna's hair? That's all, I guess.

Whssshhhhhhhh.

Borg takes the stick, thinks for a moment, or appears to think, or actually thinks while trying to give the impression that he is thinking, so looking maybe a little more extra-thoughtful than he really is:

– Invent nothing, deny nothing, stand up, speak up. That's it.

Whssshhhhhhhh.

I check Minna, can't read her reaction, and anyway am more keen to know what Tomasz will have to say. He takes the stick, the sneer now frozen on his weather-beaten face. His eyes are tightly closed, but to my alarm I watch a gigantic tear bulge from between his grey lashes and follow one of the deep smoker's lines down his cheek to the corner of his thin mouth.

– I am an artist, not a dogsbody for buffoons.

I sneak a peak at Fryman who looks as startled as you can look with both eyes shut. There is a terrible silence which Carver breaks:

– Tomasz, thanks for sharing that energy with the room.

He passes the stick to the script supervisor, to whom nobody listens as she quietly points out how difficult it is being a script supervisor when the script is changing every day but that she didn't mind because the movie was going to be so great and she thought that if the script was supervised well, then . . .

I phase out. This is an opportunity to make myself clear, to separate myself from Borg and Fryman, to make it clear to Minna who I am and what I stand for.

The script supervisor is still dumping on us.

The life lesson I am learning from the rainstick session is that everyone has something of value to say, even if it's only of value to them.

. . . that's all I wanted to say.

Whssshhhhhhhhhhh.

The stick goes to Minna, but instead of holding it upright she lays it across her lap. She blinks at the floor in front of her for a moment then starts to speak very softly.

– I just want to say I'll try to be a bit more helpful to people and not be so self-involved. It's so nice being here with you all, and I'm sorry if I'm screwing it up.

She hands the stick to me, and I am filled with some random squall of emotion. I take a moment to restrain myself, then find myself saying:

– Everybody should know how grateful I am to be doing this. I've spent a lot of time questioning whether I could ever really do this job. It's caused me a lot of pain and doubt. I've lost some things, but good things have come out of it too. I have a new resolve to do my job to the best of my ability, and to treat people better. I feel so privileged to be here in the company of people like Gideon, Ray and Minna. I think everyone should be more gentle and trusting. I'm sorry, I think I'm fucking this up a bit; I sound like I'm on daytime television. But I don't regret it. I just wanted to say thank you.

Whsssssssssshhhhhhhhhhhh.

As the rain eases, I hear Borg say with perfect clarity:

– Wanker.

I look around the circle: Fryman maintains an expression of beatific repose, Hair and Make-Up seem to be shedding little tears, Carver has started checking her clipboard and blowing out her cheeks in embarrassment and Minna, Minna makes figure-eights with her fingertips on the shiny wood floor.

Being on set is like going to another country. Nobody knows me; nobody has any expectations or preconceptions. In fact, the roles amongst the crew are rather easier to define and contrast than the characters in the film. Fryman is the aloof father who commands affection and respect. People don't fear his rage as much as his indifference, et cetera. Carver is the mother figure. Her interest is in unity, cohesion, stability. It may be the case that she is temperamentally unsuited to being a mother, but then so are most mothers. Also, in a womanly fashion, she has taken on more responsibility than she needs to, gets overly exercised about the detail. Minna, I think, is the delectable independent-minded teenage daughter who watches her parents with sullen disdain, her interests lying in other areas. Borg, of course, is the family pet, semi house-trained, curled up in the corner, hissing at anyone who comes too close. So maybe I'm the sensible elder brother: outdoorsy, the prefect, captain of swimming, three hours voluntary work a week – with an edge.

I need some comforting words, so I turn to Carver while we wait to start shooting a scene. Viragh, having said his piece, stalks the house silently, for the moment reluctantly back on board.

– What's weird is, Carver, maybe it was the stick, but I really meant it.

– It was sweet.

– Does everyone think I'm an idiot?

– No. Everybody needs that kind of bullshit once in a while. Right, new pages.

6

Even Borg defers to Fryman. It's futile trying to work out how he has attained his status of infallibility, but there's no question that he has. It might be charisma, force of will, but I experience it as a kind of love. And yes it is filial in character: any positive comment makes my heart thrill, any nuance of criticism is devastating. I look to him for encouragement and validation. I watch him all day long. There's something that I remember, a quotation about the seriousness of a child at play, and that's what he has, the air of engagement, the mind always in motion.

I am buoyant. It is so many years since I felt like this in the mornings: uncluttered, pristine, not weighed down by non-specific gloom or by the after-effects of the previous night's chemical compensation for same.

Borg and I are in make-up, two directors' chairs side by side in front of a wide mirror in one of the huge chequered-tiled bathrooms.

– How d'you like the movies, Patrick?
– Great so far.

Make-Up's movements are deft and pleasing. A brush swishes at my upturned face, occasionally a thumb dabs my skin.

– So what's with the Hare Krishna schtick?

– What?

– The rainstick debacle, Patrick. All that 'What's so funny 'bout peace, love and understanding?'

– OK, that was maybe going a little too far.

– No comment, of course, but the Betty Ford behaviour as well? I'm getting lonely up here now you've got so clean and serene on me.

– Shit, I don't know. I've told you. I'm conducting an experiment.

– But pity poor Raymond. I've got a bushel of skunk, six eightballs of cola, pills practically falling out of my sphincter and no one to share with.

– Oh well.

Hair is now doing my hair, fingers moving delicately and swiftly:

– I was also told that you've started *running*.

– Only a little.

– I'm appalled.

I open my eyes and look at Borg's reflection. Make-Up is now dusting him with the brush. I am startled to find that his eyes are wide open and looking back at me in the mirror.

– I'll have to learn how to make my own fun, won't I, Patrick?

– You'll think of something.

His eyes snap shut and I feel momentarily unsettled. Hair smooths the side of my scalp, tells me I'm done. As I walk out of the bathroom I turn to look at Borg. He seems to sense it, opens one eye and smiles humourlessly.

– I most certainly will.

Scene four today. Borg's character shows me a film of my life: scenes from school, university, graduation from law school.

– Where's my wife?

– She's with you.

– Why can't I see her?

– Of course you can't see her, she's taking the pictures. It is thought too upsetting to show you photographs at this stage. Let me just say, however, that she was a very beautiful woman.

– When can I –

– CUT CUT CUT CUT CUT.

Fryman confers with Carver for a few moments, both talk in heated whispers. Nodding at each other, they break their huddle and Carver says:

– Take ten, everybody.

Gideon walks towards me, stroking his chin, eyes still trained on the script.

– Patrick, we need to talk.

He walks by without looking at me. I follow him out of the ballroom, down the corridor and into his chaotic study.

– Sit down, Patrick. Drink?

He offers me some of his dark brown purge. I shake my head. He sits cross-legged on his swivel chair, leans back and looks at me, nodding to himself. There's no place for me to sit. I hover, faintly disconcerted.

– Patrick, I have to be straight. I'm concerned about the work.

No way no way. I am instantly drenched with panic.

– What do you mean?

– Exactly that. There's something missing. Something that I saw in the audition is not quite there right now. I don't know exactly what it is, but the way you're playing the character isn't right.

I feel my throat drying, a fidget possessing my hands.

– Can you explain a bit more fully?

– Well, the way I see this guy he's a loser, a victim.

– Yes, and?

206

– Well, you're not playing him like that.

He studies me now, eye contact. Who's going to be first to blink? Hey, Gideon, who's going to be first? Me, of course.

– Come on, I need some help.

– It's like in the audition you had this kind of, I gotta be honest, this awkward, loser type of quality. I don't know, it was kind of, I don't know, it was this quality that seemed right for this guy. Neurotic, nervous. Carver says 'tortured dweeb'. Now it's like you're this kind of slick, upright-type guy. It's not working.

– Isn't it?

– Think about it. This guy wakes up in a house with no memory, surrounded by people he doesn't know. They show him scenes from a previous life on tape, tell him his entire family's dead. He's not going to be cool, bright, taking it like it's Sunday in the park. To be blunt, he's fucked. We need some agony, some paranoia.

I don't remember being a tortured dweeb. I thought I was being myself.

– I didn't realize.

– No, no, I see that.

– I thought the audition was –

– Well, yes, but there was a quality. Carver saw it too. It's like as I say, this hunted, nervy quality. I can't say it better than that.

– But I remember the Macbeth thing I did –

– That's it, exactly! It was a joke, right? That's what made it work, right?

– Well . . .

– Yeah, kind of Dork Macbeth. We liked that element.

I try to respond.

– OK. I understand.

– Like we don't need full dork. Just, as I say, this feeling of nerviness, like neurosis, pathos. Don't overdo it, but that sense of the victim. Otherwise it's just not working.

207

– Right, I see that. I see that.

– Great. I can get Carver to do some work with you if you like? When you're not shooting.

– I'll think about that.

He stands up, starts looking for something under the piles of paper.

– Good. This is crucial. You've got to get it right, otherwise we're fucked. I know you know that.

– Yep, I got it.

– You can go now. We'll give you the rest of the day to think it through. OK?

I turn on my heel and walk up to my room in a kind of daze. I suddenly feel ashamed, lonely and deeply unfashionable. Dork Macbeth? I go to my room and try to find something that can help me through this. Nothing. I have nothing to draw on. I am an impostor, a fraud. I have been found out but nobody knows it yet except me.

There is a knock on my door and Carver lets herself in.

– You all right, Patrick?

– I don't know, Carver. Am I?

– What did he say?

– He said I was screwing it up, basically.

– No, it's not that you're screwing it up. Just different.

– Wrong, though.

– Don't think like that. We can make it work easy.

– If I become a tortured dweeb again.

– Shit. I didn't mean that in a bad way. He shouldn't have said that.

– I'm just surprised. I thought I was doing fine.

– Listen, Patrick, you're close to being excellent. Really. Just remember what you were when we first saw you. Just that.

– That's it?

– That's it.

She looks a little awkward, standing there hugging her clipboard to her chest, heels together.

– Thanks anyway, Carver. I think I'd better do some work.

– Hey, listen, if you need anything, just shout.

It is obvious to me what I need to do. I must recreate the exact physical, psychological and biochemical state I was in at the audition. The first part of this journey has been partly achieved by Fryman's pep-talk: I am now gravely nervous and utterly unconvinced of my own talent. The second part must involve some form of biochemical restructuring. I go downstairs in search of Borg.

7

Early morning. I've been up most of the night roiling in a heavy panicky sweat. Three pills, half a gram. All night I stared at the ceiling, grinding my teeth, heart banging metallically in my chest. Now in the breakfast room, surrounded by the dull murmur of communal breakfast, I'm raw and nauseous. I flick through the two pages of script I've been given, not looking at the words. I'm paranoid, exhausted, and angry. Excellent. The small rational part of my mind still able to assess things impartially is pleased with my progress towards Audition Patrick. The scrape of spoon on bowl, the insistent crunching of molars on extruded maize, is too much for my lathed nerves. I drop the script, which is blurry and hurts my hands, and go out to the porch.

Borg leans against the wall by the front door.

– Well?

– A bit better.

He looks down between his splayed knees and spits on the floor. We watch the crew on the lawn. Minna is shooting a scene. She has to run across the meadow towards the camera, freeze when she is right up against it and shout the name of my character. She wears a long blue dress that isn't warm enough for the damp weather. After each take Carver wraps her in a long black coat and feeds her something from a steaming mug.

– Forget about her, by the way.

– What do you mean?

– Minna.

– What do you mean, forget about her?

– Forget about screwing her.

– I'm not thinking that.

– Give me a break. What, you don't want to screw her? All that shit with the rainstick, the cosy little love-ins. So you're thinking, 'She's all fucked up, must want some sensitive type to straighten her out and screw her bandy till sun-up.'

– It's not about that. I don't want to screw her. I'm trying to be a friend to her.

– Oh no, Patrick! You've got to do better than that, mate. That's *piss* poor.

– It's true actually.

– Excuse me for a second . . .

Borg looks at the sky, and makes a strange high-pitched whinny.

– That's better. My lie detector went into dogshit overload.

– You think what you like. I've got more pressing concerns.

– You'll never do it anyway. She's a star, *ergo* she's a starfucker. She's one hundred per cent actress. Just wants to be loved, as long as it's by someone who's as famous as she is. Peer-group approval, Pad. I've seen it so many times. They need to be loved so bad, but only by their equals. A co-star's orgasm is the ultimate round of applause.

– And you're the co-star, of course.

– Looks like it. Spliff, loverboy?

– No. No, I'm fine.

211

We watch her do another take. She runs down the meadow, surprisingly athletic, her body making a beautiful series of shapes within the flowing dress. The freeze. She looks around, then:

– Tom? Tom?

Then she runs down past the camera, slows as she moves out of shot, pushes her hair back, grabs for the steaming mug again. We hear Fryman shout:

– Good! That's it! Good!

I look at Borg, who stops watching Minna and kicks at the gravel.

– No, you steer well clear. She's all mine, this one.

– Really.

– No doubt, Patrick. It is written. She's dead meat.

He lifts an imaginary rifle up to his shoulder, squints one eye closed.

– Yep. She's dead; she just doesn't know it yet.

Minna is walking towards us across the lawn. She looks tired, hunched into her coat, no hand visible dangling from the sleeve, just a cigarette. Borg makes a clicking sound, pretends to cock the gun and whispers.

– She's all Borg's, aren't you, baby?

I look towards Minna, who waves at us. Borg says 'ka-boom' under his breath, stuffs his hands in his pockets as he gets near.

– What were you doing, Ray?

– Just saying hello. That looked gorgeous, Min, absolutely gorgeous.

– Oh, I don't know, I had to do it about ten times.

– Naah, Min, gorgeous, my sweet.

I am unable to speak, so desperate suddenly to prevent him from going anywhere near her. We go inside. I follow as Ray puts his arm around Minna's neck, pulls her in and kisses her head.

– You're just the best, Min, trust me.

But Ray knows as well as me that you can't trust anyone any more.

In the afternoon we shoot a scene in which I have only one line:
   – I can't work out if I'm alive or dead?
We do it several times, Fryman barely paying attention, until finally.
   – OK, that's the one.
   – Was that all right, Gideon?
He is staring at his script.
   – Fine.
   – What, good fine, or fine fine?
   – Fine.
Everything has taken on a chilly and alienating air. When it happens it happens so fast. And after my sleepless night I go to bed before dusk.

Early morning, someone has brought in the newspapers, but I'm not interested in the London zoetrope. What's it going to be? Booze, football, panties, rabble-rousing and TV in the tabloids; wine, cricket, lingerie, liberal-baiting and Asian cinema in the broads, don't need it.
   – Hey, Patrick. Your old bitch, right?
Borg is a vision of rawboned confidence, feet on the table, reefer on. He holds up the front page of *The T——*, a picture of Susie with a sharp new haircut, a severe little smile: 'Susie Fisher's Smash-Hit Column: Now in *The T——* Weekend'.
What smash-hit new column?
   – Jesus, let's have it.
   – In a moment, Patrick.
He finds the Weekend section, hurriedly flips to the right

page and starts to read. As he does so, he makes small excla-
mations – Ouch! Oof! Oh dear!

– Come on, Ray, hand it over.

– I'm really not sure you want to read this, Paddy.

– Come on, give it.

– A woman scorned. Is there any other kind?

I take the paper. Ray smiles without humour.

The headline: 'IS THAT THE BEST YOU CAN DO?'

I start to read:

*So, OK, is it just me or is something horrible happening?
With men, I mean, of course. I can understand why there
was a change in the early 1990s, when guilt receded and
porn, alcoholism, football and wanking became acceptable
and – in certain situations – mandatory. Being a man at this
time must have felt like being a woman during the early years
of feminism. There was a basic but touching honesty about
it all, a sense of new freedoms and dropped inhibitions.
Women responded with mindless hedonism of their own. It
was childish but maybe for a time it was a bit of fun.*

*But now, there's something else in the air. The repercus-
sions of the men's lib movement are becoming crystal clear:
men get older younger, then stay younger for longer. I'm
tempted to call it retarded acceleration. Or accelerated retardation. Either way, men are acting retarded and they're doing
it quicker and quicker.*

Where is this leading? I feel a lurch in my soul:

*My own ex-boyfriend, a failed actor, is a particularly fine
example of this phenomenon. Usually drunk or stoned, often
wearing the vapid grin of the superannuated ecstasy taker,
he blamed the world for his inability to get his career together.
He was an adolescent convinced he wasn't responsible for his
own predicament.*

What the pathetic-little-boy act in fact concealed was a des-
perate attempt to seek refuge from reality. That's what it is,
all the beer, all the drugs, all the porn, all the football – an
unwillingness to engage with the world as it is.

I had a moment of clarity one rainy afternoon, coming
home to see him fast asleep in front of the snooker, three
roaches in the ashtray and a men's magazine open at some
pre-teen crotch shot.

Enough already.

I kicked him out there and then and thankfully haven't
heard a word since. Good riddance.

Over the weeks since I started this column, I have had a
fantastic reaction. What this tells me is that other women feel
this way too. I do not expect to cause a revolution. All I sug-
gest is that my women readers interrogate their relationships
a little. If they find my experiences ringing true, then maybe
it's time to do something about it.

For example, kick the bastards out.

I read it, re-read it in a kind of fascinated misery. I check
the byline picture: she has tried to make herself look crazy
sexy cool, the lipstick lesbian schtick vamped up, thick black
mouth, kohl around the eyes, the hair an aggressive black
bob.

And also: 'I kicked him out there and then'. Is this how
history starts to deviate from reality? And why does this
feel important to me, that the record is set straight and that
the world knows that I left of my own free will?

Another question: if happiness writes white then what
emotion has caused this screed of black betrayal?

And what does she mean 'over the weeks since I started
this column'? I go down to the office, where Carver is, as
usual, at work on a list of some sort.

– Carver, I need to use your PC.

– What is it?

– Family problems.

– Sure.

I am mad with impatience as I connect, drumming the table through the atonal toccata of the dial tone, the howls of cyber wind as the computer attempts to mesh with the net. I get to *The T——* site, type her name into the search engine.

At random, from four weeks ago:

Feminism relapsed into arcane intellectualism and over-compensation: it basically headed for the universities and became marginal. Masculinism has dragged its knuckles into a dimly lit cave hung with porno spreads. From this dank and brutal place it has become a central force in the culture.

My eye hops from paragraph to paragraph until:

A twenty-minute tour of The Creep's cookie folder yielded a fascinating look into the modern man's erotic landscape: amateur blatino cum sluts, all anal all the time, six-on-one high-school gang bang, oral humiliation.com, lolitasixteen the youngest legal babes on the web, and of course battalions of asian girls in kiddie clothes, so friendly, bendy and anony-mous. Also, in case you were interested in knowing, it appears that there is an inexhaustible well of pornography on the web that consists of – get this – cartoon representations of tiny young girls being attacked by imaginary beasts with giant octopus tentacles. I'm not joking. In fact, what's the opposite of joking? Maybe I'm grieving.

Did I do this to her? Is she really doing this to me?

I feel caught in a crossfire: on the one hand, my director is telling me that I'm a lousy actor, on the other my ex-girlfriend is telling me that I'm a lousy person. What else is there? After the man and the work, what else is there from which to draw solace? I'm a lousy cook as well, for Christ's sake.

In ten minutes I'm supposed to be shooting a scene. I return to the kitchen with some degree of purpose and drag Borg into the lobby.

– I need some more drugs.

– Ahh, it's so nice to have you back, Patrick.

I do half a pill and half a gram, suck back two fat spliffs, feel the bump and grind the moment Fryman says, 'We're rolling.' We do four scenes in one day, me all the time a quivering wreck. Just before we wrap I drop another half an e, ask the first a.d. to rustle me up a strong lager and get through the last scene on toxic fumes as my body attempts to deal with the doctorate-level chemistry experiment I am conducting within it.

Fryman is quietly impressed. Quite often as he peers into his camera he is heard to say,

– This is all so much better, Patrick.

8

The next morning, me dosed again on insomnia and anguish, we do three scenes in what seems like either twelve minutes or nine hours. What the hell? I'm slapdash, headachey, filled with kamikaze courage.

Thankfully, Fryman has a problem more pressing even than me. Tomasz is in full revolt. Any time Gideon talks to him he shrugs and inclines his head and blinks, a motion which, depending on context, means either a) sure, whatever, you know best, b) OK, you're the boss, or c) OK, do what you like, what the fuck do I know, I'm only one of the finest DPs on planet Earth.

During lunch, Carver walks into the kitchen clutching a hank of paper and I see her whisper to Gideon, who nods and shakes his head sort of simultaneously.

As Carver walks by I grab her.

– What was that?

– I found Tomasz on the internet. Singing like a canary, in perfect English. Here.

She gives me a copy of the printout. It's from some Euro film magazine. The great man has made a point of talking only in English, and rather silky and eruditely polemical English at that. He makes the statement that 'all directors are hyperactive children who understand light no more clearly than a baboon understands Proust.'

– Funny.

– Yeah, Gid can barely contain himself.

I re-enter the kitchen. Tomasz has apparently discovered what has happened, tries to stamp out of the room trailing indignation. He ends up in the pantry. Instead of making a somewhat ignominious re-entry into the kitchen before making another attempt at a fabulous exit, he merely closes the pantry door and holds tightly to the knob as Gideon pulls on it from the other side.

Carver tells us to break for an hour, but Minna, Borg and I are keen to overhear how the conflict might resolve itself.

– Look, Tomasz, I'm not trying to screw you over, I'm trying to break through with you.

– You treat me like a Jew.

– Look, I just want to be friends.

– Do you insult your friends? Do you shame them? Treat them like Jews? Do you destroy their work? Do you destroy them?

At which point, Gideon, both hands clasped around the doorknob, feet braced as if we were trying to hold a boat to its mooring, makes what is evidently his biggest error so far.

– Jesus, Tomasz, it's only a bunch of freaking lights.

There is a moment of silence followed by the sound of a pantry being demolished from within by an angry, late-middle-aged Hungarian man. The racket of tinned peaches and bags of flour being swept from shelves and hurled against walls still leaves Tomasz's voice extremely audible.

– You are all American shitheads, trying to humiliate me like some Jew.

Gideon spreads his palms at the closed door and shakes his head in disbelief.

– What is it with the Jews, man? I'm not trying to do

219

anything to anybody like they're a Jew. Listen Tomasz, *I'm* frickin' half a Jew.

– I knew it! The Jew is destroying my work!

Gideon comes over all calm and badass. He lets himself into the pantry and closes the door behind him. I stand up to leave, Borg and Minna do the same. Amidst the clonking and scraping we hear Gideon's voice become charged with the proximity of violence.

– Let's talk about destruction, asshole! Let's talk about a fucking superfluous Balkan asshole trying to destroy my movie!

Again a moment of silence, this time entirely unambiguous. They are undoubtedly wrestling. Borg, Minna and I let ourselves out. In the gloom of the hallway outside the kitchen there is a huddle of anxious crew members. A quiet and nervous voice asks me:

– Did Gid like the hair?

At the end of the day, Carver takes me aside.

– Hey Patrick, you OK?

– Yes and no.

– What happened?

– What do you mean?

– You're being great again.

– Am I?

– In fact it was nearly miraculous. Like you just flipped back to normal.

– Really?

– Yeah. What happened to you?

– Lots of things all at once.

– Well, it's all good.

Carver is the governing principle of this movie – everything that happens happens because of her. Still, despite the nineteen-hour days and the forcefields of ego that make

220

it difficult to move around, she is always fresh, clipped and absolutely on it.

– Thanks. I try my hardest.

– You look more yourself as well.

Sweaty, paranoid, appalled. I've been typecast.

– What's happening with Viragh?

– Oh nothing.

– Meaning?

– Gid fired him.

– But I thought he was the only person holding the money in place?

– Listen, relax. Let me look after money. You've got other stuff to think about.

This, like everything Carver says, is very true.

Tonight, to clear out the toxins, I commit myself to a longer run in the eerie late-p.m. sunlight. Thinking time. At the end of the drive, I turn left onto the road, then follow a gently inclining path through the woods. Two things in balance. First of all, of course, Susie. What is she trying to say to me? I struggle to imagine her thought processes, but my mind balks at the step between wanting to express hurt and resentment and being prepared to express it to as many people as possible. That ambition of hers, is it really prepared to incur any cost? Or maybe I deserve it, and it offers me an opportunity to reassess. Maybe the running, the abstinence wasn't a fresh start at all, but instead an implicit acknowledgment of the need to perform a kind of penance. Susie, look at me, toiling up this hill, the turf at once springy yet sapping. I'm killing myself for you.

Of course, I need to speak to her as soon as possible, tell her that I understand and bear her no ill will. Maybe I need to demonstrate that I've changed, but that doesn't mean I expect anything to happen as a result.

221

I complete the ascent, only to find another steeper slope rising in front of me. I rest for a second, relishing the loneliness.

Then, Minna. There is one thing that must not be allowed to happen. Borg must not get anywhere near her. All forms of sabotage are to be allowed in this mission. There may be an element of altruism involved, really, maybe a little, but also there is certainly quite a lot of sheer, straight-up, ugh ugh cudgel-wielding Cro-Magnon competitor-hatred. I decide against another climb and turn back towards the house. I restrain the desire to lean down the hill and hurtle into the gravity. I get a sense of it every so often, if I take a big stride or jump over some obstacle on the path, the centre of the earth relentlessly pulling me in. It's a curious skill, one that lies latent in everyone: self-preservation. I make it down to a five-bar gate, vault over it, jog slowly back to the house, go straight up the stairs to Minna's room and knock softly.

– Who is it?

– Patrick.

There is a moment's silence, the sound of a stumble, then she opens the door, looking as if I've woken her up.

– What do you want?

– I want to talk.

She looks impatient, wraps her robe more tightly around her.

– Can't it wait?

– I only want a few minutes.

She turns away from the door and pads back to her bed. Her room is underlit, musty. There's a smell of cigarette smoke, spilled alcohol, even bad sweat. She sits on the bed, lights up, sorts through a few bottles on her bedside table, holds them up to the light one by one. There's a gin bottle with about two inches in the bottom. She unscrews the cap and pours the gin into a mug.

222

– Minna, are you all right?

– I'm cosmic. How are you?

– No, I mean, it's worrying.

– What is?

– The drinking. Your mood.

– Don't you know who I am? I'm always like this.

– Well, that makes me more worried.

– Well, don't bother, there's nothing you can do.

She belches, rubs one foot over the other. I realize that she doesn't give a damn.

– Is that it?

– There's something else actually. Just be careful, all right?

I still have this stupid idea that I could save her or change her in some way. How many people must have tried that, or wanted so badly to achieve it?

– About what?

– I don't know. People on set. They're not bothering you, are they?

– I don't know.

She is playing child now, shrugging and batting her eyes in feigned indifference.

– I'm just a bit worried that you're, I don't know . . . I just wanted to make sure you're OK.

– I'm cosmic I just said.

Her face becomes ugly, on the verge of tears.

– Don't cry, Minna.

– Don't drink, don't smoke, don't cry, Minna.

I move closer to her as she starts to sob.

– What is it?

– Just go away, go away.

– Can I get you something or do anything?

– Tell everyone else to go away as well.

I open the door. Borg is in the corridor, he looks straight by me. I put my arm across the space.

– She doesn't want to see anybody.

– Are you sure?

– That's what she said.

– That's because she's seeing me.

– She said no one.

He walks through my arm and says:

– All right, Min. I've got it.

There is a murmur of assent. I grab him by the shoulder.

– Got what?

– Fuck it, never you mind, loverboy.

He closes the door behind him. I go back to my room, lie on the bed and try to find solutions in the cracked ceiling, my hands over my ears to block out anything that wants to get in.

Next morning, I'm back on Carver's PC. First I need to check my e-mails. My original intention was to leave all that behind for the time being, but I need to know if Susie's written to me, some apology or initial steps towards a reconciliation, or at least a ceasefire. E-mail is the perfect form for tentative steps towards peace, no direct confrontation being necessary.

But nothing from her, just the following, dated weeks ago:

From : Hillary Kelly
To: pmoon109@hotmail.com
Subject: [No Subject]

Dear Patrick
Still expecting a response to my impertuous request! Maybe now is the time that it is politic for me to 'flesh out' my proposal with some more of the 'grisly details', if you will.
As I mentioned, I have been writing a play which is the

fruit of my deep and fond study of the theatre across all
these years of happy theatregoing. It is provisionally entitled
'The Love Game', as I am aware that I may have already
related to you.

The general flow of the piece – its 'high concept' if you
will (dread term!) – is about the real possibility of 'love at
first sight' and how and if one can truly 'love' somebody
one hasn't met before.

'Scenario'/'Theme'

A famous actor is considering his future. Why am I what
I am? Is this thing at which I excel of any lasting value? Or
are the achievements I possess merely effervescent? Do I
really affect people's lives? Or bring joy into those lives? Or
am I just a clown?

He pursues these questions along their tragic arc to a
bloody, tragic death!

As I have outlined, I think I can attract 'some fiscal
interest as it were from some of the many people I know in
the various realms of the theatre all over the country' as I
put it in my last missave.

I would like to suggest a meeting of some sort, hopefully
lunch, at a venue of your choosing.

As ever, I await your response once again with relish
and no little anticipation, and look forward to that lunch!

Respectfully and expectantly yours,

Hillary

Hillary is one part of my recent history that really has to
go. I press delete, think of writing to Susie, but I can't find
my voice. Carver comes in holding new pages:

– Right, Patrick, you're needed.

For the moment that sounds good.

9

We're deeply into this movie now, Viragh forgotten, Gideon rarely seen outside shooting hours, off somewhere with Carver figuring out what the hell they're supposed to do next. But tonight out on the patio, the Talent don't care about all that, there's something else going on.

Borg is on lager, Minna on wine, me back on mineral water. I am trying to get him to theorise. None of his theories is likely to be popular with girls like Minna. However, Borg has decided on a different course:

– Well, you know, the thing about [famous actress] is she's gay . . . the thing about [ultra-famous producer] is that he's a pervert . . .

And so on and so forth. Gratifyingly, Minna seems uninterested, keeps her nose in her wineglass.

– And [mega-famous actor], of course. He does this family man schtick but he's the biggest pervert of them all. He pays girls to vomit on him. He spreads chocolate on the floor, they run around on all fours eating it up, then he lies down and they throw up on his naked body while he masturbates.

Is this conversation really suitable for female company? Borg seems to have no scruple in this regard, which I reckon has to work to my advantage. He continues:

– Actors, I've figured it out. All these terrible backgrounds. For most of them the act of sex is an act of violence against their parents. This is why they're all so neurotic. Every time someone in show business has an orgasm he hears his mother weeping. This also might help explain why they're all perverts.

Minna seems disquieted.

– I think it's so sad. Hollywood people are always so sad: drugs, craziness, divorcing all the time.

– Yes, but of course it doesn't make any sense to get married any more. Now everyone breaks up, forty odd per cent or whatever it is. It's a gamble you're bound to lose.

The point has lost some of its zip said by me rather than by Borg. Minna looks hurt:

– Don't say that.

Borg turns to me, adopting a camp look of admonition.

– Yes, Patrick, how cynical of you. That's a terrible thing to say.

Double take. Triple take.

– What do you mean that's a terrible thing to say? You said it to me about two months ago.

– No I didn't. He's being silly, Minna. No I didn't. What I said was that it's sad that some people think like that. I don't. Prenuptial agreements, I ask you. Marriage is a sacred thing. It's one of the last dreams we have left. It can't be just a matter of playing the odds.

– How can you say that?

– Well, call me old-fashioned, Patrick, but isn't marriage about committing to someone for the rest of your life? It's about good faith, that's what it is. Marriage is an act of good faith.

I am staggered at the Saturnian scale of the man's testicles. Minna, meanwhile, is looking at him with a certain terrible fondness.

– I hope you're right, Ray. It's all anybody wants really, isn't it? One person to share your life with.

– Absolutely. But I can tell you, that idea has caused me some heartache in the past.

He looks ruefully into his drink.

– Oh dear, Ray.

– Sometimes I think I'm the only man of my generation who thinks like that. I know it sounds crazy but once in a while it seems that everyone I know is out for what they can get.

Minna sneaks a guilty look at me. Why? What does she know?

I am roused to sarcasm.

– Hey, I really want to hear this, Ray.

– Hear what? All I'm saying is, I've always tried to give things a go, stay loyal and try my best, whatever the relationship, but now I wonder what's the point.

– You've never told me about any relationships.

– Well, as I say, I try to forget. Some of them have been pretty painful, I can tell you.

Borg sighs and shakes his head. Minna is rapt, her head inclined away from Ray's so she can look at him more intently.

– The worst thing is – you just never know what to say. So many of my friends are in these relationships that look stable on the surface. You know, it's all mortgages and holiday brochures. But the men, Minna, the lousy men. I can't think of one who isn't in some way on the cheat. If it's not their wife's best friend it's porn and prostitutes. I mean, or driving slowly past girls' schools, who thought that we'd be reduced to that? Or this new thing, this big new thing: lap dancing. What must be wrong in your life that you pay desperate girls you can't touch to jiggle around in your face? It's beyond sad; it's humiliating for everyone concerned, Minna. I think men have lost touch with something sacred

228

within themselves. The good masculine qualities: curiosity, bravery, loyalty.

I try to make a frantic gesture of disbelief at him without Minna noticing.

– Oh, I'm sorry, Patrick, I'm not trying to make judgements if that's what you're into. I just think it's, well, as I say, it's all so sad.

He winks at me. The motherfucker winks at me.

– Well, not everyone's like that, Ray.

– No, of course. It just seems so bad that relationships after all this time are still about keeping secrets from one another. I've tried to be brave before, but it's difficult. Some people have a terrible time with honesty.

Minna is nodding ardently.

– That's so true. Leaving yourself open to someone can make you feel so vulnerable.

Borg looks as if he's just realised something terribly profound about the universe.

– God, Minna, that's so right.

– Yes, I think it is.

– Yes, you know. People *think* showing vulnerability is showing weakness. But surely that's wrong. Being vulnerable with someone isn't necessarily weak. It can be the bravest thing in the world. Some people, they see weakness and all they want to do is stamp on it. I don't understand that mentality.

Now Minna is dancing around on her seat in frantic agreement.

– Yes, you're right, you're right. It says that in this book I'm reading. Almost exactly that. Showing vulnerability is the bravest thing.

But Borg nods judiciously, takes a wise, contemplative swig of his lager. Minna gets up and gives him a squeeze on the shoulder.

– If you do want to talk about it, then I'm here, Ray. I've

had my fair share of disasters too, you know. You should read this book.

– That's really kind, Min. I'm not sure I'm quite ready yet, the pain's a little raw – but that's really kind.

– Wine. Let me get some more wine.

Minna walks back to the kitchen door.

– Ray, come on, you must just leave her alone.

– Why? I'm getting in your way?

– No. Just leave her. She doesn't need this. Either of us.

– I thought you'd welcome the sport.

– It's not a competition. I'm trying to protect her. Even if it were –

He swivels toward me, sneering with surprising vehemence:

– Hold on a second, loverboy. First of all: you want her, don't fucking kid yourself. And guess what? I want her too: so it is a competition.

– You're out of order, Ray.

– No, Patrick, I'm fully operational, mate.

I shake my head, not sure what I'm trying to communicate.

– Where did you get this crap, anyway?

– Read the books they read, think the way they think.

I feel disgusted but outclassed as well. Minna is coming back, a bottle of wine swaying between her fingers. Borg leans over and whispers into my ear:

– Relax, it's just a game, darling. May the best man win.

I feel a faint spray of his spit on my neck. He sits back.

– Hey, Minna. We were just talking about you.

I get up to leave and walk out into the lobby.

I go to the drawing room, intending to spend the night staring into the fire. Every so often, the door opens, people look at me and decide to leave me alone.

*   *   *

230

Later, I walk up the stairs, past Minna's room. I can hear a murmuring from within, a female voice, maybe she's learning her lines. There is silence, a slight scuffling, then a man's voice, gentle but insistent. I am rapt and disheartened. More silence, then the man's voice again, with almost a pleading tone. Minna makes some response, there is another faint scuffle and the door handle turns. Startled, I skip down the corridor towards the bathroom. I look over my shoulder and Borg is closing the door behind him. He looks at me, waves, a low grin sliced into the shadowy face. He puts his forefinger to his lips for a moment and walks down the stairs whistling softly.

I don't take it well.

10

After dreaming of Ray I wake up to the sound of his voice. He is standing over me, a copy of *The T——* open in front of him.

    – News from the front, Moonie. You're mentioned in dispatches.

    – What is it?

    He clears his throat through his fist, pinky delicately raised.

    – Ahem. You sure you want to hear this?

    – No.

    – Oh what the fuck, I'll read it anyway: 'They start screwing and planning careers when they're thirteen, they still attend raves and fail to do their laundry when they're thirty-five. They marry then seek a divorce before a settlement with marriage can be arrived at. They pretend to know everything when they're eighteen, then pretend to know nothing in their thirties. British men are giving a big collective shrug and then going to the pub.' I think she's talking about us, Patrick.

    – What's this?

    – Your missus, who else? Anyway, shut your face, it gets better. 'Amongst the most pitiful scraps of evidence was an item on our phone bill: Las Vegas Leisure Services. Five full

232

minutes of investigative journalism later it was clear that less than a month before I finally came to my senses and evicted him, The Creep –' That's you, isn't it, Paddy?

I don't respond.

– Thought so: 'The Creep was inviting prostitutes into my house and paying for them. Paying for them, I might add, with my money, as he had none of his own.' Blah blah blah, more ballbreaking garbage et cetera, ah, here we go, my favourite bit: 'Of course, the thing that makes this activity farcical rather than just pathetic is that he has been impotent for a year, as good as impotent for six months before that.' Patrick you should have told me, mate.

– Oh my God.

– I feel hurt you couldn't share that with me.

– Fuck off, Ray.

– Don't shoot the messenger, creep. You were right. You're not much competition after all.

He drops the paper and leaves me. I get up and go downstairs. Carver is in the lobby on her mobile:

– Yes he fired him . . . Because he was an asshole, that's why . . . Yes, I know who he is . . . I know they're anxious, I understand that . . . Listen, it's all going beautifully. Trust me on this.

She never stops: ceaseless servile competence. She stops in mid-sentence, looks startled and holds the phone out in front of her:

– And I hope you fucking drown.

I look at her consolingly, which she obviously finds no consolation.

– Patrick, I need to take a break.

– Then talk to me, Carver.

We go to my stream, and each of us squats on a rock. She has some time off for the first time in weeks. Gideon's

233

rewriting, everybody's waiting. Carver is in a cream parka, the fur-lined hood pulled round her lilac-tinted shades. She looks as if she's been beamed down from Aspen or Pluto.

– It is quite beautiful here.

– I guess. I haven't had much time to think about it.

– I would do anybody's job but yours, Carv.

– Thanks, that's a mood enhancer.

– No really, especially on this – you're doing everything.

– It's OK. You don't get bored, at least.

– How do you know Gideon?

She fidgets, knits her hands in front of her. I can't see her face, just the parka and the stanchion of her sunglasses.

– How do I know Gideon? That's a long answer.

She says nothing more.

– Which you're evidently not going to give me.

– Maybe not just now.

We are at the shallow valley less than a mile from the house. The dun hillsides slope up towards the teal sky, nothing but earth and grey air. There is no evidence of humanity visible from here apart from the beanpole actor and an alien in a Yamamoto parka.

– I'll tell you some things but not everything.

– OK.

– So. Hmm. We . . .

She tails off.

– Sorry, Patrick. I'll try again.

But she says no more. She slides her shades off, looks at me for the first time and shrugs.

Ahh, I see: love, the unspeakable thing.

– All right, I understand.

She turns away again. But I don't really understand. If I were her I'd want to permanently absent myself from the source of the pain.

– So what do you get out of the job, then? Kicked around all day long by everybody?

234

– You know, Patrick, you may not get it, but you don't know what it's like to have no imagination.

– That's a ridiculous thing to say.

– But it's true. I don't have one. I'm not self-pitying about it. It's why I do what I do. I couldn't do anything else.

Her voice is very cool about all this. I can tell she doesn't want to be persuaded out of it right now, she just needs a little understanding.

– I don't believe you.

– Let's leave it, actually.

She looks at her watch.

– I should probably make a call.

– No, no. No reception up here. Use that fact.

– Sure.

We are silent for a moment, and it feels a little awkward. Being on set makes relationships move at funny speeds. I know nothing about her, yet in a way too much. Finding out that someone's in love with someone shouldn't be amongst the first thing you know about them. She must have sensed the awkwardness too.

– How's it going with Minna?

– What do you mean?

– What I mean is, how far have you got?

– I've got nowhere, and I don't want to.

– If you want my advice, I'd say keep away.

– Because?

– Just trust me.

– Why?

– Anything I say would come out wrong. I'm supposed to be the person everyone can trust. I don't want to screw that up.

We are silent for a few moments. She is actually of course so kindly. All that brittleness, I've seen it before, it's just the way she gets through the day.

– Carver, can I ask for some advice?

235

– Of course. I'm everyone's servant. I am happy to be everyone's servant, it's what I just told you.

– Not professional advice. Personal.

– What's the difference?

Maybe this is a trick question, but I don't have time to think it through.

– You know what my ex-girlfriend's doing, don't you?

– Ray said something about it.

– Well, I want to know why.

– Sure you do.

– OK then, I'm asking you – why?

– I don't know.

– Somebody must.

She looks into the sky for a moment, then raises a finger.

– I know, let's try something. Let's movie-ise it.

– What do you mean?

– Give me some backstory, Patrick. What I mean is, I need to find some little bit of her past, some tiny little moment or action that everything turns on. The key element in her movie, if you were going to make a movie about her.

– Where should I start?

– Way before opening credits. Getting bullied in the schoolyard or losing her virginity to a close relation – wherever.

– I'll try.

And I tell her my version of the Susie story. Admittedly, I tend to emphasise her character flaws rather than my own, but I go all the way back. How we met, her book, the golden couple phase, the steady dissipation of feelings, even a sketchy if slightly expurgated précis of the sexual disaster. She listens well, occasionally asks a question to clarify some issue or sequence of events, seems to be interested. Then I remember the collapse of Susie's relationship with her father, start to talk about it and Carver lets out a shriek:

– Stop there – we've got it.

– What?

– Her movie detail. Here it is, this is it, this is all we need to know about her backstory.

– Really?

– Yeah, of course. Think about it. What kind of freak makes out Daddy's a child molester to sell some books?

– Did she do that, though?

– That's how you told it to me. She writes this autobiographical novel and it's basically a vendetta against her father, right?

– I'm not sure it was a vendetta.

– Well, she's got *some* problem with him. Who'd do that?

– I never gave it that much importance.

She's excited, waving her arms around as if to say 'you're not getting it'.

– No it's perfect, it explains everything. In fact it's backstory 101. Gets you out of so much trouble, narratively. Bad Daddy – he drank, he beat the shit out of Mom, he raped me up the ass when I was twelve, that's why I'm now a bitch or totally screwed up or so terribly lonely or whatever.

– He never did that.

– No, but you get my point.

– Sort of.

Carver gets off the boulder and stretches briskly. She is precise and efficient in all things.

– And you say he didn't do anything?

– No. She said he never went near her.

– It's perfect. All this ambition, this ability to hurt other people, it's faraway Daddy who never gave her the love and admiration she needed. The only way she can get attention is by lashing out. Some people are quietly hostile all their lives, but she's this expressive type, novelist, journalist, so she goes public.

– Do you think that's true?

– I'm not saying that it's true. I'm saying it's plausible motivation. It's the movies, Patrick. It doesn't matter if it's true as long as it's credible. Come on, let's go. All this fresh air's creeping me out.

– What? I should make an effort to see him?

– Why not?

– I'm not sure I buy it.

– Oh my God, I do. I buy that the answer to every clever girl is something to do with daddy. Or anyway I'm prepared to buy it for two hours in a movie theatre.

We walk back to the house and I go to my room. Susie's dad Harold Fisher is an indistinct presence to me. I remember his overtight V-neck sweaters stretched over a respectable gut, his laconic right-wing observations, the collection of muddy golf gear in the utility room at their house in Surrey. She always told me not to bother trying to create a relationship with him, and I was relieved. I have little or nothing to say on the subject of carpet wholesaling and tend to be very much opposed to golfers' politics. But now he is suddenly of vital interest. I ring his office and ask for an e-mail address. The first piece in the backstory perhaps: HaroldMFisher@HaroldMFisher.co.uk

11

So now this bright morning my love scene with Minna.
Gideon comes to see me in my room.

– Listen very closely to this. I've been watching the
dailies. Somehow you got there. Something happened, you
wobbled, but then you got back on it. You're doing some
really good work. The dweeb is back and it's a beautiful
thing.

– Really?

– Yes, really. Would I lie about something like that?

I try not to show any evidence of the elation that rushes
through me.

– So really it's good?

– Excellent. It's all getting so much better.

I nod with conviction. Praise is what I'm in business for.

– I'm pleased I'm not fucking it up for everyone.

– If you listen to me, Patrick, listen to what I say: everything will be just excellent.

– I'll listen.

– And here's a ticket to London. Take a few days out, go
get fucked up, whatever. You deserve it.

He leaves the room and I give a little dance of delight.
Then I remember that I seem to have improved because of

the drastic return of my neuroses, so I think about Susie. A couple of minutes later I'm chewing my knuckles and ready to go down to make-up.

The light is soft and warm in the bedroom. I arrive early and slip into the bed shower-fresh, my mouth impeccably sweet after hours of work in the bathroom: scrubbing, flossing, gargling, swooshing, spraying.

– Relax, Patrick. Relaxation is the key to a good bed scene. That and a beautiful girl.

I close my eyes, go over my lines and wait for her to be beside me. Fryman continues to give orders with a quiet urgency. I hear the occasional clink and thud as the lights or props are moved around and then the sheets are pulled back and I can sense the shivering animal bundle herself in.

– Remember the sequence, Patrick: wake slowly, turn to her, I'll move in for close-up, kiss her awake. It has to build slowly, your only thought, 'This is the high spot of my life, I'm finally in bed with this beautiful woman.' And you, Minna, you start real slow, hesitant, but build it up. I want to see you really get hot with it, then once you're going you're on your own, make like you haven't seen each other in years, or you're breaking some fast, some five-year sex fast. It's got to be that good a fuck, yeah, you got that?

OK, not five years, but if you exclude Putanesca, who was effectively assisted masturbation anyway, then what, a year? God, without knowing, I was doing the Method all along.

– I'm ready.

– Just wait a few seconds then we'll go with it. When I say go.

Under the sheets I feel Minna's hand reach out for mine and squeeze it. She whispers:

– This doesn't mean anything.

I swallow and feel as if I'm being filled with some kind of unfamiliar gentleness.

– Of course.

There is a moment's complete silence, then the faintest sound of the button on the camera being pressed.

– OK, Patrick – go.

I continue to pretend to sleep for what seems like too long, then open my eyes. The light is offensive, I hold my forearm up to my brow, prop myself on my elbow. I look at Minna and there is no need to act the look of tenderness that I must adopt.

I start to kiss her slowly. Because of the make-up her skin is waxy and cool. I reach across her tummy and pull her closer, still kissing her slowly, moving my lower body towards hers. I am so tall, she so small, that in her fetal position her feet could rest on my knees. She starts to respond. I can sense that underneath the sheets she is naked apart from tiny cotton panties. She moves towards me more ardently, kissing me all over my face. Her breath is like wine vinegar, she even smells unshowered; milky, stale perfume and sweat, but, my God, this is terrific.

I hear Gideon's voice:

– Like it so far.

She pushes against me, we are now kissing properly, her hands moving down my back, my chest pressing against her small but immaculate breasts and *this is it I'm back, fully returned to humanity, to wit, a collection of inflamed nerve endings on a stalk, pulling a compliant body around the world, dog-selfish, hungry, unselfconscious, demanding release, satisfaction, anything to put an end to the crazy singing or to make it last that little bit longer, forget love, money, success, everything outside the here and now, a tall guy with a furious, exquisite appetite that demands to be gratified, no artificial stimulants and most of all no acting necessary.*

241

We tumble and cavort unreally, seemingly half for ever, Minna Howard and I, naked apart from the filmy-thin fabric re-shaping itself to our blood-fattened genitals, it's exquisite, the filthy tension of the real bodies and the faked desire that somehow becomes real, down inside me the unfightable rage of the sex-instinct, a millimetre of sodden cotton between us and the fuck, but her dry-mouthed panting, my arching and bucking maybe it's a fuck after all but better because remember it's not real, doesn't have to go any further, it's just a scene – and I think she comes, I certainly do.

Rapid breathing in the silence, the shift of sheets, and then Fryman,

– Perfect, absolutely perfect.

Later, I am running in the twilight, pounding the tarmac with my big flat feet.

Oh Susie! I think how close I was to going the other way. Now I'd be calling her every day, talking about, I don't know, wedding arrangements, sharing excited analysis of what's happening up here, telling her what it's like doing a love scene with Minna Howard, leaving out only what happened and how it felt. I know we could have rubbed along, muddled through with some educated half-truths and tactical omissions. What relationship doesn't involve some measure of suppression? There is a feature in *The T——*, they ask some sleb, 'On what occasions would you lie?' and every time the same response: 'To avoid hurting other people.' That's what relationships consist of: the continual preparedness to lie so the other person isn't hurt.

Everyone assumed that we had taken the simplest option, staying together that long. As if, in fact, it wasn't an achievement overcoming the recurring bursts of desire to get out because a different part of the soul was able to perceive that those moments recur whatever the situation, and that mediation is the best way to resolve disputes unless something fundamental has gone. Of course, it's possible that it had. Certainly, the obvious manifestations of 'sexual love' went long ago. Sex and pure delight and the rest of the world not mattering – they had all gone, but the deep imprints made on the other's heart persisted, persist still, that must be right, because look at me, Susie, slogging along wet moonlit roads, the rush of air drying tears into my face.

I try to identify the origins of our catastrophe. But each time I start to consider something that might be interpreted as the first cause, suggestions of previous first causes accompany it like fast-receding echoes. No: don't look for a first cause of war in the past, look for a first cause of peace right now. If it's impossible to identify who threw the first stone, then the alternative is to let the other person throw the last. Just one attempt at holding back, one act of grace and courage (more likely not an act but a Stoical non-act), an opening of the arms, an unconditional amnesty, that's all it could take. Yes, Patrick, shock with gentleness. Most of all, try to understand. That's it. If you have to look back, then look back on yourself. Never stop asking questions in pursuit of the cause in case you stop one question short of finding yourself responsible, and therefore capable of making amends.

The narrow road that leads to the house is unlit, the woods alongside are alive with tree monsters and wind devils. Fear as well, from nowhere suddenly. I sprint down the drive, pursued by voices in the trees, their stage whispers of blame and threat. The house is fully illuminated, squares of orange, yellow, white. Minna's room is above the front porch. Shadows move behind the curtains, but, curiously, I can stand it.

12

Back in London for my mini-sabbatical, the cell in Holborn feels uninhabitable, bleak beyond expression. It needs the movement of bodies to warm it up. I can't sit still so I go to an internet café to check my e-mails:

From: Hillary Kelly
To: pmoon109@hotmail.com
Subject: A Modest Proposal

Dearest Patrick
Hello. It is now some time since I sent my last missave (including, you may recall, the detailed ground-plan of my idea for a stage play).

I am not trying to bother you, but I thought I should give you an update as to the status of the project from both its artistic side and, if you will, its more practical ramifications.

To metaphorically put the cart before the horse, perhaps, logistically I have made emphatic progress!! Two or three established directors with glittering pedigrees have already expressed an interest in seeing how the work could 'develop' going forward. In particular they have asked me to think about the 'overarching structure' of the piece, in terms of its story and plot, as well as some of the finer brushstrokes of the characters.

With such exciting news in hand, I really do beg you to consider your response and to respond accordingly to me about this project. What with the imminence of the 'green light' for production, I would hate it if you missed out on another Great Role for your illustrious career.

Now I think would be a perfect opportunity to have that lunch we have talked about so often and really get into all the nitty gritty in an interpretative sense!

Yours desperately impatiently (in a good way!),
Hillary Kelly

I type a brief reply and hesitate for a second: letter-writer's remorse, the indistinct sense of wrongdoing every time you drop an envelope into the postbox, or press 'send'. Part of it is a feeling that you may have misspelled something, but it's not just that.

From: pmoon109@hotmail.com
To: Hillary Kelly
Subject: A Modest Proposal

Just get lost will you, you freak.

And then I read:

From: Harold Fisher
To: pmoon109@hotmail.com
Subject: Your suggestion

Patrick
I'll meet you, but it won't do any good.
Harold M. Fisher

Chairman and CEO
Harold M. Fisher PLC

I arrive at the golf club early. The clubhouse is a large
Edwardian structure, a super-sized suburban house, bay windows, ivy. Peacocks stalk the lawns like pre-revolutionary
French aristocrats. I wait in the hallway, which is lined with
wooden boards inscribed with past club champions, captains,
secretaries, treasurers, all of it evidence of the human need
to organise, extol, reform, commemorate. Harold Fisher is a
dominant figure: you can trace his migration through the
mythology of the club: 1970s and 1980s club champion,
then treasurer, chairman of the greens committee, now club
captain. A large, heavy-framed photograph of him in blazer
and striped tie hangs halfway down the corridor next to a
full-length portrait of the Queen. It strikes me that he is the
prime minister of this tiny statelet.

– Can I help you, sir?

An elderly man in a braided maroon jacket appears from
a side door and looks at me with polite concern.

– I'm meeting Harold Fisher.

– Excellent, sir. If he's not playing, he'll be on the range.
And vice versa.

The man directs me to the driving range. I pass a series
of men in couples, shoes crunching the tarmac. They study
the ground in front of them, pulling trolleys loaded with
softly clinking golf bags. I can only hear the tone of their
conversations, but there is a sense of comfort, peace and
friendliness. Maybe this is what marriage should sound
like.

The driving range is a long, low shed facing out to a field
throughout which are scattered tiny slender flags, three
large archery targets. There is only one golfer, in the booth
at the far end of the range. I have time to watch his strange
nervy ritual as I walk towards him. First he stands behind

246

the ball, spinning his club, peering into the far distance. Then he pulls at the wrist of his ladylike glove with his teeth, hitches his trousers with the heels of his hands before taking up his odd sidelong crouch. Finally, after several minuscule adjustments of shoulder and hands, and twitchy glances out into the field, he makes his swing, which culminates in a balletic pose, on one tippy-toe, hands clasped over his shoulder, head in noble profile as he peers into the dull white sky.

– Wow, looks good.

– Shows what you know. Caught it fat.

His body is slightly buckled by age, rounded shoulders, bulging torso on legs made to look unreally thin by his tight houndstooth check trousers. His white hair is blown in wisps around the lumpy bald head.

– Here, you have a go.

– I don't think so.

– Come on, don't be stupid.

– I'm hopeless, I've tried before. The ball's too far away from my brain.

– Nonsense. Come on.

He gives me his club and throws a dozen balls at my feet.

– Right. Knees bent back straight chin up let the arms hang from the shoulders splay the feet a little.

He taps at me as he says this, chin, shoulders, kicks my feet into the right angle. I feel that if I make one false move I'll collapse on the floor in a riot of compound fractures.

– Relax, lad.

I drag a ball towards me with the head of the club. The ball seems vast, a grapefruit next to the slender knife-like blade of the club.

– Is this even possible?

– It's easy.

– Can't they make the end of the club a bit bigger?

– No need.

I shuffle stiffly, trying to make my arms hang, feet splay, back straighten, whatever.

– Either everything you just told me is wrong, or you're supposed to feel like you've got all-body arthritis.

– You're fine. Just remember – slowness.

I look down the field, take aim at one of the archery targets. I try to visualise the outcome: an effortless syrupy motion, a sound like snapping chocolate as club meets ball, a purposeful receding purr, the ball rising to its apex, dawdling gracefully before dropping to earth with precise reluctance. I look at the ball, feel my hands tighten round the rubber grip, move the club back and feel my body pivot and buckle and extend. I hear myself yelp as if punched as I bring the club down with tremendous force, feel my own shoulders somehow pressing at my windpipe and I look into the air expecting the ball to soar into the flat grey sky, but instead become aware of a scurrying around my ankles, as if a fieldmouse were tying my shoelaces. I look down and see the ball snuggling against the instep of my shoe.

– Damn it.

– You didn't listen.

– Wasn't that slow?

He moves me aside, takes the club. As soon as he touches it, it seems to become part of him. He swishes it a couple of times with oily wrists.

– So what was it you wanted to talk to me about?

– I don't know exactly. Susie, I think.

– Huh. Here, watch.

He knocks another ball into position, resettles himself, and this time if anything he is slower, more graceful. There is a juicy sound as the club connects with the ball and it catapults away from us, a white smear, then a fast-receding grey dot against the sky, then a slowly circling distant eagle, then a tiny greyish dandelion head falling lazily to earth,

248

until finally it becomes a tiny egg, impeccably white and silent not three yards from a gracefully bending flag that looks as if it's drying its hair in the wind.

– I don't know what you expect me to say.

– I don't either.

– Let's go and play a few holes.

He has fitted me up with spiked shoes, a lemon polo shirt and a set of clubs. We ride in a golf buggy, the slightly unsettling intimacy of my thigh pressing against his. He points out some features that are new on the course, some that need to change. All I see are trees, grass, the occasional bunker shaped like a cartoon mouth. It must be boring to be as good as he is – one shot into the middle of the fairway, the next on or near the green, a little chip and a putt or a couple of putts. On every hole that's it. Meanwhile, I spend most of my time brushing back thorny shrubs, peering into ditches or treading through reeds and bulrushes. I feel as if I'm doing a screen test for *The Wind in the Willows*.

The third tee. I try my hardest this time. As I take the club back, I hear myself making an oddly sexual rumbling noise in the back of my throat, and really honestly try to be as slow as possible without reaching full stasis as I swing back, but as soon as I need to bring the club down I feel a murderous violence begin in me again and with bulging eyes and stiffening arms I scythe at the ball with a strangled grunt and the club javelins into the soft earth fully two feet behind the ball, which appears to oscillate. Fear perhaps, or laughter.

– I think I made it wobble.

– You don't listen, do you?

I get back into the cart. The course is deserted. Rain starts to fall and he manoeuvres the buggy under a stand of oaks. He pours me some coffee from a thermos flask and we look out ahead of us, listening to the rain sputter in the trees.

– Right, I've thought about it, and I'll say what there is to say, OK?

– Fine.

– As you know, I'm a rich man, Patrick. Did it all myself. I'm a successful man. I never did anything that I wasn't responsible for myself, never bought anything I didn't pay for myself. Whatever I've done in my life I've done it to the best of my ability, and if I thought it was worth doing, I've done it well. Same with people. You either like me or you don't. I've never worried what people think. I let my achievements do the talking. I've got no time for arse-lickers or silly people. Take me as I come, and I'll do the same for you.

– I understand that.

– With Susan, it's very simple. I said what I thought, left it up to her. Very fair. People know where they stand with me. Take it or leave it. When I left school, I said, I'm going to be my own man, and everybody laughed. Now look at me. These people who come in and try to tell me how to run the business I set up and made successful, same there. Listen, I say, when you've taken something from nothing and made it successful, I might listen. Until then, you don't know what you're bloody talking about.

– Yes.

– I gave Susan as many opportunities as possible, and she knows it. She didn't do anything about it, so that's that as far as I'm concerned. Finished. That's what I said, and once I say something, I mean it.

He stares straight ahead, such certainty to him.

– It must be difficult for you, though. Her being your daughter. To say that it's finished.

– Doesn't matter who she is. Some people are born daft, silly people: nothing you can do with them. So I've been unlucky, and one of them's my daughter. She had everything she wanted. A horse, all the clothes, cars she wanted. As you

250

know, I paid for her all through school and university, gave her everything. She wouldn't have been writing any silly books if it wasn't for me. I never expected anything back but a bit of respect due to her father.

He takes a sip of his coffee, peers up at the sky from under the buggy's roof.

– Yes, Patrick, finished with her.

– She said it was fiction.

For the first time, there is anger in his voice as he turns to look at me.

– Really. Fiction, was it? So the father, the bald golfer, the carpet wholesaler who sings in a choir and reads military history, who the hell else was it?

It's difficult to know what to say. I remember now, she even got his voice right, the vestigial Yorkshire accent barely concealed by the piss-elegant vowels. She has his jawline, his set of the eyes, even something about the hands. I shudder for a reason I can't identify.

– Her mother pretends not to understand, of course. The women stick together.

He spits out of the side of the buggy.

– You know what they called me here by the way? Behind my back, of course, for years, until someone told me and I stamped them out.

– No, I can't imagine.

– Well, no you can't.

– I understand.

– Do you?

– I don't know.

– She's a fucking disgrace, if you'll excuse me.

I am shocked by his choice of words. I look at him, and it is anger that's suggested by his attitude, the slouch over the steaming plastic mug, mouth gripped by a resentful smirk. Anger, but also disgust.

The rain is getting harder.

251

– Right, let's go. You're not enjoying yourself anyway.

– No, I'm not at all.

Back at the clubhouse he asks me in for a drink but I decide to leave. He disappears into the fug and murmur of the men's bar. I wait outside for a taxi back into town. It's possible that I've found out something, but I don't know what it is.

One more day before my flight back to Scotland and I get the idea to go to The Circle. First time in a while. As I pass through the lobby I notice a short handsome man in a baseball cap arguing with the girl behind the reception desk.

– Donachie.

He is pale; his face has lost the Californian burnish. He's even getting pouchy around the mouth and chin. He looks English all over again.

– Patrick.

– Tim, what are you doing here?

– I'm in London.

– Since when?

– Since last month.

– What are you up to?

He looks uncertain, his smile watery, his eyes restless.

– I'm back. Working, trying to get some work over here.

– That shouldn't be a problem.

– No, of course not. Getting the right kind of thing, though. You know, getting the right script.

– Yeah, that's the important thing. Just don't take any old piece of shit.

– Too right, the stuff I'm offered sometimes. Even now. What about you?

– Still doing the film. You know, the Minna Howard, Ray Borg thing. The American guy I was telling you about.

– Right. Great. Minna Howard, fuck, nice. Sort of little, low-budget indie thing, that's right, isn't it?

This is what he must tell himself in order to stay sane.

– Yeah, I guess so. I mean, it's not a blockbuster or anything, but there's a bit of interest in it.

– Great. Shepperton?

– Shooting in Scotland. Getting a bit of advance press, apparently. You never know.

– Great.

– Shall we get a drink? I'm a member here.

– Actually, you know what?

He looks at his watch, does an engaging little cameo of a man who'd love to have a drink if every other circumstance on earth wasn't just a little bit different.

– Actually, I'm up for something. Audition. Something pretty meaty.

Which is presumably why a moment ago he was begging to be let into the club.

– Good. Write me an e-mail. We'll have to meet up when I'm back.

– 'Course.

The personification of evasion, he inclines in the direction of his imaginary audition, but my will is strong:

– What about that little . . . the American chick?

– I moved on. Had a bit of a messy one with her.

– Sounds fantastic.

– Well, yeah sure. She's all yours. And I'm sorry about all the Susie stuff by the way.

– Oh, you've been reading that too?

– I'm afraid to say everyone is. Right, must dash.

I am riveted by his behaviour. Has he really gone that far? Am I really no longer even worth a quick drink, a bestowal of gentle condescension? Apparently not.

– OK, Tim, keep in touch.

– Of course, mate. Any time.

I walk into the main bar but I can't bear it. This place is Susie. And besides, people look up when I come in, as you would when The Creep walks in during your cocktail hour.

13

I get back to Scotland late. The house is still alive with activity, the crew bustling through the lobby as I get through the door. I go to Carver's office. I've thought it through, I write as follows:

From: pmoon109@hotmail.com
To: susie_fisher
Subject: not much

dear susie
i need to talk to you. i've been thinking a lot. i totally forgive you for everything, even the things you don't think i need to forgive you for. listen, i'm not in the least angry.
this is not an attempt to get you back. you wouldn't have me, i don't want you. i just want to recover something, make a plan that says we don't hate each other — strange that we spent all that time together but never really talked about it, just stayed day to day, never did enough maintenance on the memories or tried to understand each other enough. i'd hate to think all of it will be allowed to disappear. i don't want nostalgia: just

some acknowledgement that there was something that was valuable to both of us, and come on, for years most of it was interesting, fun, complex, all the best kind of things.

just a reply, that's all i want.

p

I mooch around downstairs, watching Gideon. In the three weeks since he fired Tomasz he's taught himself how to make a film. It's one in the morning and he's in the ball-room at the top of a stepladder trying to get a lighting set-up just right, Tomasz's men listening closely, exhausted but amazed at his single-mindedness. Whatever else, you have to give him credit for desire, effort and ego, 24/7 energy, sheer force of will. There is something religious about his dedication – childlike and deeply devout – and also about his certainty. I watch him balancing on the ladder, looking intensely between the script and the lighting. The techs stare up at him, rapt, mouths a little open, awaiting their instructions. They are his now. I am filled with admiration. Close up, everybody loves a dictator.

Out in the lobby, Borg sees me and smiles.

– How was London?

– Confusing.

– Beautiful. Let's have a smoke.

Borg takes me to his bedroom, way up in the attic. The room has a sloping roof, no natural light, just a mattress and a bedside lamp. I ask him where his clothes are; he looks briefly confused and pulls at his shirt.

– This is them. The rest are in there.

He points to a small grey canvas knapsack in the corner of the room. There's a sound of scratching from overhead. Borg looks at the ceiling for a moment, then back at me.

– Rats? Bats?

Now we both look up as if we expect to see them emerge

256

through the ceiling. It sounds like rats and bats are fighting and fucking.

We squat on the floor, Borg rolls a joint, all grass, passes it to me to light. I sense him watching me exhale up to the rafters. I pass him the joint. It strikes me that maybe he's got an element of gayness to him, the way he's so vigilant with men, the odd kind of feigned disgust with women, but now's not the time to go into this.

– Things have moved on.

– Well, we were pretty behind.

– Not with the filming, Patrick. That's not what I mean at all, loverboy.

I feel unease. There is a despicable confidence to him. He takes that moment too long over drawing on the joint, runs his tongue around the inside of his mouth, inspects the end of the joint, blows on it slowly.

– As we suspected.

– What did we suspect?

– She's a slut.

– Who is?

– Come on, Patrick, stay with me.

– OK, how do you know?

– The crew, everyone, it's well known. She has this method, they tell me, which is basically she always works her way through vertically up the credits. Starts off on the sandwich delivery boy, through the focus puller, up to the first a.d. and co-star. Then one day she accidentally on purpose finds herself sitting on the director's face. In fact, more likely, kneeling in front of him expertly unbuckling his jeans and telling him in so many words exactly what she's going to do to him and how and over what time period and how he's going to feel afterwards.

– Really?

I try to look as if I'm fine with it, or even as if I'm bored by it, but inside there is a kind of sadness.

– In the last two weeks she's humped the sound guys and the lighting guys. One at a time, then, it is said, all at once.

– Huh, that figures.

– Don't be so upset about it, Patrick. It's just sex. It's not as if you can't be her friend, right.

– I'm not *upset. I'm* not upset. No, you know I think it's pretty obvious.

– Cocksucker. As I said.

A mannish shrug, he tips the ash from the joint into the ashtray.

– So she's a slut, hey Ray.

– Too right.

– Won't be the first.

– Oh no, you're right there.

– You twisted fuck.

– What was that, Patrick?

– I said 'you stupid twisted fuck'.

– Love hurts, loverboy.

– So presumably you too, right?

– Sometimes you can't help yourself. I tell you what, though: I was wrong. No bucking bronco under the sin. Sack of spuds, mate. My old grandmother. The crew agrees: she's a corpse.

– Are you enjoying yourself?

– It's killing me.

He smiles at me through a miasma of bluish smoke.

– Good night, Ray.

– Good night, Patrick. Sweet dreams.

I go back to my room. First of all I'm gripped by unwanted images: Minna, splayed in frantic want, pounded senseless by the boys from the crew any old how, her heart banging like a deer's within her tiny ribcage, something akin to oblivion pulsing through her veins, and it hurts for a time. But soon, the gothic imagescape fades away. I stare into the darkness and start to receive a feeling of resignation or acceptance, and even a kind of calm. I fall asleep counting the ways in which I'm different from Ray Borg.

It's the middle of the night, and I'm in a hot, sheet-twisting dream about Minna or Susie or Marinara or some hybrid, a face above mine, lips thick with blood, hair brushing my face, my guts pulsing, Borg visible over her shoulder, smoking, grinning. I start to shout. The light goes on. Carver is pulling back the curtains.

– Hey, Patrick, get up. We've got some freaky light. Gid wants to shoot.

– What time is it?

– Five.

– Five? I can't get up yet. I've only been asleep two hours.

– Get up, Patrick, now.

And she leaves. I am in a fog as I dress and go downstairs. Borg is in the hallway shivering, barefoot. My throat is sore, my voice reedy.

– What is this all about?

– Let's just do it.

I am so angry I nearly hit him. He looks at me with contempt, all the more wounding for being put on, as if I don't justify genuine contempt. Carver, the furred hood pulled tight round her face, opens the front door.

– Strip to boxer shorts, wrap yourself in a blanket and get out here.

There are two horse blankets on the porch. I give one to Borg wordlessly, wrap myself in the other. It is stiff with cold, abrasive and damp. Fryman is standing on the lawn in a ski jacket and mittens. I can hear his voice as he abuses the three or four crew who are moving the gear.

Borg and I walk through the knee-high grass, blankets trailing in the sopping tangle. The ground is so cold it feels hot. It is a silvery morning, the light seemingly generated by the mist. There are animal noises, distant, prehistoric, as if orcs might scud through the low cloud as brontosauruses graze in the nearby valleys. Freaky light. I hear some creature beating and writhing in the grass near my feet before it slithers to safety.

Fryman looks at us.

– Quick, we've got to be really quick.

I try to sound pained but reasonable.

– Can I at least get a coffee?

– Later. Give them the pages.

Carver gives Borg and me two pages each. I can hardly focus on the words. 'Your wife is dead, Robert,' says Borg. 'So who's that in the house?' I respond. 'I can't tell you yet.' Then I must pause 'like the pause when a train is about to come to a halt in the station, loaded with momentum', and run at him and we fight until Gideon tells us to stop.

– Are you ready yet?

– Look, Gideon, I can barely even see it. Give me a minute.

Borg speaks quietly but with intensity.

– Oh, come on, Patrick, it's one line.

– How long do we fight for?

– Just keep going.

I throw the page of typescript down, let the blanket drop. It feels good suddenly, this nakedness, the light, the time of day. I feel authentic and uninhibited, the coldness making me feel wild. Borg's blanket slips off him like a snakeskin. He shakes his hair down, won't look me in the eye yet. Carver guides us to a place in the grass, Borg looks at me and I realize how easy it is for me to want to fight him. We do the lines. I pause, watch him for a moment and sense his derision. I tear into him. I try to get him to the floor but he's strong, his rear leg braced, his forearms fending me off. Then he throws his foot out and sends me heavily onto my back, thrashing in the long, wet grass, feeling the stones and twigs digging into my back. Instantly he's on top of me, trying to pin my shoulders down, but I get him onto his side. Gideon has his handheld camera, is near us one second, moves away the next, circling us in a crouch. He has another camera running from a stand.

– Stay in this spot, no closer to the stand, stay here. Fight harder.

Borg whispers:

– Good morning, Patrick.

I start trying to punch him, but am too close to get any leverage. He is rubbing his head into my face like a boxer, trying to get my wrists behind me. We tumble a couple of times. I can feel the cuts in my back and legs from the detritus at the roots of the grass. My body is now slicked with dew and sweat. Borg momentarily gets me on my back, wrists pinned. I pause for a second, panting. Borg, moving more quickly now, shouts:

– Sorry, Pad. No need to be jealous. I told you. She's nothing.

I bend one of his arms behind his back, overturning him. He is now cursing me, one of his hands reaching for my mouth. He scrapes at my nose and eyes. I can feel that my boxer shorts have come off, torn by the frantic effort, and I have found a position where I can get short punches in at his ribs. Fryman is now pulling away a little, still going round us. I hear him shout to Carver to move the stationary camera. Borg looks me in the eye.

– Useless. Horrible. Lousy. No fuck at all.

He lunges upward. Now I can hear his breathing in my ear, can smell sheep shit, peat, sweet grass, the smokiness of the morning. Then I feel a tear of pain in my shoulder. He's bitten me, deeply, and now he's shaking his head like a pitbull and growling. I scream, shake him off by summoning everything I have left, get my legs alongside his

261

skinny dog-ribbed torso and land my fist and forearm in his face. He smiles at me:

– You soft-cocked fucking nonce.

Fryman is now maybe twenty yards away. Borg and I are panting desperately. I look down at him. He is still smiling, hair plastered over his neck and face. Only as we start to relax and I loosen my grip on his wrists am I conscious of my cock and balls pressed into his belly. He purses his lips, spits up at me deliberately.

– Easy, loverboy.

We stay stock-still, panting, gazing at one another.

Carver throws blankets over us.

– OK, good. Get showered and get some food. We're back inside in two hours. New pages.

Borg and I disentangle, say nothing. We walk back to the house, muddied, freezing, sore. Borg goes his way, blanket held up over his mouth, childlike; I walk at a slow pace up the stairs to my room. I inspect my body in the mirror. Streaked with earth and blood, it glistens with dew and sweat. I rub my hands over my body, marbling the skin with dirty brown swirls. My balls feel heavy and tight. I stand in front of the mirror, pull faces, smear myself until I look like an Amazonian indian ready to stalk monkey.

I walk down the corridor, in boxer shorts, get to Minna's door, turn the door handle without hesitation. She is sitting on the edge of her bed, her long hands supporting the small, delicate face, naked, looking down at her toes, which she wiggles and bunches.

She looks up slowly – unsurprised, perhaps; I can't see her expression properly in the deep-shadowed morning light.

– It's me, Minna.

Her voice is thick, soft with tears.

– Oh no. Oh no, Patrick. Not you now.

I am instantly ridiculous, lose my purpose.

– I wanted to say sorry.

She looks at the floor, her head lolling as if she's still drunk. I leave her, go back to my room, and stand in the shower letting the sweat and mud stream off me.

14

The last weekend, and Susie has set the mood for me. No response to my e-mail, unless the following in *The T——* is her attempt at reconciliation:

> *Then of course the heroic struggle to reclaim the language of sexism from the working classes.*
>
> *Bitches. Whores. She wants it. Splitarse. Bint. Take it, you slag.*
>
> *Maybe the phrases make men feel like they're part of a movement. Every movement needs slogans, even one consisting largely of regression. Or indeed stasis. Yes, maybe that's it: 'masculinism' turned out to be a movement whose ultimate objective is for everything to stay the same and for people to acknowledge that this is just the way things are. Men and women are equal but different. That's the deal. It has recently been discovered that what men like is screwing and fighting and football and porno and getting fucked up. This truth now established, women must learn to cope with it whatever way they can.*
>
> *I suggest they cope with it by not standing for it.*

I'm not interested in the politics, I want the personal. I don't have long to wait:

And, of course, there was a final act of hypocrisy that still
amazes me: The Creep told me right at the end that he knew
that I'd been sleeping with someone else, and so my desire
to turf him out was hypocritical and lousy. Unfortunately for
him, I had known for several years that he had conducted
an on-again-off-again affair with his agent. I had never
bothered to censure him on this point, because it seemed
largely irrelevant and even quite sweet. He never had the
guts to talk about it, let alone run off with her. My view was
that eventually one or both parties in any long-term rela-
tionship commit an act of infidelity. The question is, how
does an adult respond? The Creep responded with a frantic,
confused, ill-thought-through lurch into emotional violence.
At the risk of sounding priggish, I would have quite liked to
talk it over.

This combination of pussy power and ritual humiliation
is working. Her byline is bigger, she's now on page three
of the supplement, half a page a week. I check Google. As
suspected, her mentions are up considerably. In, what, two
months? she's become national rent-a-gob, a spokeswoman
for her generation of impatient, man-fearing, kid-hungry,
dried-up, teary, confused, utterly lost women who hate their
own minds almost as much as they hate their bodies. It
became clear to me, when I saw her name on the list of
panellists on some late-night arts review show, that in fact
she's got exactly what she's always wanted. She will dance
and skip with joy round the apartment to bunny-boiler
rock. Isn't it ironic? Don't you think?

But I don't have any anger; in fact for the moment I
seem to be spectating on it all, asking rational, regretful
questions: Why didn't I sense that I was capable of causing
such pain? Why can't she sense that she is?

*   *   *

The work has become so easy. Mostly I'm done in one or two takes, no drugs, no anxiety necessary to help me out. My scenes with Borg now crackle with tension, with Minna a kind of defeated wistfulness. Gideon comes up to me after my death scene and announces with American certainty:
– Patrick, you have become your character.
– Is that a compliment?
– Oh yes. You are finally fucking excellent, my friend.
– I thought I was going to get fired for a while.
– That was always a possibility.
– Well, thanks for giving me a second chance.
– Oh don't thank me. I had you on the plane home. But that's what Carver's for. She's my conscience. She's also my patience. All my bad qualities.

Early morning, our last day, I'm standing at the top of the central staircase, looking down into the hall. Minna appears, staggering into the space, then she tentatively begins to climb the stairs. At the same time Borg enters through the front door, freezes, watching her for a moment, looks up at me, makes no gesture, walks through the hall into some darkened part of the house. Minna falls halfway up the stairs and collapses, one arm through the banister, hair spidering over the deep red carpet. I go back to bed, all done.

The night of the wrap party. There is a strange air to the place. It isn't the usual wrap feeling: euphoria, adrenaline drained away, the body ill-equipped to deal with the imminent rapid influx of alcohol and outflow of hyperactive conversation. It's as if some panic has abated or some crisis has been averted. The atmosphere is essentially post-hysterical.

I'm in the drawing room sulking, pretending to read,

praying for tomorrow morning to come, the taxi out of here. Some of the crew have driven into the nearest town for alcohol. There is a sense of a party building, generating itself of its own accord without anyone really wanting it. Borg is up in the rafters, Carver and Fryman are doing whatever it is they do alone together at nights, Minna is somewhere, not here, likely with anyone.

It is ten p.m., maybe ten-thirty, but it's still dusk outside. I hear the thwocka-thwocka-thwocka of a helicopter moving in and out of earshot way above the house. It seems to be circling. I move to one of the drawing room's tall bay windows, the glass rippled with age. I can't see anything. I can just hear the continuing thwocka-thwocka-thwocka, which could be getting closer, it's difficult to tell. I walk into the hall and out of the heavy double front doors onto the tarmac outside. I can see the helicopter now, banking around towards the house, its front a bubble of glass, the skinny thorax held high behind, a giant wasp or locust. It dips its head, races to a spot directly above the house, hovers for a moment, then moves out over the overgrown lawn and starts to descend. The gorse bushes and long grass are tugged and flung around crazily before splaying away from the vortex of wind created by the rotors. Close up the helicopter looks like the skeleton of a helicopter – just thin struts of metal and the skull-like globule of glass up front. It reaches the ground with a little waver, blows a handful of dust into my eyes. By the time I turn back, Stephen Buha is visible hanging out of the door, trying to make himself heard over the slowing rotors.

He dismounts, holding his hat on with one hand, yelling into a mobile. He is dressed in a deerstalker, plus fours, tan brogues and a dark green *Mitteleuropean* cape. He walks towards me, bawling into his phone. He stops, looks around, seemingly annoyed. The helicopter's blades start to slow and the pilot rushes after Buha leading a terrified-looking

267

hunting dog and carrying a shotgun. I begin to hear Buha's voice:

– No, Scotland, I just got in a couple hours ago. What? No, it's a fucking hellhole. It's just all these beat-up old hills and then a tract of frozen tundra, like, in frackin' June. I love it.

Buha walks by me, lifts his chin.

– Hey, what's your problem, nigger? I'm here for the party. No, no, not you – there's some asshole looking at me like I'm some sort of freak. Anyway, what you said about the money? I nearly shit myself. It's great.

He grabs the gun from the pilot and swings it by the barrel. He is having a conversation, it appears, about some money issues related to a film he is producing.

The scrawny pilot walks up the steps to the front door, leading the gundog. It looks terribly ashamed, ears hugging its skull, making a noise like a rusty gate way back in its throat. I have a sudden wave of dog empathy. The pilot, dressed officiously in a white shirt with epaulettes and pale blue uniform trousers with a military crease, looks at me and shrugs. He tugs on the dog's lead and speaks in a Scottish accent,

– It's rented. It's a rented dog.

Buha snaps his phone shut and thumps me on the back.

– So, gook, what can I shoot?

– I don't know, I'm not much of a hunter.

– Can I shoot some Scottish people? Are they all Mormons or something? Or Amish?

– He had a run-in at the airport. About the gun.

– That's it, they're all Amish Nazi gun control hippy Democrats. What the fuck. Where's Fryman? Is it a grill? Have we got steaks?

Buha stalks into the house like some gigantic swollen emu, and the pilot shrugs at me and makes the money sign between finger and thumb. I watch them recede into the darkness of the hall. I walk over to the helicopter. It is a beautiful thing, so light and capable. I step in and pull a couple of levers, tap a couple of dials, sit back, pretend to be driving. Just think, two people in the bubble and the whole sky to fly through: me and my baby.

I stand on the tarmac in front of the porch. The house looks as unfamiliar as it did the first day I arrived, some really old-fashioned way of living, no longer tenable with people like Borg and Buha around. I look up to see Minna staring down at me. I don't even wave.

The party is starting. Everybody congregates in the drawing room, and overlaying the post-hysteria is suddenly a mood of camaraderie. I don't know what it is, but maybe it's related to freedom, all of a sudden everybody conscious that tomorrow nobody will owe anything to anybody for a while, all responsibilities discharged. Borg has joined Buha and Fryman by the fireplace, and I move over to join them too. Borg has adopted his charming persona, of course he has, what with being in the presence of the power and the money:

– Stephen, I think now is the time to say what a great job Gideon's done. It hasn't always been easy, but he's obviously a genius.

– He has a genius for spending my money, that's true, the asshole.

– Well, it's all been worth it. We've done some great work, I'm confident of it.

– Yeah, well, that better be fucking right. My cock is on the block here, Gid. My cock is *always* on the block. That's why I love it. When am I gonna see a cut?

Fryman is buzzing. He's fully in touch with his gaia, or his chakra, or he's smoked some of Ray's grass, or Carver has eased him off in the shower.

– Six weeks. I think we can show something in September. What do you think? Bit of pre-press, distributors about then.

– Yeah, yeah, whatever the fuck. Let's stick it up a parrot's ass and see if the cat miaows.

Ray moves in.

– Stephen, have you met Minna?

Minna has wandered over, her eyes unblinking and wide, the pale brown irises the thinnest of rings around her dilated pupils. She clings to Gideon's elbow. He shrugs her off. She tries to light a cigarette, holding up a lighter, closing one eye at a time until she brings the flame to the right place.

– Minna Howard, this is Stephen Buha, our sugar daddy.

She is slightly unsteady on her feet. Her head nods, she grabs for my elbow this time. I keep it firm so she can rest her weight against me.

– Hello, I'm Minna. I'm so sorry, I think I may be just a little trashed.

She puts her head on my shoulder and makes a humming noise. Buha looks at her without emotion.

– Another fried chick. Just what the movies need.

Gideon rolls his eyes.

– Can you talk to her, Patrick?

I take Minna out of the drawing room. There is a chaise longue in the hall where I sit her down. Her forehead is hot, she keeps rubbing her hands together as if she were running them under a tap. I kneel in front of her.

– Minna, look at me. What have you been doing?

– I'm drunk.

– What else?

– Nothing else. Don't start at me again.

– I just want to make sure you're OK.

She drops her head. Her ankles are crossed at a messy angle. She drops her cigarette onto the carpet.

270

– He said that when we got back to London I could stay
with him.

– Who said that?

She is trying to pick up the cigarette, but can't. I take it,
and throw it onto the tiled floor.

– So that I don't have to go back to him.

– Who said you could stay with him?

I can't stand the thought of her on that barge with Ray;
I can't stand the thought of her with anyone.

– You're all the same, Patrick. You think you know what
I want, but nobody does.

– Look, I just want to know you're OK, that's all.

– Just leave me alone. I'm going to Spain with Alice.

– Yes, of course you are.

– We're going to get totally fucked up.

– Yes, good, good.

– You can fucking piss off and leave me now like everyone
else does.

She starts to rub at her eyes.

– I'm not going to leave you until I think you're all right.

– Oh, do leave me alone, Patrick. All this rubbish. I just
need a bit of sleep.

– Do you want some water?

– Let me sleep, for God's sake.

She tries to lie down on the chaise, as awkward as a foal,
all useless limbs. I try to get a look at her eyes, but she
bunches her fists in front of her face again. Her breathing
is heavy and fast, but I think that might be because she's
upset. Her dress has ridden up around her waist. I pull it
down, trying to make her decent, and slide off her shoes.
I move to kiss her head, but she bats me off in an hysterical flurry and whimpers:

– Don't kiss me, please please, don't kiss me.

– I'm sorry.

I stay on my haunches, watching her for a minute, feeling

271

more helpless than she looks. Then I hear a gunshot and a loud cheer.

I go back into the drawing room, and everybody is standing on the patio outside the French windows. Another shot and another cheer. I walk across the room. Buha is standing in the twilight, aiming his shotgun into the middle distance.

– Fuck! I missed! Fuck!

I move outside, stand next to Wardrobe.

– What's going on?

– Stephen saw a deer.

Buha swings round to us, batting a fat hand from beneath his cape.

– Shut up! Shut up!

He reloads and holds the gun up to his shoulder. He aims into a gorse thicket by the stream. He fires again, the recoil almost knocking him over. Everyone cheers or laughs. Borg is leading the crowd, clapping loudly, a cigarette in the corner of his mouth, eyes squinting.

– Yeah, Stephen!

Buha wheels round, breathless and exhilarated.

– Jesus, I need a bigger gun.

Borg calls out:

– No, you just need a stationary target.

He braces the gun at his shoulder, looks through the sights and rakes it across the group.

– Hey, look! He's right! You're all stationary.

Everyone laughs, more nervously this time. Buha opens the gun and two spent cartridges leap out. He reaches deep into his cape, and slides in two new cartridges. He snaps the barrels back into place and once more points them at the group.

– OK, you motherfuckers. Here's your movie right here. Here's your movie. This is the movie. The producer, right?, turns up at the strike party of this movie he's funded – and he goes insane, OK?, and he chases everyone through the

fucking haunted house, all these smartass little movie fag-
gots shooting them one by one. And he's looking for one
thing, just one person, right?

Buha holds the gun at hip level now, and starts to walk
towards Fryman. Even Borg has lost his jaunty aspect. Buha
starts to speak more softly.

– All this bigshot producer wants – because he's got everything else, money, sex, drugs, fame – all he wants is . . .
gratitude. Everyone thinks that this guy doesn't need praise
or affection or reassurance or gratitude, right? because he's
such a bigshot asshole. Everyone thinks that they know
what this guy needs, what he can handle. But maybe they
don't.

There is silence now. Buha moves his feet into the brace
position.

– Everybody say, 'Thank you, Stephen.'

Nobody says anything, too weirded out.

– Come on! Come on! It's not too hard. Say thank you.

There is a murmur of unsynchronised thank yous. He
starts to walk towards the group, eye still squinted over the
sights.

– Come on, you ingrate assholes! You gotta do better
than that! Say, 'Thank you, Stephen, for letting me be a
part of this movie.'

– 'Thank you, Stephen.'

– 'For letting me be a part of this fine motion picture.'

– 'For letting me be a part of this fine motion picture.'

– And you.

Buha now has the gun barrels resting in Gideon's
stomach. Fryman is smiling, but barely. He lifts his arms
in mock surrender. Buha gestures with the gun for him to
kneel.

– This is the movie, folks, right here. Here's your movie,
right here. Yeah, all this big guy wants, this bigshot producer, who everyone thinks is such a big tough guy, all he

wants is some thanks, nothing more. For his time, his effort, his support, but most of all for his love.

Fryman is now kneeling. Buha has the barrels of the gun against his cheek.

– Thanks from his director for all that love. The movie hinges on this moment, Gideon. Does he get it, Gideon? Does he get the love he wants? Does he get it?

Fryman looks Buha in the eye.

– Thanks, Steve. I love you.

– Did everyone hear that? Say it again, louder.

– Thanks, Steve. I love you.

Buha begins to look tearful. He turns the corners of his mouth down as if suppressing sudden grief. Buha looks at Gideon with a kind of yearning, drops the butt of the gun to the floor, rests one hand on the muzzle and strokes Fryman's hair with the other.

– He does, I think. I think he does love me.

– Dad, can we stop this now? It's kind of embarrassing.

– I'm sorry, Gid. I'm sorry I'm such a fuck.

Later on, things are getting worse. They're drunk, they're all so drunk, and everybody is as horny as all get-out. Hair is preparing to go into Make-Up. Sound is involved in some assistant producing. Script girl grips grip. There has also been lights/camera action. Wardrobe is sucking a guy's cock.

Being reconfirmed in my abstinence, I just want to get out and as soon as possible. Borg, Minna, Buha, Gideon, I don't have a word left. Carver would be OK, but she's working even now. I see her sitting on the stairs curled round her phone, presumably talking to the US, quoting figures, dates, making convincing rationalisations to some distant money-man.

So now I'm trying to talk to the helicopter pilot about something unrelated to the media. He is talking to me about

274

helicopters, but not just about helicopters. The conversation is centring on the fact that he did a bit of acting when he was younger and that some people thought he had a bit of talent – quite a bit, in fact – and in addition to this he writes poems and short stories, mainly about a helicopter pilot's life and how it's not as glamorous as one might think, and there is no little emotional power, not to mention quite a bit of pathos and human interest, attached to flying people around in helicopters and would I like to read some of his stuff because he's always thought that there might be a TV show in it, or radio perhaps, or even a movie . . .

Why, yes, of course! But what about devolution? Is it a step on the road to independence? Or has it in fact drawn the sting of Scottish nationalism and allowed a lasting settlement within the context of the Union?

– And maybe it could be about a fleet of helicopters. You know, in Aberdeen there are all the ones that work the rigs, then there's mountain rescue and then more corporate work like me, so there could be a different focus every week. Lots of contrasts.

– It sounds as if it could be really good, Alex. What could we call it?

– What about *Pilot*?

– Nice.

– But mightn't people think it's about planes?

– We can't have that.

– *Copter*? *Copter*'s good. *Chopper*, maybe.

– I prefer *Copter*.

– What about *Heroes*?

– Alex, I simply must urinate now.

Minna is not on the chaise. Her shoes are on the staircase, looking as if they've been kicked off in haste. I walk along the dark corridor looking for evidence of her. Nothing.

Then more gunshots. I head back to the drawing room. Another gunshot, this time accompanied by a shattering of

275

glass. Alex is sitting on the edge of a sofa, one or two people are crashed on the floor, another couple are trying to kiss but are too gone to get it together. Everyone else is outside.

– What's happening?

– I told the big guy that they're knocking the place down next month. He said he wanted to get started on it right now. He's an ignorant shite, right enough.

Another boom, another shattering, another whoop of scandalised delight. I walk outside but the group is moving round to the front of the house. I follow them round. There are a couple of lights illuminating the front tarmac. The group is gathered around Buha who is now in shirt sleeves. The group steams in gunsmoke and mist.

– Hey, look at this.

Buha is gesturing at the staircase window, the leaded stained glass, the intricate and mysterious vignettes invisible in the darkness. He lifts the gun to his shoulder.

– This is going to blow!

And the noise is amazing, the crash of the glass then a seeming eternity of subsequent smaller shatterings as the glass falls into the wooden stairwell.

– Holy shit, this is the fucking best, man!

He pops the cartridges, reloads and lifts his gun towards a small window on the first floor.

– You're next, baby!

He fires and I remember in the same instant:

– Minna! That's Minna's room.

The group is instantly silenced. I hear Carver in the darkness:

– Oh shit.

I run up the steps to the porch, break through the double doors, sensing there are people running behind me but not caring to turn round, I pound up the stairs, crunching over broken glass, once losing my footing, falling onto my hand.

I try to open Minna's door, but it seems to be stuck. I throw
my pathetic limp body at it but nothing happens. One of
the crew does the same and it slams open. There is a dull
yellow light in the room, spikes and slivers of glass are
everywhere and there is a hump in the bed, a clump of
black hair visible over the top sheet. This is where my nerve
fails. I stay in the doorway and watch as the crew member
throws the sheet back, provoking another hail of glass
shards. He reaches for her neck with two fingers, pushes
her eyelids open.

– She's fucked up.

– Shot?

– No. Drugs, I think.

– Is she alive?

– I think so, I don't know.

– Somebody get an ambulance.

– No. Let's get her in the helicopter and take to her hospital.

I volunteer in an unadmirable blaze of courage, and help
the crew guy drag her out of bed. She hammocks between
us, her dress soaked with sweat, her blue-white limbs glistening. When we get her through the front door, the pilot
is in the bubble of the helicopter. Most of the crowd has
stayed in the house, a couple are still alongside us. Carver
is one of them. I can hear her mumbling under her breath:
'Please don't die, please don't die.' As we struggle to get
the limp body into the bubble, Fryman pushes through the
crowd, as I sit in the passenger seat and a couple of people
pile her on top of me. The pilot starts up the blades, I get
Minna into position on my lap and pull the door closed as
Fryman holds his handheld camera up against the glass.
Then as the rotors increase in speed he holds his hand up
to his mouth and shouts:

– We're all praying for her.

15

The ascent is noisy and slow, the insubstantial machine fighting the night winds. Three of us in a two-man helicopter: Alex silent, Minna collapsed in my lap as if filleted, and me terrified half to hell. Three of us pressed up against four thousand feet of vertical drop, a pitch-black night. In my mind the darkness teems with peaks, invisible crags rear up all around us. Minna has made no movement since we boarded. Her flesh is cool, but so is mine. I remember one thing clearly as we got her into the helicopter, Borg's moving around on the periphery of the panicking group, his face for once fretted with a genuine emotion. I couldn't tell but it looked like fear.

We seem to have reached some stability. I notice Alex has relaxed. I can see a town in the distance, a sprinkle of lights thickening into a glowing reef, then utter black beyond.

– The coast?

Alex nods. He has adopted the mannerisms of magnificence. He is alert, competent, he talks to air-traffic control and the hospital management with clarity and purpose. The idea is for us to get to an Aberdeen hospital where they have more experience with drugs-related incidents than they do at a smaller place that's closer to us. We can land in the car park, empty because it's so late, and we'll be met with an emergency crew who'll take her straight into casualty.

An English doctor or orderly interviews me over the radio:
– What has she taken?
– I don't know. She used to do heroin.
– Describe her state before she collapsed.
– I don't know, she was alone.
– Can you tell me anything?
– Three hours ago she seemed to be drunk, or maybe tripping.
– Has she vomited?
– I think so.

The radio appears to have gone dead. The streetlights below have started forming themselves into the arcs and grids of suburbia. Cars are visible sliding noiselessly up and down the narrow roads. I pull Minna more tightly towards me and begin to feel a sense of peace. The radio crackles.
– Still there?
– Yes.
– We just want to know, well, the doctor wants to know –
– Yes.
– Is it really Minna Howard?
– Yes it is.
– Wow.
– What do you mean?
– Slebs. We don't get many up here.

Minna has been in casualty for two hours. I'm seated in the waiting room staring at the floor. A woman in jeans and a black suit jacket is pushing a microphone under my nose.

279

– So can you tell us what happened?

I can see the knees of the cameraman as he genuflects in front of me, trying to get a shot of my face. I am in the camera's forcefield. It is simultaneously repelling me and drawing me towards it. I have bunched my fists at my temples to box myself in. I can feel the tiredness and anxiety building in my eyes and lymph glands.

– She was taken ill. We think it might have been food poisoning.

– Then why did they need to airlift her out?

– I don't know.

– Ms Howard has a history of drug-related problems . . .

– Look, fuck off, no comment.

– Are you Ms Howard's boyfriend?

– No comment.

– The pilot mentioned a wild party at the house, and a shooting incident. Can you tell us any more about this?

– No comment.

I hear the woman's tone change.

– Tommy, turn the camera off for a while.

As he stands up I take my hands from my face and look at the woman. She is young, early twenties, a provincial hairstyle, cool, milky-brown eyes. There is something about her that reminds of me someone.

– Thanks for that. Turning the camera off.

– No problem. What d'you think's wrong with her?

– I don't know. Alcohol, probably coke, and then other stuff. Ecstasy, maybe, she must have done a lot of something.

– Heroin? Wasn't she on heroin at one point?

– I don't think there was heroin at the house, I don't know.

– Were there other drugs available?

– A couple of people probably had drugs. It's a movie set, for God's sake.

280

– Heroin you say, maybe?

I look at her. She isn't taking notes.

– This is off the record, isn't it?

She doesn't respond.

– Look, can you leave me alone. I've got nothing to say. I don't want to talk any more.

She holds out her hand and places it on my arm, gives me a motherly squeeze.

– Absolutely – your name?

– It's Patrick. Patrick Moon.

– Sure it is. I'm sorry.

– And you are?

– Beverly. Beverly Lewis.

We shake hands. She smiles without smiling with her eyes and I realize exactly who it is she reminds me of, all that taut ambition, all that need.

After two hours' sleep in a waiting-room bucket chair, they tell me to leave. She's still in intensive care, seriously ill, nothing I can do here. I get a taxi back to the house. Fryman, Borg and Carver are slouched around in the drawing room, all looking in different directions. Most of the crew have left, the rest are packing up about the house. Buha flew out a couple of hours ago. He had a meeting at Burbank first thing tomorrow, had to make Heathrow by noon. Just another fried chick anyway, right?

Minna is in a coma induced by alcohol, tamezapam, Xanax and aspirin. All members of her family have not yet been informed, so nothing has been announced to the media. Her father, apparently, is no longer in contact with the rest of her relations. He is thought to be living in Spain.

Carver has stopped crying. Her shades are on to mask the puffiness, redness, downright ugliness that shock and sadness cause. Borg is in a different kind of mood. He's flicking through a copy of *Sleb*, one leg hooked over the arm of a chair.

Fryman is difficult to read. He gets up, starts pacing the room.

– Holy shit. Do you think she's gonna die?

– The doctor said fifty-fifty.

He looks out of the bay windows, something on his mind; he's courting attention.

– Wow.

Borg doesn't lift his head from *Sleb*, but the pace of his browsing slows.

– Yeah, I know.

– This movie, this happens on my movie.

Carver takes off her sunglasses, rubs her eyes.

– I just want to get out of here.

There is something more to Fryman now, a new energy as he stalks the floor. He looks at each of us in turn, a challenging brightness in his eyes.

– I mean we obviously gotta use it.

– We've got to use what?

He looks at Carver and spreads his arms.

– What happened. Whatever happens.

– Gideon, stop right there.

– No no no, listen to me, hear me out. She doesn't die, we're OK, we use it anyway, no problem, some good publicity way in advance, get some buzz about the thing going early. She does die, well, she's an actress, right? So she dies being an actress, making a movie, dies in the process of fulfilling her dream, right? So this movie is her memorial. This movie commemorates her beauty and her talent.

– But what do you mean use it?

– When we're selling the film.

– You're saying *what*?

– Listen, it's obvious. Everybody will know she died on the film, we just make sure it's bumped up in the mix a bit.

– What mix?

– What do you mean, what mix? The fucking marketing mix, Carver. To say to people, this is the movie she was making when she died, look at how beautiful and talented she is, use that thought when we're talking about the movie.

Carver stands, gazes at him in disbelief.

– You sick sick bastard.

– No no, Carver. What's sick? It'll happen anyway, the people who like her will mythologise it and all that shit. The feeling will be out there, the knowledge will be out there, so what I say is, let's be in control of it.

– Somebody dies and you're thinking how it will help your movie?

– Carver, take it easy. *If* she dies. What I'm saying is we should acknowledge the truth of the matter – that this is her last piece of work. And the themes of the movie, dis-placement, alienation, distrust, they're kind of picture per-fect as the backdrop to what happened to her. That's how we position it in relation to how we talk about her on the movie.

– What did just happen to her?

– What do you mean?

– What happened to her? Say it. Say what happened to her.

Fryman is silent, pretends to look as if he doesn't know what she's talking about.

– Nothing's happened to her yet. All I'm saying is how best to handle it if it does.

– What is this thing that might happen?

– Don't be an asshole. You think if we don't talk about it no one else will? We have an obligation to use it.

– Say what you're really saying, Gideon.

– Look, if you're going to get moralistic then fuck that, Carver. There's no moral here, there's no wrong or right about this. This isn't moral, it's about what happens and what doesn't happen and who should control that.

– So some girl you're screwing dies and you can use that to sell your movie.

– Shut up.

– I know you're an asshole, Gideon, but I never thought you could use someone's death as a movie promo.

– You have no idea about anything.

– You freak. I'm leaving.

Carver leaves the room. Fryman looks at Borg.

– Hey, Ray, did I say something wrong?

Borg looks up from *Sleb* as if he hasn't been listening.

– Yeah, what? I don't know. What is it?

I get up. Fryman makes a silent appeal to me with his hands. I shake my head, walk out into the hall. Carver is sitting on the stairs, knees brought up under her chin, hands wrapped round the ankles.

– That was the right thing to say.

– Was there anything else I could possibly have said?

– No, probably not.

– Let's get out of here.

– Let's do that.

Back in London, the threshold of my flat. I have a prepared statement in my hand. I survey the hungry faces pressing towards me on the gangway. One TV girl, three press, two photographers. They were there when I arrived with Carver, crowding us like casbah beggars. We went inside and wrote a speech, tried to write something that was utterly true in itself, stripped of anything that was reminiscent of self-aggrandisement, disrespect, sentimentality. I look down at the paper, screw it up in my fist.

– Patrick!

– Patrick!

– Patrick!

284

– No questions. Nothing to say. It's all too sad; I've got nothing to say.

I close the door softly. I'm back in my barren little bachelor pad. Carver is on the sofa staring at the ceiling. I turn on the TV, just to block out all the other stuff, get myself a beer, flick through the channels until I see the helicopter pilot, a grim, regretful face adopted, secretly having the time of his life:

– When I got there, it was carnage – drink and drugs everywhere – it was a horrible scene. Then, after the shooting incident, I found the young lady and tried to get her into the helicopter. Most of the people were too drunk or I don't know what to help, but I managed to get her into the chopper and get her to hospital. They said there was nothing more I could have done. I just wish I'd known about her condition earlier, because I could have saved her life.

Now I'm on the screen, head between my hands, Beverly's clipped Presbyterian voice introducing me:

– Patrick Moon, who features in the film and who sources say may have been Ms Howard's boyfriend, was also at the party.

Cut to me, head bowed.

– I don't know. Alcohol, probably coke, and then other stuff. Ecstasy, maybe, she must have done a lot of something.
– Heroin? Wasn't she on heroin at one point?
– I don't think there was heroin at the house, I don't know.
– Were there other drugs available?
– A couple of people probably had drugs. It's a movie set, for God's sake.
– Heroin you say, maybe.

A jump cut.

– Look, can you leave me alone. I've got nothing to say. I don't want to talk any more.

Then, to camera, Beverly's head tilted a fraction to the right, brow knitted in concern.

– Police and doctors have yet to confirm exactly what happened to Miss Howard to put her into this coma, but it is certain that she had been drinking heavily and taking drugs at the end-of-shoot party at Barrie Lodge. The latest information we have is that drugs were definitely involved in this incident and in large quantities, but the results of all the tests being done on Miss Howard are not yet being made public. This is Beverly Lewis, in Aberdeen, for the BBC.

Then the anchor:

– Raymond Borg was also a member of the cast and he gave the following statement when he arrived today at Heathrow Airport.

Borg, jostled by the pack, speaks to camera:

– The entire cast and crew are obviously distraught at what has happened to our poor Minna. [PAUSE] She is a fine actress, a beautiful woman and a good friend. [PAUSE] I extend all my sympathies to her family, her friends and her admirers. She was on the way up, of that there is no doubt. Of course, we all hope against hope that she's going to pull through. For now, though, can I ask everybody to remember that what she really wanted – that what she undertook – was really just a search for a little bit of peace. [PAUSE – HE LOOKS UP FROM CARD] Let's just try to give her [PAUSE] a little bit of peace.

A faltering, unconvincing, performance, Ray. Just a B-movie talent, after all. You must be able to do better than this. We've all got to do better than this.

I sit on the sofa next to Carver and turn the wretched thing off.

– What I don't get, Carv, is how anybody could.

– Anybody could what?

– Sleep with Ray Borg.

– No human could.

– So why did Minna?

Carver looks puzzled:

– She didn't.

– What?

– She didn't. To my certain knowledge.

– How do you know?

– No. She's been sleeping with Gideon since the first day of rehearsal. I know, I spent many hours trying to pick up the pieces.

– So she didn't sleep with the whole crew either?

– No way. She's Gideon's girl, poor thing.

I must look bereaved. She strokes my head.

– Hey, Patrick. Don't worry. There's nothing you could have done. And think how I feel.

I look at her. Once so exotic and strange, now suddenly so comforting.

– I look at these people and think there's got to be more to life.

– Than what?

– Movies, ego, bullshit, whatever.

– Patrick?

– What?

– Give me a break.

– What?

– Well, I'm serious. What else you going to do? Work?

part three

1

So finally, two months after the end of the shoot, today I did
my last voiceover session on *The House of the Mind*. Gideon
contrived to be elsewhere each day I recorded. He's still doing
his twenty-hour days. Carver tells me post-production is his
favourite part of the process, because of the total control. No
inconveniences like lighting men or actors to foul up his in-
effable vision. Apparently he's never been so happy.

Minna is still in *Sleb* every week but now with a fixed
grin, usually with a yoga mat rolled up under her arm. They
loved her when she was down but, give them credit, they
love her more now she's on the way back. She is God's gift
to them, of course: beautiful, frangible, the line graph of her
life with its high peaks and deep valleys. And who knows?
Next month she might crash again.

It is still a source of pain to me that she's with Gideon.
OK, he's a hot young film director, so has excellent career
prospects; secondly, he's Tantrically attuned, so presumably
terrific (if slow moving) in the sack; thirdly, he's rich and
(everybody keeps telling me) good-looking. Still, it's unbearable when beautiful women choose to sleep with other men.
I've never fully come to terms with Elizabeth Bennett
passing me over for Mr D'Arcy.

I asked Carver why she was still working with him.

– You've got to separate the work from the life, Patrick, otherwise you just end up hating everything.

I agree. I stopped reading biographies of people I admired a long time ago. I discovered that when I knew the truth, the only person I hated more than the subject was the biographer himself for destroying my dreams.

I stopped reading *Ulysses* as well. I realised there's no point. I now read what people around me read: the red tops, *Sleb*, the 'now a major motion picture' books. You've got to be part of the conversation. *Ulysses* is for freaks.

Straight from the last VO session to The Circle to do some pre-press for *House*, as I unfortunately find myself calling it. I am late, but that's OK, because I'm in the movies.

The journalist is showing me a photograph of Susie, which is mildly coincidental as she has finally agreed to meet me. The photograph is in *Sleb*'s Out and About section. Susie is pictured on the arm of a tall, sleek, middle-aged man. They are walking into a restaurant. The caption reads: '*Susan Fisher, writer and broadcaster, with beau Martin Threlfall, editor of* The T—— *at their engagement party.*'

The results of her diet and exercise regime are obvious. The results of her recent elevation into solid, low-ranking celebrity are yet more obvious. She looks content. Of course, I want her back.

– Haven't you seen it?

– I don't read the magazine. I hate it.

– Don't be daft! Scrate.

She is here to interview me for the other *T——*. She is nervy and wiggles around a lot and smokes awkwardly with the same hand she uses to hold her pen.

– I've always hated that type of voyeuristic crap. As if it's enough simply to print the photograph, namecheck the clothes designer; as if there isn't any more to say.

– Yeah, it's great though, innit? It's just like, y'know, a comic for like grown ups, in't it really?

I have inadvertently adopted a cultural-purist persona, and find it difficult to retrace my steps:

– Can't grown-ups get along without comics?

– This is what they said, this is what I heard when I was phoning around. You're like y'know, a bit of like a brainbox like?

I vaguely know her. She's a lot younger than me but she's been in and out of The Circle for a couple of years, drunk and incapable a lot. She's from the North.

– Who did you speak to? My agent?

– Just a few people, y'know, around?

– And what's this about? Why do you want an interview?

– Cause like y'know like everything that's happened really, y'know?

I have become warm. Someone made some connections and they figured out I was also the guy in Susie's columns, The Creep, the one suffering from accelerated retardation (AR is now a media cliché, used any time a man does anything related to drink, drugs or sport), the porn freak, the john, the impotent wanker. This, added to my inexpert but arresting performance on the news media around Minna's emergence from her coma and the (not immediately denied) misconception that I was her boyfriend, gave me some specific gravity. In addition, Susie's getting her own show, *Agenda*, late-night cable, way down the dial (maybe even digital), but the media whores are agog. It's gonna be a bawdy, candid mix of forthright, brutally honest discussions, chats, features on the new sex war with slebriddy guests and loadsa slebriddies. And now *The House of the Mind* is getting attention, on the back of Gideon's heartbreaking PR offensive, the informing theme of which is how the film proves that Minna

293

Howard is a very special young talent who is going all the way, especially now she's conquered her deadly addiction to drugs and booze, and found love with Gideon Fryman himself, as well as jivamukti yoga, soy and plenty of water, and the sub-theme of which is how the whole process has allowed him to achieve a rapprochement with his father. Apparently, it's been a very healing experience all round.

Of course they want an interview.

– Well, OK, I know why you want one, but what's the focus?

– My angle? I don't know one hundred per cent, but it's like a sorta how you came from obscurity a bit and how it's like really ironic?

– Ironic in what way?

– You know, the irony of the fact that you've become well known like out of these bad things, like that actress nearly dyin' and your girlfriend y'know trying to slag you off like in the papers an' everythin'?

– In what way is all this ironic?

– Like, the irony of it.

– But in what way ironic? It's actually inevitable, isn't it?

– Yeah right yeah got it yeah.

– I'm not sure about irony. There's no point fighting it any more, is there? Haven't we all just given up and joined in? Am I sounding like George Steiner yet?

– Y'what? Oozee?

– Never mind.

She knows perfectly well who he is – she read English at Cambridge if I remember right. She has a tape recorder running, but is scribbling away in a notepad anyway, smoking, gripping a huge glass of drywhywhy.

– So right, what was it like when Susie was writin' those things about yer in the papers?

– I loved it. I loved every minute of it, especially the stuff about the porn and the prostitutes and my criminal invasion of her privacy and the impotence, because I thought 'this might make me famous'.

She's looking at me strangely, slowly nodding her head. There is a moment's silence while she tries to compute.

– That was irony.

– Riiiiight, I get it, riiight, got it, riight. All right, what's it like, y'know, not bein' able to get it up?

We decided to meet in neutral territory. When I suggested The Circle, she said:

– Jesus, Patrick, *nobody* goes there any more.

She's at something in the West End early, then she's got something later on in Holland Park, so she suggested we meet in town around eight. So here I am on a hot mid-week night drinking cranberry and soda in some hip hotel bar where they're trying to prove to the world the excellence of their air-conditioning. They're playing loungecore and, although it's early, there is a celebratory feel to the place. This is a new form of drinking. Well-presented groups of men and women stand with glistening hair in the chilly spotlit piazza holding luminous cocktails: Aegean blue, burnt umber, cloth of gold, sunset over Tucson. They are all laughing or on the verge of laughing. The joke is something to do with the fact that they live in a golden age of health, wealth and sexual possibility. I kind of get the joke but can only assess it as being funny rather than being able to laugh myself. They all look as if they have just stepped out of the shower, breezed through the hairdresser's and clad themselves in box-fresh Voyage, or tatty jeans and thrift-store T-shirts, or agnès b for the post-preppies. The sheer volume of prosperity is uplifting. I think of the old days of English drinking: damp-haired, shadowy-mouthed people gesturing through the fug of underlit pubs at deaf-mute barmen, beer the colour of canal water slopping over your sleeve while

295

you rummage for a soggy fiver, the smells of tobacco, dry cleaning fluid and old rain everywhere. Actually, I hated the old days.

And in she comes, cigarette twirling, not looking in the least bit nervous or ashamed. We do a little stuttering dance as we kiss. I grip her elbow, give her a strange little pat on the waist, which is probably some vestigial primal sex-related bullshit, and which she tries to evade.

– God, you look great.

– Thanks. It's killing me. I did it on professional advice.

– What the doctor?

– No no. The flack. The PR woman. You've got to be thin to be on TV.

– And congratulations. On the engagement.

She has no comment, looks around for a waitress. Close up, I can detect the effort in her new shape. There is a sense that it's all precarious, she might blow any minute, but that just makes me want her more. No controversialist T-shirts now, just an open-neck black blouse showing a freckled brown chest (the Hamptons, I remember from the column), good black trousers and too much make-up. She orders a still mineral water without lemon, and wriggles on to a barstool.

– How weird does this feel?

– Well, what did you expect, Patrick?

I eye her neckline, there is a sliver of black bra cup visible. What are the odds, I wonder, if I make a play now, book a room in a sweat of desire, get her upstairs and it's 1992 again. I remember how she felt, wonder how different she would feel now with her TV body. I notice she's had her teeth whitened. I always loved her mouth, the small lips, the fat translucent tongue, how clean it always seemed. I reach into my jacket pocket for my Altoids tin: two little blue diamonds within.

– You know I've forgiven you.

– I never did anything wrong, Moony. Sorry, I mean Patrick.

– What, not at all?

– I don't think so.

This makes me angry, and for a moment I can't control it.

– So sleeping with your boss, that was fine?

– Will you never grow up, Patrick? I had sex with someone once, I instantly regretted it, told him I regretted it. It was a stupid one-off mistake.

– That lasted three months.

– You know what I mean.

– And now you're marrying him.

So much more difficult when she's there in person than when she was an imagined recipient of an e-mail:

– I realised I liked him a lot more than I thought.

She has changed: all these bristling defences. I expected some of her old self to resurface, try to coax it out with a modulation of tone:

– Listen, Susie, this is not why I came at all. In fact, it's the opposite.

– What are you on about?

– I think I've got it.

– What have you got?

– I went to see your father.

– Yes.

She looks uncomfortable and wary, shimmies on her seat.

– Well, I think I got some understanding of how you must have felt.

She lights a cigarette and tries to look as if she's not listening.

– Oh, come on, listen to me, give me one chance.

She neither agrees nor disagrees, so I continue:

– I don't know, I always thought you were culpable for cutting him off, but when I read your columns I had the thought that it was so disproportionate that there must be something else going on. So I went to see your father to see if it would make sense of my thoughts one way or the other – you know, either you were acting knowingly, or there was something else underlying it all and you were expressing some deeper hurt that you couldn't get across in other ways. So I met him and, guess what, he's this distant, hard, self-obsessed lunatic who never leaves the precincts of his golf club, and presumably never made any attempt to communicate with you apart from to give you money, never gave you any affection or whatever. And now I say it, I admit it sounds a bit simplistic, but I thought that I was getting close to something. I couldn't believe we'd been together so long and never really even talked about any of this stuff. And also, I acted so appallingly that if I were you I might have done the same thing or maybe . . .

She stops me dead with the derision in her eyes.

– Have you finished?

– Yes.

– Good.

She starts to look around the bar.

– She should be here by now.

– Who should be here?

– Ah there she is. Norma! Norma!

She summons someone from the crowd.

– This is Norma Kellaway.

There is a young woman now standing at her elbow, a tiny crop-haired dyke-alike.

– Norma will be your literary agent.

I am confused.

– What are you talking about?

– I'm putting a deal together. I write my side of the story, you write yours – we publish simultaneously next autumn.

I look at her. She's dead serious.

– I'm having a seizure.

– We'll time it so it comes out at the same time as the film. If you can do it – tie in a bit of Ray Borg, Fryman, Minna Howard – we're away to the races.

Norma draws on a cigarette and says:

– We've got HarperCollins, Penguin, Little, Brown all lined up for the meetings, fifty grand each as a going-in point, depending on how much you'll spill.

– I think I may be going insane.

– Look, it's all a farce, Patrick; that much I now know. Just cut yourself off from it, let it happen.

She looks impatient, shakes her hair back, holds her hands up.

– Really, trust me. I understand it now. Don't let anything affect you, keep the life separate, and you can get away with anything. First of all it's a rush.

– I'm not even going to think about it, of course.

– Well, I thought you might say that. But just keep thinking about it. We've got a month before we have to say yes or no.

– Say no now.

– No. No way. I know you, Patrick.

Norma smiles at me, as if she knows something I don't. Susie speaks again, affecting a tone of blasé tedium:

– By the way, while I remember, that stuff about my father is horseshit, misses the point entirely. I never liked him enough to care that he was never around.

– You're a very strange woman, Susie Fisher.

– I never tried to hide anything. You know what I wanted. The fact that I've got it shouldn't change what you think of me.

– So is it worth it?

A couple approach us; the man has a look of glee on his face. He taps Susie on the shoulder. She turns round, instantly composing her face into a smile.

299

– Hi, Susie Fisher, right? We just want to say that we really like your work.

– Thank you.

– And you're Patrick, right?

– Yes.

– Nice.

They both just hover around us, not sure what to do next, because once you've moved towards the light and said hello, what else is there to do? Until tomorrow, when you can tell your friends that you introduced yourself to a stranger and found out you had nothing else to say. They shuffle away, embarrassed. Susie checks her watch. I try to catch her eye:

– What's in your book?

– We haven't decided; we're waiting for you.

– And if I say no I won't be mentioned, right?

– You'll feature, obviously. You're the reason it's happened.

– And you can do this without asking me about it?

– As long as I don't say anything libellous. Which I won't.

– So you can be hurtful as long as you're not libellous. That's almost a moral system.

– Look, Patrick, I can't teach you anything about hurting people.

– Do I get to play me if there are film rights? I'm joking, of course.

This time she looks at Norma and raises her eyebrows, then looks down at her lap and rummages in her handbag for something.

– Hold on a second, Susan. Are you saying there are film rights?

– No, not yet. There may be a couple of people interested if the book comes out right, but it's all a long way off. They're saying it needs a central thought to get people interested, which it doesn't yet; we don't really have a central concept.

I study her in silence. There's no talking to her. I close my eyes, decide to start all over again:

– Are you coming to the screening?

– Martin wants to see it. He's heard Fryman's a genius.

– Don't you want to know how I am?

– Of course I do, Patrick.

– Well, I'm fine.

– That's good.

She hesitates as she gets off her stool, then kisses me quickly on the cheek and walks out with Norma. Man, who would have guessed that underneath it all she still had such an incredible ass?

Carver has come round for dinner and a movie. Dinner was green slush, orange slush and beige slush. We are now on my sofa, suppressing our flatulence, half watching *Adam's Rib*. Carver is into the classics, but to me the rules they are governed by no longer seem to apply.

– It didn't work.

– No.

I turn down the volume a little: the dialogue is so shrill and abrasive, it's not a screenplay it's a constant bicker.

– The backstory thing didn't work. In fact she's way way ahead of me.

– Oh well. You tried.

– Shall I try again?

– No way. It's OK to make the first gesture of peace, but if you make too many you end up looking like a jerk.

There is something in her eyes I almost can't bring myself to believe. All the way through the kindest, the steadiest, the most hard-working, honest, never complaining, the most acute and wise.

– Carver?

– Yes.

– Can I ask you something?

– Of course.

– Are you what you seem?

– What do you mean?

– What do you think I mean?

She looks at me, kindness again in her soft brown eyes.

– What do I think?

– Yes.

She pauses, bites her lower lip and squints as if trying to remember a sequence of events that occurred years ago.

– I don't know. What do you think?

– I think you know what I think.

– I think that you're thinking that I might be your love interest.

– Am I right?

– I don't know. I mean, movie-wise speaking, narratively and so on, it makes perfect sense.

– I suppose so.

– But maybe the only way to find out would be for you to kiss me.

Shocked but not at all surprised, I kiss her on the cheek, then on the eyes, bring my hands up to her face. I feel something beyond acquiescence in the way she angles it up towards me.

– Well?

– So far I'm buying it.

2

The screening is in a small new cinema in Shoreditch. I decide
to walk from Clerkenwell. I've checked Ray's barge a few
times since I moved in, but he's never there. I decide to try
again tonight. I walk down the shadowy twilight street of
council blocks, through the gate and across the patch of scrubland that leads to the canal. Three homeless people are lying
around blotto in the twilight, their clothes the colour of river
water. I walk down the steps to the bank and try to look
inside the barge. Nothing. I turn back, climb the steps and see
someone jogging across the scrubland. He seems to notice me.
He stops and tumbles to the floor. The silhouette seems
familiar. I go towards where he fell to the ground. He is curled
up, one arm shielding his face, wearing old jeans and a black
T-shirt.

– Borg. What's going on?

He lies motionless, so I squat down next to him and shake
his shoulder.

– You OK?

He looks up at me.

– What are you doing here?

– I just came to look for you. So we could walk down
to the screening.

– Why did you do that?

– No reason. What's the problem? What the hell are you doing?

– I don't want to see anyone.

His voice is an urgent whisper.

– Why not?

– Just leave it right? I've got to pick something up. I'll see you there.

– Don't be stupid. I'll wait.

– You can't wait. I don't want you to wait.

– Christ, what is it with you?

– What is it with me? Nothing's wrong with me. I've got to go.

He gets up from the floor, looks back towards the road in panic. There is a minivan parked by the entrance to the scrubland. A figure waves at him from within.

– Look, Patrick, you've got to leave.

– Are you in trouble?

– Will you stop fucking interrogating me and show me some respect?

I look back towards the minivan. Someone is getting out of the driver's door. She walks round the car and slides the rear door. Two children get out. The three of them walk towards us. The woman is tall, about a mile wide with a severe black page-boy haircut. The children, two girls in matching shorts and shirts, are also equipped with the hyper-severe haircut. It looks as if it's been affixed with a central screw. The woman waves, cups her hand to her mouth:

– Raymond? What's going on?

He looks at me, his face filling with panic.

– Look what you've done now, you bastard.

– What is it?

The girls run the last twenty yards towards us.

– Daddy, Daddy, why did you fall over?

304

I look at Ray in bewilderment. The woman speaks, her voice stern and matronly.

– What the devil are you doing, Raymond?

– I'm not doing anything, right?

– Who's this?

She is near enough to see clearly now. She looks like a farmer's wife, soft, mountainous, built for comfort not for speed. Ray is lying flat on his back staring up at the sky. The woman continues to look between the two of us. She is wearing some form of floral teepee, black ankle socks and slippers. The girls move towards her, looking warily at the now-vigilant homeless men.

– Raymond, who is this?

– I don't know.

He gets to his feet and stands with his hands on his hips, looking into the distance.

– What are you talking about? Of course he knows. I'm Patrick Moon. I was just in a movie with him.

– Oh, hello, I'm Carol, Raymond's wife.

– Good to meet you. Are you coming to the screening?

– Oh no, no, no, I don't go to things like that. We come up from Hampshire with him. We'll drop him off and I'll take the girls to a show. Not my sort of thing at all.

– So you don't live here?

– No, no. We live down near the coast. He stays here once in a while. When you're stuck in town – right, Raymond?

– Right.

– And this is Merry and Lola. Say hello, girls.

They murmur hello and push themselves further into her big fleshy body. I look at Ray. He summons the girls. He has now surrendered.

– Come on, girls, let's go down to the boat.

He leads them away, one on each hand.

– How absolutely bizarre.

– What's bizarre?
– Oh nothing. I'll go now.
– Could we give you a lift down there, Patrick?
– No, it's OK, I'll walk. Hey, Ray!
He half turns.
– Only collide.
He lifts his head in reluctant acknowledgment and makes his way down the canal steps, one hand on the shoulder of each of his little girls.

Fryman wants to show the cut to the cast, distributors, some money-people, a few key press, 'select other invitees'. Carver told me a month ago that there's buzz. She comes back from the edit every day with a fresh piece of encouraging news. It's all looking fine, I'm looking fine, everything will be just fine.

The cinema is in a converted church. There are a couple of Klieg lights outside the cinema, a bunch of photographers, maybe six or seven standing around the velvet rope. Fryman and Buha have invited some A-listers, but even I have to pause on the carpet for pictures. I try to look as if I've done it a million times before. I smile and shrug a lot until some soap star turns up in a limo and I'm instantly old news. I walk into the cinema and Carver frantically waves me over. For three days round the clock she's been in the edit suite.

– Have you seen the whole thing yet?
– This morning, honestly, it's just so terrific. You're terrific.
I feel my heart expand, can't hear enough suddenly.
– Really?
– Honestly, you're brilliant. So's Ray, so's everyone.
– My God. Really, did I come out OK?
– Fantastic, honestly.

I stop pretending I don't feel nervous and ride the adrenaline.

– I still don't believe you.

– Trust me, you're going to love it, everyone's going to love it.

I look around the lobby, see familiar faces, but want to avoid everyone. I've got nothing to say until I've seen the film, won't be able to concentrate on anything anybody else says.

My seats are in the front row, next to Minna and Gideon. The rest of the row has been kept clear. I sit and gaze straight ahead as I sense the auditorium fill up behind me. Despite Carver's reassurances, I am possessed by terror. I believe, of course, that I will be lousy. I replay some of the scenes in my mind and can only think of the missteps, bad rhythm and gaucheness. I don't even listen as Gideon stands facing the audience and gives a short speech, although I'm aware that his mood is manically positive and that he talks about me a little. Borg slips in and sits on the other side of Minna, looking straight ahead. The room goes dark and I grip the armrests, fear binding me up like a mummy. It starts. The credits, a long helicopter shot of the highlands, no music. My name appears on the screen, then fades out, melting into clay-white sky.

I sit still through the closing music, trying to deal with my exhilaration. I don't think I'm mistaken.

– *My God, Patrick, you've fluked it . . .*

The awkward, distracted, paranoid individual up there on screen, the misfit, the fish out of water – in other words, me.

– *My God, Patrick, you've fluked it, but you were brilliant.*

There is a feeling that's something like joy within me and a strange tearfulness as the last lines of text scroll up, the music fading. Then Minna appears on screen, close up, slow motion, monochrome, her eyes blinking heavily, that exquisite face hollowed and blanched by the grainy light. A jump cut. She talks but there is no sound, throws her fringe back, draws from a thin black cigarette, rubs her black eyes with the back of her delicate hands and laughs silently. The camera watches her as she breathes in deeply, looks out of frame, still slow motion, and she freezes, the only movement her childlike blinking, luminously beautiful. Then a cut to her being bundled into the helicopter, me holding her head to my chest, looking resolutely heroic; a shot of the helicopter rising against the night sky. Then in the hospital, still grainy, the camera moves in on her, wired up to banks of machines, then finally in a convalescent's gown walking on the lawn outside the hospital, laughing into the camera, the head thrown back, freeze-frame on this image of triumph over adversity, of damaged beauty having survived against the odds.

Then, a single line of text across the foot of the screen: 'Now do you know how much we love you?'

The image fades to black. Applause starts in the back of the room as the lights come up. By the time the room is fully lit, half the people are standing, clapping ardently but with solemnity. As Fryman and Minna stand, the applause increases. They turn to face the audience. He nods briefly, she looks winningly humble before they both walk out of the fire exit at the front of the theatre followed by Borg. I stand to follow them, and the applause gets louder, it's now like sizzling fat. I turn and notice with a kind of panic that they're doing it for me. My face is expressionless as I look around the crowd: Susie, Threlfall, Hair and Make-Up, Carver, Buha, Mary, all showing the same smile of admiration, the one that looks like savagery.

So this is it, this is how it feels to get what you want. But the freaks, the brutes, the betrayers, the self-obsessed, the confused, the

lonely and the lost – why should anyone want what they have to
give in the way of love and respect?

But instead of disgust or indifference, I feel light and fiery,
overcome with unmediated pleasure. I am incapable of any
self-deprecating gestures, any ironic shrugs or humorous
mugging; instead I notice that I'm tearful. There are no
ambiguities or vestiges of moral doubt, just a kind of ugly
joy of vindication. I am awesome, brilliant, I am fantastic,
excellent. I have the admiration and envy of my peers, who-
ever the hell they are. And more, it's just as I remembered
from over a decade ago now: it isn't a hollow feeling, it
isn't in any way illusory; it is sweet all the way through, it
is a surpassingly gorgeous feeling and it is the realest thing
on earth. The applause continues as I walk out of the exit.
Borg and Fryman are in the black corridor whooping and
hugging, Minna hanging onto Fryman for dear life. Fryman
sees me, spreads his arms towards me. I can say nothing as
he claps his bony hands onto my face.

– You see, Patrick, you've got to trust me.

I don't say anything, but mainly because I am choked
with self-love.

I walk between him and Borg, through a fire door and
into the wet London air. The street is quiet under the
yellow streetlights. I stand still for one moment, feeling
a kind of sweet anger rise within me. Then I gallop and
yelp, swing myself around a lamppost, one hand holding
me on, the other gripping the air. I see my reflection in
the blacked-out car window unleash a scream which
nobody hears.

The after-screening party is three streets away. The building
is a converted what? It's hard to tell, although the lift could
accommodate fifty people or twenty head of cattle or two
Cadillacs. It moves at an almost imperceptible pace. My

fellow travellers, a group of seven or eight New London exotics, are largely silent, eyes raised to the roof, tugging at their lapels and skirt hems. Three girls, three renditions of perfection: a shaven-headed black girl, legs like a stork's, culminating in an impeccable fist-sized ass; a blonde, hair falling in offset glossy parentheses around a small-jawed face, a tiny distension of the belly visible under the tight minidress; and a Japanese girl, square purple-tint no-frame shades and, against the possibilities allowed by her gene pool, not just long-limbed, not just bubble-butt but *zaftig*. Zaftig Japanese girls, for God's sake: it's almost too much to bear. I reach for my Altoids tin, rattle the blue pills quietly. I notice with a creep of pleasure that the boys are all short, so actors, no doubt, and going places, too. I loom behind them, no longer conscious of my indifferent past, only my recent successes. The lift door opens and immediately the muffled boom of generic London media party music, some new sub-genre of a side-genre – glamour-core or mediabag, maybe.

The party has already attained its cruising altitude, the vigorous judder of the music, the competing, ceaseless clamour of the crowd. I sidle round the walls strangely peaceful, attentive. I don't recognise many people. I see Mary, she waves me over.

– Listen, Patrick, this is all good.

– What do you mean?

– Everything, it's great.

– How do you know?

– Fryman's doing something else. Something a bit bigger, early next year, shooting in Canada.

– So.

– He called me. He wants you in it.

– Why didn't he ask me straight?

– He said there was something between you.

– Did he?

– Well?

I look around the room. I see Fryman, in a group with Buha, who is wearing a three-piece chalk-stripe suit, watch-chain, hanky billowing from the breast pocket. Fryman makes a face as if to echo Mary: 'Well?' I try to look indifferent and scan the room.

And in the corner, to my shock, Tim Donachie is standing on his own, looking over at me.

– Hold on a second, Mary.

As I walk over to Donachie his face brightens a little.

– Tim, what's up?

– Hi. I blagged an invite from Susie.

– Great to see you.

– And you. Well done, mate, by the way. Everyone says you're brilliant.

– Don't believe what everyone says. What you up to?

He smiles, it's still stunning.

– I've got to be straight. You know I haven't worked in two years, don't you?

– I assumed you were just about to happen.

– No, well, it didn't happen.

– Sorry. I know the feeling.

– You won't for a while now.

His saying this allows me a brief revisitation of the euphoria I felt in the auditorium. Maybe he's right.

– So really, you've got nothing at all?

– Well, I just got a little fringe thing. You know him actually. Graham Furnish.

– You're joking.

– No. We're doing *The Tempest*. Studio in Hammersmith.

– Oh my God, Furnish. Still doing Shakespeare.

– Right. I'm Antonio.

A juve lead still and maybe nothing else.

– Furnish is great, you know; you'll like it.

– Well, that's why I'm here in a way.

311

– What is?

– I told him I was coming and he said, if you want, he's got something in it for you.

– Jesus.

– Prospero, in fact. He doesn't want to talk to Mary in case she rejects it out of hand, after all this, you know?

– Hey, Patrick, mate, Paddy boy!

A skinny, ginger-haired man in clown wear – yellow polka-dot shirt, tartan trousers, a bandana round his neck – smiles at me with gappy, discoloured teeth.

– What?

– I'm the snapper from *Sleb*. Can I do a couple, boy?

He's already taking pictures, pushing me back with an outstretched hand, trying to get me to stay still.

– All right, boy, great, nice, thanks, Paddy boy, put you in the paper, yeah? Lovely, great stuff, mate.

I look around the room, listen to the permanent buzz, the hacking laughter cutting through, all these known faces, all with some claim on me.

– Listen, Tim. I'll let you know. For the moment, I've got to get out of here.

The clown dances round me as I wait for the lift.

– Come on, lovely, smile, this is your night, yeah? Lovely jubbly.

Outside the party I stand still for a moment, wishing I had a cigarette, then start to walk west. The city seems quiet; I buzz with energy. It isn't long before I begin to shade into those other regions of vindication, self-pity and martyr-dom, return to press on the pleasure nerve, the moment when I turned to the audience or the moment before that when I knew that I'd done some good work. I am a greedy little lab rat and back and back I go to that pleasure nerve until I forget where I am, but now as I walk along an empty,

312

paper-blown street I can sense a second shadow, and each time I walk under a streetlight I feel it circling the pavement closer to me until it sweeps in rhythm with mine, then a thick gloved hand is over my mouth, and in my kidneys the dull pressure of a weapon.

– I'd never hurt you, Patrick, you know that.

There is a cloth over my nose and mouth and I'm asleep.

3

When I wake up I'm slouched on a battered wing-backed
chair wrapped in a coarse grey blanket. It's somebody's apartment, probably a bedroom. The room is dimly lit and musty,
feels as if it's high up. Thin orange curtains are pulled over
the windows. I try to stretch my feet, but they're tied to
the chair legs. The room I'm in has lino on the floor, an
old chest of drawers. There are rows of lighted candles on
all the surfaces. I can hear faint noises from the kitchen,
which opens off the narrow corridor. One of the walls is
painted black, there is a saccharine representation of the
Virgin Mary hanging on the wall opposite me, airborne,
robes flowing. The flat is cold, smells damp and musty.

He appears in the doorway.

– You know who I am, don't you?

– Hillary, right?

– That's right. Your freak.

– I'm so sorry.

– Yes, I'm sure you are.

An impossibly thin, tall, gangly, nervous-looking man,
Patrick's spooky fan looks uncannily like spooky Patrick. He
is dressed in a stained white polo shirt and black trousers
that hang two inches above his battered sneakers. I notice

as he leans against the doorjamb, hands clamped under his armpits with his ankles crossed, that he's not wearing any socks. His voice is high-pitched and tentative. He smooths his hair, which is a wet black smear across his scalp. I speak thickly:

– You're not going to kill me, are you?

He looks disappointed. Shakes his head slowly.

– I told you, Patrick, I could never hurt you. Would you like some tea?

– That would be nice. What time is it?

– Time for elevenses.

He disappears back into the kitchen. I notice that I'm not afraid and close my eyes. I try to remember his play. It was about an actor, right? Not about an actor who gets skinned alive by his freaky fan, or at least that didn't make it to the synopsis.

Hillary re-enters wearing an apron. The tea tray is an unsettling parody of gentility: a white milk jug, a cracked teapot patterned with pink roses, the matching cups, their lips rimmed with gold, little side plates, sugar tongs in the bowl, a toast rack with four slices, two pats of butter (one for me, one for him) on a chipped dish, jam decanted into a ceramic pot with a spoon in it. He puts the tray on the floor and gets a chair for himself from another room.

– Ooh, I'll put some music on.

He leaves again and a radio comes on. He comes back in and starts to pour the tea, strains of easy listening from the other room.

– Did you enjoy your party?

– Yes. Well no, not really.

– Oh, that's a shame. Sugar?

– No thanks.

– Toast?

He looks at me, head cocked, one of his ridged bony hands wielding a tarnished silver butter knife.

– Sure, thanks.

– There's more where that came from.

– Thanks, this will do me fine.

He passes me tea and toast. I balance the saucer and plate on my knees, try not to look at him, although I'm conscious that he continues to gaze at me. I can hear distant buses outside, growling, blowing air like whales, the whelp of their brakes.

– Where am I?

– You're at my house.

There is very little tone to his voice. It may be irony, but now is not the time to find out.

– It's a nice place.

He doesn't say anything, spoons some jam onto a slice of toast. I strain against the ropes that tether my ankles.

– I won't keep you tied up for ever. I just didn't want you to panic and try to run away.

– I wouldn't have tried to do that.

– Actually, you wouldn't have been able to.

He indicates towards the corridor.

– I had to lock it up in case you got a bit cheeky.

He smiles, but regretfully. I nod and eat in silence, him studying me, me studying my plate. I look at him. He sits back on the sofa, smooths his hair again, smiles primly. His ankles are ceramic white, the shins like raw bone.

– You told me to get lost, Patrick. Called me a freak.

– I know, I'm so sorry.

He smiles again.

– I didn't want much, you know.

– I am so sorry. It was very rude of me.

He gestures towards me.

– And then I have to end up doing this.

As if kidnapping and incarceration were inevitable. He moves himself to the edge of the sofa. It's strange, but what is at least clear now is that he wouldn't hurt a fly.

316

– We all want the same thing, Patrick.

Oh, but I beg to differ, Hillary. There's almost no one who wants this thing. I try to keep some humility in my tone.

– And what's that, do you think?

– I don't know if I know what the name of it is.

There's a knock on the door. He looks at his watch.

– She's early again. Time for lunch, Patrick!

– We just had elevenses.

He gets up and looks at me with what looks like fondness.

– She has her lunch earlier now.

He goes out to the corridor, closing the bedroom door behind him. There is a clatter, a small commotion, the squeak of wheels. The radio is turned down and I hear Hillary making reassuring noises, the front door opening and closing again. He re-enters my room and starts to untie my ankles. Still crouching, he looks up at me, nervous, desperate even.

– All right, Patrick. Just this one thing. I'm really sorry, but can you just do this one thing for me?

– I'll try.

We walk into the sitting room. An old woman is crouched in a wheelchair, surveying the Formica table with a look of bemusement. A mismatched collection of plates are piled with chicken tikka pieces and mini samosas; there is a tub of taramasalata, pitta bread cut into quarters, a bottle of San Pellegrino. The table is set for three, paper napkins folded into little tents.

– Mum. This is my friend Patrick Moon.

She looks at me mistily and smiles.

– Oh yes, I've heard a lot about you. An actor, aren't you, very nice.

– Yes.

She reaches out her lizard-like hand, I shake it awkwardly. The room is ill-furnished: a black vinyl sofa, a dilapidated bookcase thinly stocked, four bucket chairs around

317

the small dining table. The windows look out over what looks like far west London, blocks of council flats, slick grey roofs, the sky dingy and squally.

– He said you were coming over some time. Said he'd do you a bit of lunch, didn't you, love?

– Yes that's right, Mum.

– He's good really.

– Yes, he is.

– Not every lad would do what he does, making me lunch every day.

– Ooh, Mum, that reminds me.

Hillary is in a sprightly mood now, flits into the kitchen and comes back with a plate of sandwiches with their crusts cut off. He places them in front of her.

– Here you are. Nearly forgot.

– Bovril. He knows I like Bovril.

– Right, we're all here now. Let's sit down.

I follow his instructions. He pours me some water, strokes his mum's head. Then he deftly reaches under his chair and produces two copies of his play.

– Yes, Patrick, as we were saying before Mum turned up, I think you're right, I could probably do some more work on the opening scene.

Something happens inside me. I start to act:

– Yes, Hillary, you're right. I think it could be a little bit more direct maybe.

– Direct. Yes, interesting thought, Patrick.

– And I was thinking maybe, the opening speech, we could do that from offstage – build the sense of, of . . .

– Of drama?

– Of drama, that's exactly right, Hillary.

His face is filled with pride. I do my best, Hillary responds with eagerness and the old lady looks on throughout, an indistinct smile on her face. So here we are then, actor, writer, audience, colluding in the same sweet and necessary lie.

4

Carver Finstock, thirty-four, once married, once divorced, no children. Born on Long Island, educated at NYU and USC. That's all I need to know. If anything else is important then I'll get to find out in time, no reason to force it. Carver Finstock, line producer, mild eating disorder, teetotal, drug free, as many hang-ups as she needs to hold my interest, she's borderline perfect for now. OK, no Nubian or Swede, no Inuit, Aztec or Polynesian, but Jewish, which isn't bad. I call her The Jewess, because it has connotations of lioness, princess, empress – some kind of grandeur, at any rate.

Today she's wearing a tartan miniskirt and what might be described as a tunic. She's grown her hair into a quick-moving bob. Tonight it's in bunches (which is very very good). I like the way she dresses young, it gives me an eager hard-on. Viagra now is only employed for extra entertainment, perhaps the second time round the block. Like everything else, once a necessity, it's now an optional extra.

I watch her get undressed and draw the curtains in my white, box-like bedroom.

– Do you think I'd make a good Jew?

– No, you'd be lousy.

– You're such a kvetch.

– What what?

– I'm being Jewish. Get your tuchus over here.

She's getting into her pyjamas now. Baby blue, shorty shorts, the top has a chubby yellow Pokemon stretched between her breasts.

– Ahh, such a shmendrik, Paddy.

– What does that mean?

– It means you're a silly alter kakher.

– You're making it up.

– Such a farbisener, but such a mensch.

– What does that mean?

– Bubkis, bubele.

She jumps on the bed and kisses me. Carver has many things going for her: she's organised, full of energy, gets things done and has honed her sexual technique over several years in many of America's most testing environments. She's older than is ideal, but she's fighting the years with real tenacity. Also, if I narrow my eyes slightly, then through the blur she looks just fine.

The flat is too small for two, so next week we move out. She's bought a place in Soho. Larry Finstock wrote the cheque. He's some US network higher-up who reportedly likes my work. I haven't told Carver yet, but I have started to notice that certain young actresses are taking an interest in me. Things are just fine.

Tonight, we're settling in to watch the television, upon which I will be appearing. It is an interesting feeling. Carver is sitting on the bed now:

– So how did they do it?

– I don't know how they filmed her, but they did me here in the flat, then some moody exteriors around Clerkenwell.

– So you haven't seen her bit yet?

– No.

– Isn't that risky?

– We're about to find out.

The title sequence, twenty-cuts-a-second MTV-style, images of books flying by, film cameras, newspaper mast-heads, yapping mouths, theatre curtains opening, cds whizz across the screen, the music some generic big-beat thing, then the title: *Agenda*.

The presenter is some columnist standing in for Susie just this once: she stands on a large circular set, more media images back-projected onto the orange, blue and purple lit screens behind her.

Man, it's just so *now*.

– Hello and welcome to Agenda. *Tonight we'll be examining the ever-shifting barriers between the public and the private, how personal lives are increasingly finding their way into the public domain.*

Camera two: close-up now on raddled old hack.

– Susie Fisher is one of Britain's foremost newspaper columnists. Her weekly analysis of the breakdown of her relationship with Patrick Moon, her actor partner, became one of the most widely read and talked-about columns of the past year. She was accused variously of betrayal, hysteria and amorality, but she also provoked a considerable debate about the mechanics of the modern relationship as well as the appropriateness of conducting a personal vendetta in the public prints. This debate was furthered by the news that emerged last week that both she and Moon have signed a book deal with HarperCollins, for what is believed to be a six-figure sum, each to tell their side of the story. The fact that the books are also due to be published to coincide with the launch of Moon's latest film, The House of the Mind, *which comes out next September, has added an additional flurry of questions,*

ranging from Who are these self-obsessed media freaks? to,
Why didn't I have that idea? Often, of course, asked by the
same person. Tonight Agenda *presents an interview with both*
parties, and we invite you to judge for yourself. Yes, the media
really is eating itself.

Cut to Susie in her office, the blood-red womb, the piles
of newspapers, the rows of photographs of her, a professional in her milieu. She looks really hungry, she starts
to talk:

– I suppose when I started I didn't realize what I was get-
ting into. If I think now, with the benefit of hindsight, would
I do it again? I say absolutely.

The phone next to my bed starts ringing.
– Hi, Patrick, it's Mary.
I get up, take the phone into the sitting room so Carver
can watch me in peace.
– Hi, Mary.
– Sorry to call you so late, but it's the time difference.
Gideon's in LA.
– No sweat.
– Anyway, I think we've done the deal.
– Great.
– Six weeks' shooting, partly in Canada, partly in London,
starting February. He's sending you a script next week.
It wasn't even close. Prospero may be a great part and
Gideon may be a terrible guy, but he will keep casting me
in motion pictures.
– Great.
– Now, on the other thing, the Susie and you thing.
– I'm listening.
– The Americans say they want an American.
– What for Susie?

322

– For both of you, I'm afraid.

– No, nothing to worry about, really.

– Are you sure?

– Absolutely. The literary agent warned me something like that might happen.

– Well, it's happened.

– No worries. We still get paid.

– That you do.

Mary's buying me lunch next week, the sweetie. I'm thinking maybe Mirabelle.

– Have they got a title yet?

– It depends on what angle the final script takes. If they end up making you the central character then they're thinking 'Cracked Actor'.

– Yuk.

– If they end up making Susie central, then they're toying with 'You Wouldn't Like Me When I'm Angry'.

– Double yuk.

– Then they've got this last one.

– Well, go on then.

– 'The Chancers'.

– That sounds perfect.

– I'll tell them you said that.

– Great. And Mary?

– Yes.

– Thanks for everything.

– No, thank you, Patrick.

I hang up and go back into the bedroom. Carver shushes me and points at the TV. I am on screen, down by Borg's canal. A moody location, I thought, industrial but with a kind of urban romance, a whiff of escape, a place where men might gather to construct illicit plans. I watch me put my hands in the pockets of a big black coat (three takes to get the timing right) and hear my voice doing the VO:

– It's funny, at the time it nearly broke my heart, but now I just see the funny side. It's basically a love story, well, a falling-out-of-love story, I suppose. People can't get enough of love stories.

The edit is glib: my voice tails away to coincide with me stopping on a footbridge, looking back down the canal, a close-up on the side of my face as I consider the slow, black water, trying to look as if I give a damn.

– Hey, Patrick, that's great.

– Is it?

– Yeah. You could almost be an actor.

I watch the screen: a cut back to Susie, a cut back to me, a talking head, a cut to break, dumb nothing music, then saturated ad colours, actors moving around, doing what they're told. Pixels form in my eyes, white noise in my ears, and I feel a rising, indistinct desire never to be on television ever ever again.

I'll get over it.